What's
Left
is
Right

By
Irving Munro

Acknowledgments

Cover design by ebooklaunch.com

Original Austin skyline photograph by imagesoftexas.com

Disclaimer

Sherlock Holmes:

When you have eliminated the impossible, whatever remains, *however improbable*, must be the truth!

Prologue

RAUL HERNANDEZ WALKED ACROSS THE parking lot adjacent to the Gold's Gym on Lamar Blvd. in Austin, feeling exhausted. It had been a ninety-minute workout on the treadmill and another twenty on the weights. This was his normal routine at least twice a week. He also ran 20 miles on the weekend. For a 42-year-old he was in great shape and he meant to stay that way.

He had just pressed the remote for the BMW when they hit him from behind and everything went black. When he came to he realized that he was in the trunk of a car, tied up, with a hood over his head.

I guess this is it, he thought. *I missed them in the parking lot. How did I miss them?"*

It was stifling hot and the smell of gasoline was overpowering. His sweat was soaking the sackcloth of the hood. Raul closed his eyes and slowed his breathing. His military training had taught him not to panic in these types of situations. He was not in any great pain, but his head throbbed and he knew that he had been knocked unconscious. His weapons were in the BMW; he never took them into the gym and he guessed they must have known that.

An hour went by before the car stopped and the trunk flew open. Two men hauled him out, dragged him across a dirt track and yanked the hood off. There were about a dozen of them standing next to several trucks parked off to the side of the road. They were all dressed the same, all in white sheets and hoods. Raul recognized them immediately. The Klan!

"A bit elaborate, boys. If you're going to kill me just do it. But why don't you untie me and let's have a little rock and roll first, or are you not up for that?"

1

"Who the fuck do you think you are talking to us like that, you piece of shit!"

He recognized the accent. It was the Honduran with the scar.

"You come over the border and take our jobs. We round you up and send you back. And what do you know, you're right back here again. Well, no more. This will be a lesson to all of your kind."

Raul quickly processed what he had just heard. *This was what the Honduran had told this bunch, that he was muscling in on their turf and going to steal their jobs.*

"I'm not here to steal your fucking jobs! I'm not Mexican and not illegal! This lying Honduran has told you a pack of lies! Do I sound like a fucking Mexican to you?"

He could see Rodriguez standing by his limo watching all of this go down.

Raul's mind raced with anger. *Just untie my hands, you fuckers, and before I eventually go down, I'm going to rip your head off, Rodriguez.*

For a second he thought the guy behind him was untying the rope around his wrists, but in fact he was securing a second one to a trailer hitch on one of the trucks. The engine roared into life and he was yanked off his feet. He felt his shoulder joints snap. The pain was excruciating as he was dragged across the gravel road and the truck gained speed. His head slammed into a rock and all the pain was gone.

Raul Hernandez died there that cold night in Texas.

He had tried to explain to his killers that he wasn't Mexican, and that was true. In fact, his name wasn't Raul Hernandez, but that didn't matter. Those who had taken his life wouldn't have cared about the details anyway.

Chapter 1

Whispering Hollow

"ALMOST FOUR INCHES OF rain forecast in the next twenty-four hours!" announced Marie Mason as she walked into the Travis County Police Department office in Hudson Bend in Austin.

"Need to look out my wellies!" replied Tommy Ross, referring to the Wellington boots he used to wear growing up in Scotland.

It had been three months since the death of detective Jack Johnson. Jack had been the head of the cold-case unit and had died at the hands of serial killer Luther Fisher. Now Detective Sergeant Tommy Ross was the new head of the unit and Marie was his second in command. They were still trying to get their arms around the enormity of task.

Travis County is part of the Austin-Round Rock Metropolitan area. With a population of close to 1.5 million it's the fifth most populous county in Texas. The county is named in honor of William Travis, the commander of the Republic of Texas forces at the Battle of the Alamo. The Travis County cold-case unit is a part of the major crimes division; with close to forty murders in the county each year many go unsolved, so Tommy and Marie had their hands full.

"We need to try to get additional budget to get all of these in electronic format," said Bill Ross, sitting opposite Tommy and buried in the mounds of files, some going back twenty years or more.

Bill Ross was Tommy's father and, with the approval of Police Chief Bill Dunwoody, had joined the team as a volunteer officer. Bill was a retired Scottish detective, now living in Austin. His nickname in the London Metropolitan Police had been "Sniffer" for his dogged determination and research. He was able to sniff out inconsistencies in evidence and identify where pieces didn't quite fit.

"I'll talk to Chief Dunwoody about the budget, but right now we need to concentrate on putting the files into some sort of order of priority," said Tommy.

~

Almost on cue, Bill Dunwoody burst into the room.

"Good morning, everyone," announced the chief as he strode across the room with a thick folder tucked under his arm.

"Got another one for you and I would like you to give it top priority." He threw the thick file on Bill Ross's desk and it perched on top of the other files, threatening to fall and spill its contents all over the floor. Bill Ross grabbed it just in time.

The chief flopped down on the only free chair in the room, leaned back and put his feet up on the desk.

"Ten months ago a body was found laying beside a dirt track in a remote part of the county: Whispering Hollow in Leander. The Leander fire department crew found the body following a call out from local residents. They had seen what looked like a large bonfire down by the lake and, given the county burn ban, they had called 9-1-1. By the time the fire tenders got there it had almost burned itself out but there was no mistaking that it was a wooden cross, and the badly mutilated body of an adult male was laying beside it. The crew was given strict instructions not to discuss what they had found, and up until now they have obeyed those instructions."

"We can only imagine the effect on the Travis County community if this information got to the press. Tommy, I want your team to take over as the original investigating team has reached a dead end on the investigation of this horrendous crime. I would like that you consider this as a cold case and look at the evidence with a fresh set of eyes. You must not discuss this with anyone, including the original team. I don't want any of their speculation to influence your work. You can all appreciate that speed is of the essence here. The governor has been briefed and has approved your involvement. So please drop everything else and get to work and keep me updated on progress." And with that Bill Dunwoody got up from his chair and left the room.

~

They all stared at each other waiting to see who might say something first.

It was Bill Ross. He was staring at the crime scene and autopsy photographs that he had extracted from the file. "It looks like every piece of skin has been flayed from this guy's body. What a mess!"

Tommy chimed in, now that Bill had broken the ice. "The governor has been briefed," he parroted the words that Bill Dunwoody had used. "We better get our act together on this one."

"Let's take the rest of the day to wrap up the other files we've been working on. In the meantime, I'll go speak with the chief and see if we can get a temporary resource to accelerate transferring them into electronic format while we work on this new case. That will make it easier for us to get back into them when we're finished with this new assignment."

"What's the dead man's name?" asked Marie.

"They haven't been able to determine that," replied Bill.

"Well, we do have a lot of work ahead of us, don't we," said Marie with a grin.

Chapter 2

The burning cross file

THE FOLLOWING MORNING MARIE AND Bill meet in the conference room and spread out the contents of "The Burning-Cross File," as they had christened it, over the table. Tommy was delayed, as there had been excessive flooding in the Cedar Park area caused by the torrential overnight rain with many roads closed and morning commuters stranded.

As they spread the contents of the file out, they could see other members of the department pass by the room. The floor-to-ceiling glass would have to be blacked out if they were to use this room as their center of operations for the duration of the investigation. Bill Ross could sense the tension in the air. He had experienced this many times in his work in the Met in London. Detectives were fiercely competitive and hated it if another team had to be brought in. This was a high profile case and Chief Dunwoody was briefing the governor regularly, so the members of the original investigative team were doubly agitated. They would have to tread carefully.

~

When Tommy eventually arrived in the office, having navigated the street closures, Bill and Marie had blacked out the conference room windows and had arranged the contents of the file into manageable sections.

They began with the photographs. They were horrific. As Bill had previously stated, it was as if every inch of skin had been removed. Both hands had been severed and there were no signs of them at the scene. The face was unrecognizable and it looked like someone had taken a baseball bat and set about the head. The bottom section of the jaw was missing and had not been found at the scene. All the teeth on the top section of the mouth were gone.

Marie was first to voice an opinion on what she saw laying on the table.

"I think I've seen something similar to this a few years back. It was the James Byrd case in 1998. He was an African-American who had been dragged behind a truck. The murder had been committed by three white supremacists. Their ring-leader, Laurence Brewer, was executed by lethal injection and one of the others, Shawn Berry, was sentenced to life imprisonment. The third man, John King, still sits on death row today. In that case the poor man had been decapitated, but the rest of the body was in a condition like this."

"Then this could be another white supremacist killing?" voiced Tommy.

"The photos sure suggest that. Then of course there's the burning cross," replied Marie.

Bill had not offered an opinion but just stared down at the gruesome record of the death of this man. "Marie, do you remember in the James Byrd case, was there a burning cross found at the scene?"

"Not that I recall, but I can find out," replied Marie.

"Seems like we might be being deliberately led in the direction of Klan-type lynching," speculated Bill as he rubbed his chin vigorously.

"Being from over the pond, I didn't live through that terrible time in U.S. history, but we might want to check when last there was a burning cross seen anywhere in the U.S. If memory serves, most of the Klan lynching cases ended with the lynching subject being hanged from a tree. At least that's what I remember. We should also check out if James Byrd's hands were severed. These photos tend to suggest the hands were deliberately cut off, not ripped off as a result of the dragging, if that's what happened here."

"Great stuff, Dad!" said Tommy with a note of pride in his voice. "Is this your Sherlock Homes phase?" They all had a brief chuckle at Tommy's reference to the Baker Street sleuth.

"Why would someone cut off a person's hands and take a baseball bat to the head and mouth?" said Bill.

"To make it almost impossible for us to find out who this poor guy was," responded Marie.

"Right!"

"And the over-embellishment with the burning cross to try to send us off in the wrong direction right from the start," said Tommy.

"There's something else here," said Bill, bent over the photographs with his nose almost touching one of them. "I'll be right back," and he left the conference room. He returned a couple of minutes later with a huge magnifying glass.

"Now you're taking this Sherlock Homes thing a bit far, Dad," quipped Tommy.

"No, Tommy, look at this," said Bill. "What do you see right there?"

"I don't see anything," replied Tommy, peering through the lens of the magnifying glass at the photograph below.

"You take a look, Marie," said Bill.

"There *is* something," replied Marie. "Is it a small tattoo?"

"I thing that's what it is, Marie."

"Why would someone have a tattoo the size of a dime under their armpit?"

They had been at it for a couple of hours and Tommy suggested that they take a break.

"We need to take a timeout, grab a coffee and get on the Internet and see if we can get any clues to the answers to the questions we have at this stage," said Tommy.

"Marie, you look for records on burning crosses and, Dad, you see if you can get anything on that little tattoo. It looks like the ace of spades to me."

~

An hour later they were back in the conference room. Marie went first with what she had found about burning crosses.

"I found the following on Wikipedia," began Marie.

In 2006, Neal Chapman Coombs, of Hastings, Florida, was charged with knowingly and willfully intimidating and interfering with the right to fair housing by threat of force and the use of fire, and pleaded guilty to a racially motivated civil rights crime involving a cross burning, in his own front yard, to prevent the purchase of a house by an African-American family. Coombs was sentenced to 14 months in prison in January 2007.

On November 6, 2008, a Hardwick Township, New Jersey, family who supported U.S. President Barak Obama's campaign found a charred wooden cross on their lawn, near burnt remnants of a "President Obama - Victory '08" banner that had been stolen from their yard.

In February 2010, an interracial Nova Scotia couple living in Hants County discovered a cross burning on their lawn, along with a noose. Two brothers were later convicted of inciting racial hatred.

"There is nothing on the Internet about recent burning crosses as part of a lynching. The last known record I could find related to the lynching of Michael Donald, who was murdered by the Klan in Mobile, Alabama, in 1981. I think you're probably right, Bill, that we are being made to think that this is a Klan lynching.

"In addition, I found the various reports on the details of the James Byrd death. He was dragged by a pickup truck and the rope was secured around his feet so his upper torso and head took most of the trauma. The body smashed into a culvert and he was decapitated and his left arm was torn off. When they found the body the other arm was still intact, as was his hand. There had been no attempt to cut off the hand."

"Good work, Marie," said Tommy. "What did you find on the little ace-of-spades tattoo, Dad?"

"The detective team initially assigned to the case did find the tattoo, and like you, Tommy, they speculated that it was the ace of spades. It's all in their written notes. They have been trying to track it down but to date they have found nothing. They did say that it's a strange place to have a tattoo, hidden under the arm. I came at it from another angle and found some interesting stuff."

"My first thought was perhaps a gang insignia, but I dismissed that pretty quickly as most gang insignia are large and in full sight. They are displayed as a sign of pride to be in the membership of a particular gang and also to provoke others who do not belong to their crew. My second thought was military, and after some crawling around military insignia websites I hit pay dirt. It's Special Forces, U.S. Special Operations Command, specifically Marine Corps Force Recon.

"We have to find out who killed this guy," said Bill, almost in tears.

"If we're right, this is a man who served his country and put his life on the line every day. For someone to do this to him and for him to die in this way on the very soil he fought to protect is despicable. When we find these scumbags, I'll throw the switch myself!"

Chapter 3

A strange message

BILL ROSS WAS STUCK IN the end-of-day, nose-to-tail commuter traffic that had become the norm in Austin. The city infrastructure was struggling to keep pace with the huge influx of people from all over the country attracted to the capital city of Texas by the lifestyle the city offered. The music scene was world-renowned and kept vibrant by students of the University of Texas. It was also a great place to raise a family, with excellent school systems and inexpensive housing. It was God's country, and very liberal when compared to the rest of the state.

The stop-and-go traffic gave Bill time to reflect on the day. He and the team had only scratched the surface of the burning-cross file, but even this first day of analysis suggested that it was a real hornet's nest and he guessed that in the days ahead, with continued prodding, who knew what might fly out.

It was early November, and as he drove into his neighborhood the trees were starting to shed their leaves. The rain had stopped but the wind was blowing and the leaves were swirling around like early winter snow. Bill loved this time of year and the lead-up to Thanksgiving. The Thanksgiving holiday was not celebrated in his native Scotland, so he had no experience of it until he brought his family to settle in the U.S. in the 1980s. He was looking forward to having most of his family around the festive table, but also sad that his daughter, Jenny, and her family from California would not be able to make the trip this year.

Elaine was setting the table for their supper when he walked in. The smell of roast chicken hung in the air. Bill poured himself two fingers of Glenmorangie, his favorite single malt, sat down in his La-Z-Boy, leaned back and let out a deep sigh.

"Tough day?" asked Elaine.

"Not really, just a case that we have been asked to take a look at. I can't discuss any of the details, but my sixth sense is telling me that it will be a real tough nut to crack," replied Bill.

"You, Tommy and Marie will figure it out, I'm sure," said Elaine as she added a little more butter to the garlic mashed potatoes.

~

After dinner, Bill put on his favorite sweater and went out into the backyard and fired up "Vesuvius." Bill had the huge natural gas fire pit built a few years back, and ten people could sit around it with ease. It ignited with a *whoosh*, and he put his feet up on the firewall surround, enjoying the heat of the fire, as the flames danced into the night air.

He ran through the burning-cross file page by page in his mind's eye. Tommy had prohibited him from taking the file home given the sensitive nature of the investigation, but his police training over the years had been honed into a unique ability to store relevant facts in little corners of his brain and allow the effects of the Glenmorangie to do its work. He mused that he had probably done this a thousand times over the years and it had never failed to produce a result; tonight was to be no exception.

Bill's mind raced.

The initial investigating team had searched the immediate area thoroughly. There had been blood spatter and pieces of flesh all over the gravel road for hundreds of yards. They picked up and bagged for evidence bits of clothing that had been ripped off the poor guy. They didn't find the hands, or the lower part of the jaw.

Why was there no wallet, no money, no keys, no rings or bracelets, none of the normal stuff that we all carry with us every day? He had been fully dressed when they dragged him, as the bits of clothing picked up at the scene suggested. According to the notes in the file, forensics had identified some of the clothing as being top-quality wool worsted, light grey in color, used in the manufacture of fine suits and pants. He had also worn a white silk shirt. One black shoe had been found wedged under a large rock. It was a size ten Italian Bacco Bucci sports shoe that retailed for about $300 a pair.

Bill was convinced that whoever did this had tried to clean the site to ensure that the dead man could not be identified. The fact that they had missed the shoe was a huge mistake.

Bill remembered that there had been a message left by the body. It was on a large piece of heavy-duty cardboard, the type used to package household appliances like refrigerators and washing machines. It had been nailed to an adjoining tree, and scrawled across the board in heavy black marker were the words:

Stop illegal immigration - Close the border - Kill Wetbacks.

As Bill repeated the words there was something that didn't make sense.

His mind took him back to the KKK lynchings:

Kill the Niggers! Only good Nigger is a dead Nigger!

Stop illegal immigration - Close the border - Kill Wetbacks. This was too perfect. The use of these words was strange. This was not written by some white supremacist full of liquor and spitting nails. Apart from the *Kill Wetbacks* phrase the rest of the statement could have come from a sign on the floor of a Republican convention. This was another piece of the jigsaw puzzle that didn't fit and just one more piece of evidence to suggest that this whole thing had been staged.

Another glass of Glenmorangie, then off to bed. I'm going to get you lot, as God is my witness, you are going down!

Chapter 4

The Tattoo

THE FOLLOWING DAY THEY WERE all back in the conference room. The room would now be locked off from all other officers and administrative personnel in the department. They would update the white board regularly with what they knew or, in some cases, just suspected or speculated. This would form the roadmap and audit trail for their work going forward.

"I got a call from Bill Dunwoody at home last night," announced Tommy. "I have to provide him with an update on where we are at four o'clock today. So let's get to work."

"I think that we can say with a fair degree of certainty that this was not a resurgence of the Klan. I don't think that we are going to see anyone anytime soon walking down 6th Street dressed in white and with pointy hats unless they are off to a fancy dress party," said Bill.

"Do you agree, Marie?" asked Tommy.

"Yes," replied Marie.

"Okay, so we are coming from the angle that this was a murder not a lynching. So who was this guy and why was he killed? We need to focus our efforts on establishing his identity. So what do we have?" said Tommy.

"We have DNA from blood and hair and the lab work results are in the file. The medical examiner concluded, of course, that the cause of death was blunt force trauma. There was no evidence of any drugs in his system from the toxicology screening."

"His assessment is that this guy was in great physical shape before he was killed. He was roughly six feet tall and weighed 180 - 190 pounds. The evidence gathered at the scene, which was mainly fragments of clothing and pieces of flesh, would suggest that he wore high-quality, high-end merchandize. We also have the single size ten Italian shoe, and the initial investigating team has spent hours checking sales outlets trying to find a purchase transaction for the shoes, with no success. That's all I know at this time," said Bill.

"Based on the DNA, can we check if he was Mexican or from Central America as the sign found at the scene suggested?" asked Tommy.

Marie jumped in. "I did a course on DNA matching a couple of years back and as I understand it you can't get that specific with DNA. There are basically two types of DNA: nuclear DNA and mitochondrial DNA. We inherit half of our nuclear DNA from the male parent and half from the female parent. However, we inherit all of our mitochondrial DNA from our mother. The nuclear DNA is what we typically use in law enforcement primarily; however, mitochondrial DNA is helpful in determining what group—not race—we evolved from going back thousands of years. We could get a mitochondrial DNA test done if it has not been done already. That could narrow it down a bit." concluded Marie.

"Pretty impressive, Marie, you get a gold star!" joked Bill.

~

They checked the file and found that the nuclear DNA test results had been run through the Texas State Combined DNA Index System (CODIS) and also cross-checked with the FBI's national CODIS database. No match was found for anyone in either system.

A mitochondrial DNA test had been done. It indicated that it belonged to the Type B group. Marie did some online research and found that Type B is more prevalent in North

American Central Plains Indians than in Mexicans—not conclusive but likely that the victim was Native American.

"There is also a footnote in the DNA analysis," said Marie. "They appear to have found evidence of an allele, which is a variant form of gene. It is the 9RA allele that is found in Native American DNA. It is another marker that indicates that the deceased is Native American."

"Nothing much we can do with this information at this time, but it's another piece of the puzzle," said Bill.

"I agree, Dad. I suggest that we concentrate our efforts on the shoe. We must try to find where and when it was purchased, and then we would have something to get our teeth into," replied Tommy.

"Before we completely focus on that I want to get a few other things up on the board that are gnawing at my gut and just don't make any sense," said Bill. "Why did they choose Whispering Hollow as a site for the killing? It's at the end of a long finger of land that sticks out into Lake Travis with one road in and one road out. They would have to drive through upscale neighborhoods to get there, and it's not like the general public would be driving past the site, see the burning cross and get the message. So I am going to write up here on the board *LOCATION?*"

Bill continued on, "Then there is the *MESSAGE* they are trying to convey. The way they wrote it is strange. They could have just said - *Kill all wetbacks!* So why use the words *Stop Illegal Immigration - Close the borders!*

"I don't think we are dealing with redneck types here, which is what you would expect in a lynching. I think these people are educated and articulate, at least the person who wrote the words on the sign is. This murder was not about killing Mexicans, or even Indians for that matter. This murder was about something else. So I'm going to write up on the board *MOTIVE?*" concluded Bill.

"Marie, anything you want to add?" asked Tommy.

"What about the type of clothing and the type of shoe?" replied Marie.

"I agree that we should focus our efforts on finding where and when the shoe was bought, but it's the way this guy was dressed that doesn't seem to fit. Silk shirt, top-quality wool pants, Italian shoes. What does this tell us?

"One thing is for sure, he wasn't a *wetback,* or he had just won the lottery. So not only who was he, but also what was he?

"I want to write up - *WHO WAS THE VICTIM? WHAT WAS HE?*" that's it from me."

"Then there's the tattoo," said Tommy. "Dad, your research suggested that it was Special Forces. So I would like to write up on the board - *MILITARY? TATTOO? SPECIAL FORCES?*

"I need to get to the meeting with the Sheriff. Let's meet here again first thing tomorrow. Good work today!"

Tommy left for the briefing with Bill Dunwoody.

Chapter 5

Meet the Governor

TOMMY KNOCKED ON THE CHIEF'S office door and immediately Bill Dunwoody bellowed, "Come on in, Tommy!"

Dunwoody was seated behind his huge oak desk that had been a gift from his granddaddy Harold Dunwoody, a well-known local car dealer in Austin. He sat below the Travis County state seal mounted on the wall behind him. Off to his right hung the U.S. flag and to his left the state flag of Texas.

The first chief of police of Travis County was Wayne Barton, who took the office on March 14, 1840.Since then 33 officers have served in the role of police chief to the good people of Travis County. Bill Dunwoody was well aware of the great history of the office and served in the role with great pride. Tommy held Bill Dunwoody in the highest regard and aspired to be sitting in his chair one day.

"Take a seat, Tommy, I'd like to introduce you to a couple of folks you might recognize," said the chief with a little grin on his face.

Tommy's legs almost went out from under him before he could reach the chair. Standing off to the side by the conference table was Raymond Shaw, the governor of Texas, and Gavin McMullen, the governor elect.

"Very pleased to meet you, sir," said Tommy with a quiver in his voice as he extended his hand to Governor Shaw.

"Good to meet you, son" said the governor with typical Texas informality. "Let me introduce Gavin McMullen. I asked Gavin to tag along today as he will be taking the reins from me soon."

"Pleased to meet you, Mr. McMullen"

"Good to meet you, Tommy, and please call me Gavin!"

~

Raymond Shaw had been the governor of Texas for 14 years and was stepping down to make a run at the U.S. presidency. Gavin McMullen was a Republican and the state attorney general and had recently won election, defeating Shirley Walters, the Democratic challenger. Gavin's father, Garrison McMullen, was a huge real estate developer and owner of one of the largest ranches in Texas. He was an Austin icon. Not only did he own large tracks of land in the state, he also owned the Travis Tower, the tallest building in Austin, and the entire top floor was his residence. He was listed in the Forbes 400 at number 105. He was one of the richest people in the U.S.

Tommy had only seen Gavin McMullen on TV and thought him to be very charismatic; in person he was even more so. Gavin's mother had died when he was young and it was obvious that he had inherited her Spanish good looks. This had helped him win the governor's race by carrying the majority of the vote of the growing Hispanic population. He was seen by many as an example of the new breed of Republican politicians: articulate and well versed in the issues facing a more culturally diverse Texas.

"So Tommy, what update do you have for us today?" said Bill Dunwoody.

"We have only begun to scratch the surface of this," said Tommy. "We've had the file for a couple of days and we've drawn some very preliminary conclusions that have given us a way forward for further detailed work. We believe that the evidence doesn't support the assumption that this was some type of lynching or hate crime."

When Tommy said these words, there appeared to be a collective exhale from the others around the table.

"Well, that's good news," said Governor Shaw.

"Carry on please, Tommy," said the chief.

"Our preliminary thoughts are that the killing was staged to look like a lynching. If this proves to be the case, then why did they stage it in this way out at Whispering Hollow miles from anywhere? The original investigating team did a good job collecting the evidence at the scene. There was a single shoe found wedged under a rock. It's a very expensive sports shoe and we will focus our initial work in trying to track down where and when it was bought and hopefully who bought it. There are other pieces of evidence that we will research and there is also the DNA. That's about it for now."

"Good work, Tommy, and pass my comments on to the team, please," said the chief.

"I echo that," said the governor.

"Yes, good work, Tommy," said Gavin McMullen.

"What's your plan of attack from here?" asked the chief.

"As I said, we will focus on the shoe. It's the one solid piece of evidence we have to help identify the victim. We know the original investigating team has spent hours on this with no success, but we must give it another go. We will also get back out to Whispering Hollow and re-interview the residents of the community there.

"Why did the killers choose that location? We need to find an answer," concluded Tommy.

"Great report, and as we have all said, good work, and keep the pressure on with your team. I will expect another update next week at the same time, but, of course, if there are any significant breakthroughs before then, please keep me informed," said Bill Dunwoody.

Chapter 6

Belhaven beer

WHILE TOMMY WAS OFF HOBNOBBING with the sheriff and the governor, Bill and Marie continued to update the white board in the conference room.

"Would you like to have a beer before you head home, Marie?" asked Bill.

"Okay, if it's just a quick one, I promised Shelly that I would be home before eight tonight. She's getting a bit annoyed with the long hours of late."

Shelly was Marie's long-time partner and worked as a paralegal in one of the largest law firms in Austin. It was their dream to marry and they hoped that Texas would change the gay rights statute someday that would allow them to do that.

~

"This place just opened about three months ago," said Bill as they walked in to the Bull's Head Tavern just off FM 183 and Mopac.

Mopac is a main artery of the Austin road system running north/south. The road was built parallel to the Missouri Pacific railroad track connecting Austin with Dallas; hence the name Mopac.

"Have you ever had British beer, Marie?"

"Can't say I have, Bill. I'm a Shiner and a shot gal myself."

"I never have been able to get a taste for Shiner. They have forty beers on tap here and one of them is Belhaven, which is brewed in the town of Dunbar in Scotland and imported to Texas by the Ben E. Keith Company right here in Austin. The brewery in Dunbar has been brewing beer there since 1719 and, given that Texas became a state in 1845, that's back when the cowboys and Indians were doing there thing around here. My assessment is that Belhaven is almost perfect. But there's always room for improvement through diligent quality control, and I'm a part-time volunteer in that!" laughed Bill.

"Well, with that recommendation I better have some!" laughed Marie.

~

"This *is* good!" said Marie, looking up with the foam from the head of the beer giving her a temporary white mustache.

"I thought it would be good to catch up. We haven't had you and Shelly over for dinner since Jack's death, and I wanted to ask how you were coping. His death was a huge shock to me and I'm not sure that I'm over it, and you worked with him for a lot longer than I did."

"I'm not over it, Bill, I'm tearing up just thinking about it now. Sometimes I wake up in the middle of the night and see the face of that monster Fisher again. What I went through plus the death of Jack has had a major effect on Shelly also. She knows I love my job, but she worries about me. She said that since that event in Colorado she can't wait till I get home safe each night, and the stress of worrying about my safety is affecting her job. I may have to look for another line of work, Bill. I don't want to lose Shelly," said Marie, the tears beginning to run down her cheeks.

"Have you talked to Tommy about this?"

Marie gripped her beer glass tightly and stared into the glass. "No, I haven't. I've gone to see a stress counselor to see if I could get some help, and Shelly came with me. It was clear in that session that we both needed help, not just me. The counselor also helped bring other things to the surface that I am trying to come to terms with."

"Other things?"

"If I tell you, Bill, you must promise not to tell Tommy. I need to work through all of this and I don't want it to affect the team. Do I have your word that you will keep what I tell you between us? You have to promise!"

"Of course I will."

"I still haven't come to terms with being looked over for the position of the head of the cold-case unit. I love Tommy and I want him to succeed, but I should have been given that job! The counselor is suggesting that I might have posttraumatic stress caused by the encounter with Luther Fisher and that it is being made worse by the death of Jack and by my emotional turmoil of being looked over for the promotion. She thinks that I may need many months of treatment."

"My God, Marie, I had no idea."

"There's more, Bill. Based on all of this Shelly is suggesting that I quit the unit and get another job. She said that her law firm needs someone with my experience to do investigative work and has talked to a couple of the partners already, and they want to talk with me. To be frank, Bill, I'm an emotional mess right now."

"Well I'm glad we came for a beer. Are you and Shelly free over the next couple of weeks? Perhaps before we get to Thanksgiving you both can come over for dinner? We could invite Tommy also and create an opportunity for you to get it out on the table when we are all together, and I can provide support. I am not suggesting that this be an evening for us to gang up on you to convince you to stay on the job, no such thing, but it might be good for all of us to talk it over together. Elaine really likes Shelly and I think that the feeling is mutual."

"You know what we do is a calling, Marie, it's not just a job. Elaine and I have talked about this many times over the years and she knows that being a detective is who I am, my identity, if you will, and that without that I would be lost. When we came to the U.S. and I worked for the military contractor, the money was great and I had a job with an impressive title, but I did miss the police work and I'm so thankful to Jack that he gave me the opportunity to get back in the saddle and do what I love to do."

"He was a good man, Jack Johnson, and his death sent a dagger through my heart. I will never forget what you went through that day in Colorado any time soon either. Perhaps we can find a way to support each other and get through this."

"I think it's a good idea, Bill, and worth a try, but I don't know how Shelly will react. I'll talk with her and see if she is comfortable with getting this out in the open and with Tommy being part of conversation. If she agrees that it's the right thing to do, I'll get back to you on a date that might work for us."

Marie drained the remainder of her beer, stood up and kissed Bill on the cheek.

"Thanks for suggesting this, Bill. You're a good friend as well as a great cop. Have a good night!"

Bill ordered another Belhaven, and when it came he lifted it into the air.

"This one's for you, Jack!"

Chapter 7

Needle in a haystack

TOMMY CALLED BILL AND MARIE into his office the following morning.

"You're not going to believe what happened in the meeting with the chief last night."

"Okay, Tommy, surprise us," said Marie.

"Governor Shaw and Governor-elect Gavin McMullen were there!" responded Tommy, unable to control his excitement.

"What was that all about? Why were they there?" asked Bill, somewhat suspicious of their motives.

"They were obviously concerned about the Klan link, because when I told them that our current thinking is that it is unlikely to be a Klan lynching, their relief was palpable."

"I guess that's somewhat understandable," said Bill, now a little less agitated with the motives of the two Texas politicians.

"All three want me to pass on to you both that they are pleased with the progress we are making to date. I now have a weekly update briefing with the chief."

"But we haven't really made much progress," said Marie.

"I agree, so let's get back to work and get off this political glad-handing bullshit," said Bill.

"Not had enough coffee this morning, Mr. Grumpy?" said Tommy with a chuckle.

When he saw his father glower at him, he quickly moved on.

"Let's get to work then," said Tommy.

~

"What does it say in the file about the work the team did on trying to track down the purchase transaction for the Italian shoes?" asked Tommy.

"It's a very expensive shoe. They list dozens of stores that they have talked with, including Nordstrom and DTS. They talked with both online and in-store retail folks and nothing!" said Marie.

"Anything in the file about contacting the manufacturer directly?"

"They contacted the main online retailer, it would appear. It's a site that sells both Mezlan and Bacco Bucci shoes direct from the manufacturer. They struck out there also," said Marie.

"Shit! This is going to be like finding a needle in a haystack!" said Tommy.

"Let me have a go tracking down the shoe retailer," said Bill.

"Okay, Marie and I will drive over to Whispering Hollow and start to re-interview folks there."

Bill grabbed all of the information from the file on the shoe and headed to his desk. Marie and Tommy left to head over to Whispering Hollow.

~

They must have missed something about these shoes, thought Bill as he sat down at his desk and booted up his laptop.

Bill decided that the best approach was to compare the list of stores and online retailers that the initial investigating team had contacted with what he could find with his own Internet search. It took him several hours. When he was done he concluded that the investigating team had done a really thorough job. There were only two online retail stores that carried the brand that they had missed. He called both and struck out.

"I'm not giving up on this," said Bill to himself as he stared at the screen. "I need to come at this from a different angle."

"Where are these shoes made? They may be made in China like everything else is these days, and the Italian name is just for branding and the ability to charge more for the shoes based on perception of coolness. Did I actually just say coolness? Where did that come from?" he chuckled to himself.

~

While Bill was having his coolness epiphany, Marie and Tommy had driven to Whispering Hollow. It was long a drive, forty-two miles from Hudson Bend, and it took them over an hour. They had taken FM183 north and then gone east on FM1431 toward Lago Vista. Before reaching Lago Vista they turned left on Lohman Ford Road and that took them finally to Whispering Hollow.

Whispering Hollow is a waterfront area right at the end of a finger of land on the northern shore of Lake Travis, directly across the lake from the city of Lakeway on the southern shore. It's part of the Venture Point neighborhood that has at its center the Whispering Meadows golf course.

"Let's grab some lunch at the golf course grill," said Tommy.

"It's now gone noon, and after a quick burger or something we can start the door to door. We can have a good four hours to talk with the residents before we need to get back on the road and head home."

"Sounds like a plan," said Marie as they pulled into the golf course parking lot.

It was a small grill, nothing fancy, with a few plastic tables and chairs and a small bar. Tommy reckoned that if there were more than 25 people in the place they would be violating the city fire ordinance. One guy sat at the bar and another two were at a corner table comparing scorecards and settling up their wager for the round. The place smelled of popcorn, hot dogs and beer. They decided on hotdogs and a couple of Cokes to wash them down.

"A little quiet around here today?" said Tommy, making small talk with the forty-something blond lady as she popped open the diet Cokes.

"It's midweek and it's a little cold today," responded Cheryl Brown as she poured the cokes. "It's mostly a weekend crowd here, with the retired folks on weekdays to keep the wolves from the door."

"So how long have you worked here?" asked Marie.

"Eighteen years come spring. I work Thursday through Saturday and I have another bar job in the evenings in Lago Vista where I live," said Cheryl as she headed over to the two golfers at the corner table with a couple of bottles of Bud Lite.

When she returned to the bar she grabbed a cloth and started cleaning off the bar top.

"So what brings you folks way out here then? Looking to buy one of condos over at Comanche Point, are you?"

"No, not really, we're both detectives with the Travis County Police Department," said Marie.

"Oh, I see," said Cheryl.

"Mind if we ask you a few questions, Cheryl? I assume it's Cheryl as that's what it says right there on your nametag," said Tommy.

"I guess you *really are* detectives," laughed Cheryl.

"Why did you ask us about Comanche Point?"

"Oh, they're running special pricing over there as they have a few for sale right now."

"Why is it called Comanche Point?" continued Marie.

"I have no idea, but a lot of Venture Point streets have Indian-sounding names. A mile that way is Indian Point, then there is Navajo Trace, and down toward the lake before you get to Whispering Hollow is Panateka Circle."

"Penateka, never heard of that name, Cheryl, is that an Indian name?" asked Tommy.

"I think so. I heard a couple of guys talking about the name once. I guess they were part Comanche," said Cheryl, now looking a little bored with the conversation.

"Do you remember a fire at Whispering Hollow a few months back?" asked Tommy.

"I sure do, it was like the Fourth of July that night with all the fire tenders and cop cars with the flashing lights. I guess they found some dead guy and they reckoned he was homeless and had started a fire to keep himself warm and burned to death," said Cheryl as she repeated the false story that had been put out at the time.

"It was at the end of January when it happened. It must have been real cold next to the lake."

"Do many people sleep rough down there?" asked Marie.

"I see the occasional vagrant, but not too much. In the summer kids drive their trucks down there and hang out to drink beer and watch the sun go down, but in the winter it's pretty quiet. Did you guys find out who the poor guy was? Is that why you're here?"

"No, we're still working on it and it's been a few months since it happened, so our boss asked us to come back out here and take another look. There are a lot of vagrants found dead around the county each year, but we do try our best to identify them and let their loved ones know."

Marie didn't think that her lie was all that convincing but Cheryl seemed to buy it.

"Well I hope you *do* find out. The poor man," said Cheryl, her eyes drifting off in the direction of Whispering Hollow.

~

"Well, that was a little spooky," said Tommy as they got back into the car. "We have a victim of possible Native Indian lineage found in an area where everything around seems to have an Indian name. It sends shivers up my spine!"

A couple of minutes later they drove out of the parking lot toward Whispering Hollow to begin the door to door.

Chapter 8

Raul Hernandez

IT WAS LATE AFTERNOON AND Bill had been trawling the Internet for several hours with no progress. He had gone to the evidence store and checked out the shoe, and it was perched on the end of his desk in its transparent evidence bag. As he stared at it under his breath, he whispered, "Why don't you talk to me? Who bought you? Where were you bought?"

It was a pretty fancy darned shoe and, at $300 a pair, out of the price range of most folks—real leather uppers and stylish for sure. Bill discovered that it was a Bacco Bucci Buffon sports shoe with a round toe and adjustable strap. As football (soccer) was Bill's passion, when he wasn't on the BBC website to find out how his beloved Kilmarnock FC had done on the weekend, he was studying the other European soccer results. Gianluigi (Gigi) Buffon is the current goalkeeper of Juventus in the Italian Serie A and the first choice keeper for the Italian national team. He is an Italian icon and revered in soccer circles as one of the greatest goalkeepers of his generation. This shoe was named for Gigi Buffon.

Taking a break from his research Bill headed to the coffee machine and made a quick detour into the restroom. There were only two urinals and Bill chose the one on the left. As he stood there another police officer wearing a huge Stetson came in and took the other urinal beside him.

"Why don't you fuck off where you came from, and take your golden boy son with you," said Detective Kyle Cross, the head of the initial investigating team.

Bill ignore the comment and turned to the sink to wash his hands.

Kyle Cross stood behind him and whispered in his ear. "You know in our line of work accidents can happen. Y'all take care out there y'hear. He then left the restroom slamming the door behind him.

"I guess the natives are getting restless," whispered Bill to himself as he headed off to grab a coffee.

~

It was about four in the afternoon when he finally made the breakthrough. He had been on social media websites, Facebook and Twitter, to see if anyone was talking about the shoes, and he hit pay dirt.

On YouTube he found a report pitching the shoes; the guy doing the pitching mentioned that the shoes were made in California.

Bill immediately began searching California company registrations and found the company: The Bacco Bucci Beverly Hills Shoe Company, Skylab Road, Huntington Beach, California.

"My daughter, Jenny, and her family live in Huntington Beach. What a coincidence," mumbled Bill as he dialed the main line for the manufacturer.

~

"Is this the Bacco Bucci Shoe Company?"

"Yes," said the Asian-sounding lady on the other end of the phone. "How can I help you?"

"I am Special Officer Bill Ross of the Travis County Police Department in Austin, Texas. I wonder if I might ask you a few questions."

"What about?"

"There was a murder committed a few months ago here in Travis County and the deceased was wearing Bacco Bucci shoes."

31

"Yes, so what is it you want to know?"

This conversation is a little strange thought Bill, but he pressed on.

"Are the shoes made there in California?"

"No, they are not. Some are made in Italy, some in Brazil and the rest in China."

"And you sell them through mainstream mall stores and online, is that right?"

"Yes"

"Do you sell through any smaller stores?"

"Yes," said the lady on the phone, stretching her vocabulary to the max.

The conversation had been like pulling teeth, but on the positive side he did get the information he needed.

The shoes were also sold through mom-and-pop type operations. They were small high-end clothing stores. There were several in Texas—eight in Dallas and four in Houston. He picked up the phone and started working through the eight Dallas outlets, but to his intense frustration and disappointment he reached another dead end.

~

A few minutes later Bill dialed the first outlet in Houston - M & J Fine Clothing located in The Houston Retail Center.

"M & J Fine Clothing, Martha Goldman speaking, how may I help you today?"

"This is Officer Bill Ross of the Travis County Police Department in Austin. I understand you sell Bacco Bucci shoes?"

"Yes, we do, Officer Ross, is there some problem?"

"Yes, a man was found murdered here in Travis County a few months back and he was wearing Bacco Bucci shoes."

"By chance were they Bacco Bucci Buffon shoes, Officer Ross?"

Bill almost dropped the phone and fell off his chair.

"Yes, Ms. Goldman they were, why do you ask?"

"I knew it, I just knew that there was something strange about that man!" said Martha Goldman, and she told Bill the whole story.

"It was late in the afternoon the week before Thanksgiving 2013, almost a year ago to the day, when a man walked into our store. I greeted him immediately and asked if I could help and he said that he was just browsing. As the man was the only customer in the store I kept a close eye on him as he browsed."

"In an instant, as if choreographed, he spun around and marched straight up to me and barked his needs, not in an aggressive or offensive way but in a very orderly but firm demeanor that left no opportunity for petty dialogue."

"He said that he wanted three white silk shirts, collar size forty-two, sleeve length eighty-seven and a half! He then immediately apologized that he had given the dimensions in centimeters and corrected it to inches, size sixteen and a half collar, sleeve thirty-four and a half."

"He also bought three pairs of gray worsted pants, waist thirty-four, length thirty-six. Three pairs black wool socks, half calf, and one black belt, waist thirty-four. One pair of the Hugo Boss Gettio boot, size ten, wide fit. One pair of the Bacco Bucci Buffon, the same size and fit as the boot, and one Hugo Boss Janay leather jacket, color black, chest forty-two. He didn't even try on any of items he purchased."

"He paid the bill, over four thousand dollars in cash, with new hundred dollar bills. He was starting to leave without giving his name or contact details and I stopped him. I explained that it was our policy to offer our clients exceptional customer service and could I have his name and at least a cell phone number so that I might follow up to ensure that all was in order."

"I told him that M & J Fine Clothing merchandise could be exchanged with no questions asked if there were any problems whatsoever. That in addition we also offered free laundering service if needed for as long as he owned the clothes. He was a little reluctant but did give his cell number and told me that his name was Raul Hernandez. He took his purchases and left."

"Wow! What a story," said Bill. "You have a tremendous memory for detail Ms. Goldman, perhaps you should have been a detective."

"Oh no, Officer Ross. My husband Jacob and I came her as children after the war. Jacob has worked as a tailor all of his life and we run our little shop here in Houston. We have been blessed with four children and nine grandchildren. Life has been good to us Officer Ross."

"This encounter with this man must have been quite unnerving, Ms. Goldman."

"I can say, Officer Ross, without hesitation, that it was the strangest and most unnerving transaction I have ever conducted in my forty years in the business. When I think back on it, it still gives me the chills." replied Martha.

"You still have the cell number, I'm sure," said Bill.

"I have it here Officer Ross, just give me a minute."

Bill could hear Martha opening and closing drawers and a few minutes later, she gave him the number.

"Thank you so much, Ms. Goldman. May I call you back if I have any further questions?"

"Of course you may."

~

Bill felt both drained and elated. After he hung up the phone with Martha he called the number she had given him. As he suspected the number was no longer in service.

"Well, at least we now know your name," mumbled Bill. "The name you gave Martha Goldman, that is."

Bill called Tommy on his cell to give him the good news. There was no response from Tommy's phone or Marie's, so he assumed that they were in the middle of the door-to-door work at Whispering Hollow. He left a message for Tommy to call him at home that night or just to meet in the morning for a detailed update. Neither Tommy nor Marie called back.

Chapter 9

Disinformation

NEXT MORNING, THEY ALL met again in the conference room, coffee in hand, ready for another long day.

Bill kicked the meeting off with the good news regarding the Bacco Bucci shoe.

"We should write up on the board *Raul Hernandez*. We can't be sure that this is his real name but it's what we have to go on for now."

"His behavior in the clothing store was rather odd, Dad. What do you make of it?"

"His behavior was really strange for sure, and I think we need to think about a number of issues. Why did he begin to order his clothing and shoes in metric measurements and then immediately catch himself and change to inches? Why buy all that stuff? If he was in Special Forces, was he on some kind of assignment? The medical examiner put his age at mid-forties, a little old for active duty Special Forces but not unheard of. Is he still active or is he out? If he's out, was he working for some commercial concern as a contractor? This is a little far fetched, but was he an assassin? If so, who was his target? Why was he in Houston in November of 2013, three months before he ends up dead in Whispering Hollow?

"I think we should write up on the board - *Special Forces In/Out? Assignment? Canadian? European? Houston?*

"I wish our trip to Whispering Hollow had yielded such positive results," said Tommy. "As we had discussed before, Whispering Hollow is right at the end of the finger of land that's on the other side of Lake Travis from Lakeway. There is one road in and one road out and it's a long road. You were right dad, the fact that they chose this location is really strange, and if we find out why it may lead us to the killers.

"The PR campaign of disinformation about that night seems to be holding. We talked with a bartender at the golf club grill in the neighborhood and she gave the party line as she understood it, that a vagrant had accidently killed himself when setting a fire to stay warm. We did door-to-door and most times we got no response. One of the older residents told us that with most families that live there both adults work and that the wives drop their children off at daycare in Lago Vista on their way to work in Cedar Park or Austin. Many of them don't get back home till late."

"We will have to re-plan our door-to-door and get back out there in the evening time or on the weekend. That's about it, not a great result from a long day on the road."

"You can learn a lot about a community by playing golf at the local course," said Bill with some experience in the matter. "I suggest that we get up there on the weekend, I'll try to get a tee time, and you two do the door-to-door. We can have lunch in the grill and see what information we can pick up."

"It's a good plan, but it's a little grill, Dad, twenty people max."

"That can be good, in a small place like that on the week-end when beers are flowing after the round; it can be very difficult to keep conversations private. In my experience everyone listens to everyone else's business, that's part of the attraction."

"Okay, that's one plan of attack, what else?" said Tommy.

"Does the Raul Hernandez name give us enough to pursue the Special Forces angle?" asked Marie. "Also, we could be wrong about the victim's lineage being Native American. Raul Hernandez doesn't sound like the name of a Comanche chief to me."

"I'll take the Special Forces connection," said Bill.

"As we discussed before, I wouldn't worry too much about the lineage question right now as it doesn't do anything for us until we have something to match it with. It sure was spooky though, being out there at Whispering Hollow and everything around having names referencing American Indian tribes, and here we are thinking that the deceased was possibly Native American," said Tommy.

"I should go let the chief know about the breakthrough on the shoe. He asked that I keep him informed on any significant developments."

~

"Did you talk with Shelly about coming over for dinner?"

Bill reminded Marie about the conversation they had had in the pub the other night.

"Yes, I did, and she thought it was a good idea, since she feels that Tommy needs to know sooner rather than later what's going on and getting it out on the table with your help she thought would be a good thing. Thanksgiving is on November 27th, so we thought the previous Saturday would work for us. Would that work for you and Elaine?"

"I'll have to check, so leave it with me," replied Bill.

Chapter 10

The SAS connection

THE NATIONAL PERSONNEL RECORDS CENTER, Military Personnel Records (NPRC-MPR), located in St. Louis, is the repository of millions of military personnel, health, and medical records of discharged and deceased veterans of all services during the 20th century. Bill found the website and studied the protocol for obtaining information he needed.

If Raul Hernandez had left the military, his information would be in the archives; however, the method of obtaining the data could take weeks unless he could find a way to expedite the search.

If he were still an active member of Special Forces, then the NPRC would not have his information.

"I need to find a shortcut," mumbled Bill.

"Just for the heck of it, let's try Facebook."

Bill keyed in Raul Hernandez and got over one thousand hits. Facebook provides a search filter where information can be added to refine your search, including employer. Bill was astounded that he could enter "Special Forces" in the "Employer" field It didn't provide any hits; however, when he entered in each branch of the military separately and did a separate search in each case, up popped several names. He sat back and imagined a terrorist in the U.S. sitting on Facebook and doing this to identify a hit list.

This should not be possible. Freedom of information combined with technology is immensely powerful when used for good, but in the wrong hands it could be a blueprint for disaster. There must be other ways that law enforcement can get information for both active and inactive military personnel. We need to get the governor to pull a few strings, thought Bill.

He decided to try another angle. A real long shot.

"Alex Forbes-Hamilton. I need to talk to Alex. He was in Special Forces in Iraq and is now retired. Alex may be able to offer some ideas on how to find someone who had been in his line of work. It's worth a shot and, at any rate, it's about time I called Alex. I haven't talked to him in several years."

~

Before he could make the call, Bill's cell phone rang; it was Martha Goldman from the clothing store in Houston.

"Officer Ross, I was talking with Jacob last night about our phone call together and something popped into my head. It may be nothing, but I thought I should call you anyway."

"I'm glad you did call, Ms. Goldman. Any small thing could be enormously helpful in finding out who this guy was. What did you remember?" said Bill, his adrenalin kicking in with the anticipation.

"He had one of those remote control thingies and he put it down on the counter when he opened up his wallet to pay for the clothes. It had the BMW logo on it and a plastic car rental tag."

"I didn't spot the name of the rental company but my husband, Jacob, and I rent cars from time to time and it definitely was a car rental tag."

"Wow, this could be incredibly helpful, Ms. Goldman, thank you so much. If you happen to find his ID lying on the floor somewhere that would be great too," joked Bill, and he could hear Martha laughing.

"Did the car rental tag have a color that you remember? As an example, if it had been red it might have been Avis, or green, it could have been Enterprise, or gold, Hertz."

"No, nothing comes to mind, Officer Ross, sorry. Good luck, and if I think of anything else I will call you right away."

"Have a great day, Ms. Goldman, and thanks again!"

~

"Sindhur Wadawadigi! I need to call Sindhur right now," said Bill to himself as he scrolled through his contacts in his iPhone.

Sindhur Wadawadigi was the IT person at Hertz Car Rental in charge of their big data project. She had helped him track down the car rental information in the Luther Fisher case a few months ago.

Could I be that lucky again? he thought as he dialed her number.

"This is Sindhur."

"Sindhur, this is Bill Ross, we spoke a few months ago when you helped me track down an SUV that I was looking for."

"I remember, Officer Ross, it's very good to hear your voice again. How can I be of assistance to you today?"

"I'm looking for a rental record for a BMW. It would have been rented in the Houston, Texas, area sometime in late 2013 under the name Raul Hernandez,"

"Okay, Officer Ross, let's see!"

A few seconds went by that seemed like an eternity.

"No, sorry, there is nothing that I can see where we rented a BMW to a Raul Hernandez in that time frame in the Houston area. I put in the search criteria as the last three months of 2013. There were several rentals to persons with the name Raul Hernandez but no BMW rentals. A BMW is a premium class rental with Hertz."

"I did find three records with other names but not Raul Hernandez, and all three had non U.S. driver's licenses and rented from our location at the George Bush International Airport. Not likely that they are who you are looking for," said Sindhur, disappointed that she had not been able to help.

"Thanks for trying, Sindhur, it was a long shot. You were first on my list to call because you had been *so* helpful last time. Can you give me the three names you have for the BMW rentals, just in case? We assume that the guy we are looking for used the name Raul Hernandez to rent the car, but we're not certain, so I should take the names."

He wrote down the names: one person from Sweden, a South African and a German.

"One other thing before I let you go, Sindhur. Just looking at the records for rentals from the airport in Houston for the same three-month period, how many rentals do you have for BMW cars in total?"

"Thirty-seven, Officer Ross. Would you like that I email the list to you?"

"That would be great. It was great talking with you again, Sindhur, and thanks for your help."

"Anytime I can be of further assistance just call, Officer Ross, and have a great day."

Sindhur got back to her Big Data work.

"Well, the BMW investigation will have to wait for now. It's three in the afternoon here which means it's nine in the evening in Britain. I need to call Alex Forbes-Hamilton before it gets too late."

~

Tommy had returned from briefing Bill Dunwoody about the progress on the shoe, and he and Marie were now sitting with Bill in Tommy's office when Bill walked in to bring them up to speed on his work on researching Raul.

"Martha Goldman from the tailor's shop in Houston called me back earlier. What a great lady. She remembered that when Raul bought the clothes in her store he had a BMW key fob with a car rental tag. She has no recollection of the name of the rental company, but it's another solid piece of evidence and confirmation that Raul did rented a BMW. I gave Sundhur at Hertz a call. You remember her from the Fisher case, but no luck I'm afraid."

"We couldn't have been that lucky," laughed Tommy.

"I accessed the National Records Center for military personnel on line. Typical government site. It will take us forever to get what we need from there. We need to ask the chief to get the governor to pull some strings with Washington to find out if there are any military records for Raul."

"I'll talk with the chief dad."

"I have another idea. It's a real long shot. Do you remember a case I told you about Tommy, where a banker in Scotland was murdered in the street outside his office?"

"It does ring a bell dad, but what has that got to do with anything?"

"William Forbes-Hamilton was a prominent banker in the city of Glasgow in the '80s. He had been attacked and stabbed to death outside his office on West Nile Street. Two young boys had tried to grab his briefcase. The banker would have none of it and tried to fight them off. He died in a pool of blood right there on the street, and when they found the boys they still had the briefcase. There had been no money or valuables, just business papers. A life lost for a few sheets of paper!"

"Well the banker had a son and he and I became very friendly over the years after I found his father's killers and put them away for life. His name is Alex Forbes-Hamilton. He was a lieutenant colonel with the British Special Air Service (SAS) and played rugby for Scotland. He is now retired and lives in the family estate in the Scottish Highlands. I am sure that I can get him to pull some strings and do some digging. Worth a try, don't you think?"

"Well go for it dad"

"I have his number right here. If I get him on the phone, I want you two to listen in."

~

"The Forbes-Hamilton residence," said the maid in her lilting Scottish island accent.

"Good evening, this is Bill Ross here, can I speak with Alex, please?"

"What is the nature of your call?" asked the wee girl, obviously well trained to ensure that she had the necessary information about any caller before interrupting her employer.

"Please just tell Alex that it's Bill Ross, I'm sure that will do it."

"Very well, please hold the line," said the maid and she went off to find her boss.

"As I live and breathe, Bill Ross, how the heck are you?" said Alex with genuine excitement that he was speaking again with the man who had brought his father's killers to justice.

"I'm well, Alex, thanks for asking. Elaine and I are now retired and we are living here in Austin, Texas," replied Bill.

"Austin, Texas! Don't tell me you wear a Stetson and cowboy boots, Bill. I don't picture you as the John Wayne type!" laughed Alex. "But you didn't call to have me rib you about being a cowboy, so what can I do for you, Bill? Whatever it is, just ask."

"Is it okay if I put you on speaker, Alex? I'm working with the Travis County Police Department here in Austin as a volunteer. My son, Tommy, is with me. He has followed in his father's footsteps and is now a detective, and his colleague Detective Marie Mason is also here. I'd like them in on this conversation, if that's okay with you."

"Not a problem, Bill, go ahead. Nice to meet you, Marie, and great to meet you, Tommy. If you're half as good a detective as your dad, you'll do fine!"

"If any of this conversation is uncomfortable for you, Alex, please tell me right away. It is my understanding that your stellar military service involved leadership of 22ndRegiment Special Air Service, am I right?"

Bill paused to allow Alex to end the conversation right there, but Alex continued the dialogue.

"I would not normally discuss this with anyone, but you are an exception of course, Bill. What is it you want to know? I will have to stop the conversation if I feel we are getting into anything that I might consider to be hush-hush. I *have* signed the official secrets act, you know!" laughed Alex.

"We're trying to identify a man we found dead here in Austin. It would appear he might have had a Special Forces connection. We have a name and we have a small tattoo under his armpit a little smaller that a five-pence piece. It looks like

43

the ace of spades and in some preliminary research that I did, I think it might by Marine Corps. That's all we have. Any idea how we might go about finding out who he was?"

There was a long pause before Alex responded.

"Let's deal with the tattoo first. Tattoos are not permitted in our line of work; however, I have known some men to get something discrete done after they leave the service. They just want something to remind themselves of that time in their lives.

"The ace of spades insignia does suggest Marine Corps, possibly Force Recon. How old was the deceased?"

"We think he was in his mid-forties," responded Bill.

"That would make sense, he would not be active duty now, hence the tattoo. Perhaps he could still have been working in a support capacity but not active duty. Yes, it's more likely that he had left the service." Alex paused.

Bill pictured him sitting in his lounge, taking a mouthful of single malt from a crystal glass. Bill wished that he also had his Glenmorangie in easy reach, but alas not.

Alex continued on.

"If he is mid-forties then he would have been active service and in his prime in, say, 2003. I worked with the American Special Forces in Iraq then. We were in an area that stretched about two hundred miles east of the Jordanian border. We were blowing up any sites that could be used to hide scud missiles. We were very mobile, operating in teams of four or six, with fast, agile, lightweight vehicles designed for the desert terrain. In teams of six, and living for days on end hiding in the desert, you get to know each other pretty well. A few of the Americans on my team were Marine Force Recon." Again Alex stopped and took pause.

"If I give you a name, could you make some discrete inquiries and try to find out who this guy might have been, Alex?"

"It would be a real long shot, Bill, and I don't want to go sticking my nose in where it might be blown off. Some of the guys who leave the service don't want to be found, and I don't need a knock on my door in the wee hours with a somewhat agitated individual in my face. We might end up wrestling on the lawn, and Mary just planted some new rosebushes out there!" said Alex as he chuckled and no doubt downed another glass of scotch.

"It sounds like you will do it though, Alex? We need to try to make a breakthrough on this," pleaded Bill.

"Only for you, my friend. What was his name?"

"Raul Hernandez."

"Okay, leave it with me. It may take a few days, but there are a couple of fine, upstanding gentlemen I can talk with. I'll get back to you as soon as I can. Give me your contact information."

Bill gave Alex his contact details, thanked him for his offer to try to help and ended the call.

"Well, we sure have prodded the hornet's nest now. Let's see what flies out," said Bill with a wink to Tommy and Marie.

Chapter 11

Jimmy Rodriguez

THE FOLLOWING MORNING, THEY were all together again in the conference room.

"We should plan to get back over to Whispering Hollow on Saturday for the house-to-house," said Tommy. "It's Thanksgiving at the end of next week, and I think we need to get the door-to-door completed before people go off to their once-a-year family dramas."

The couple of days leading up to the Thanksgiving holiday are two of the busiest travel days of the year as millions make the annual pilgrimage via the highways and byways to reunite with family members, who, in the majority of cases, they haven't seen since Thanksgiving the previous year. It's a joyous time but also a time of great stress. To many it's their favorite holiday, but others are heard to say, "There's a reason we only meet once a year; some of us can't stand one another."

"Would you and Claire like to come over for dinner on Saturday night, Tommy? We invited Marie and Shelly as we haven't gotten together in a while and Elaine likes Shelly's company. We could get together and debrief on the day out at Whispering Hollow over a few beers and unwind a bit."

"That would be fine, Dad, but it can't be a late night as Claire and I are up early on Sunday for church. I took her for the first time a couple of weeks ago and she liked it, and I met some really nice people, so we're going to attend regularly,"

"That's great. You didn't tell me anything about this, did you tell your mom?"

"No, not yet, I was going to wait a few weeks, but I guess the cat's out of the bag now."

"Okay, it's a plan then. Whispering Hollow during the day on Saturday and then dinner at our place Saturday night. I'll call and see if I can get a tee time. I can mix with the golf crowd while you two do the door-to-door. We'll need to take two cars so we are not seen together. I will create a cover about wanting to play the course as I'm looking to buy a home in the neighborhood. Saturday can be a tough day on most courses to get a tee time, but I'll call and see what happens. I'll get back to you both later."

~

"Whispering Meadows Golf Club pro shop, Glenn Stevens speaking, how may I help you?"

"Good morning, my name is Bill Ross and I'm looking into the possibility of buying a home there in your neighborhood. I am sure that Saturday is a busy time for you, but I was wondering if you could squeeze in a single this Saturday,"

"Yes, we're very busy on a Saturday, but let me take a look. With it being the weekend before Thanksgiving and a little colder in the mornings now, I could give you an eight forty-seven tee time, Mr. Ross. You would be playing with Bob Wilson, Herman Stoltz and Jimmy Rodriguez. They are all local residents and members of our men's golf association. They will be able to give you good pointers around the course and tell you about the neighborhood. Would that work for you?"

"That would be great, Glenn, and thank you for your help in making this happen for me. I'll see you Saturday!"

Okay, that's all set. Three locals, all members and regular Saturday morning MGA players, I should be able to get a good sense of what's going on from them boys, thought Bill.

~

The sun was just rising on a chilly Texas morning when Bill left home to make the trip over to Whispering Meadows

Golf Club. He had checked his golf bag to make sure he had enough balls, as playing a course for the first time can be tough and the Texas Hill Country courses are particularly challenging. These courses have hundred-yard force carries over the many canyons that cut through the hills around Lake Travis.

Bill loved the early morning, as the sun cast long shadows through the canyons. He drove along the Balcones Fault, a geological rift that was created millions of years ago and was responsible for what is today called the Texas Hill Country. The rivers that cut through this region—the Colorado, Brazos and Guadalupe—exposed the harder white limestone that formed these deep canyons. The Native American Indians considered the fault a sacred place and buried their dead in the many caves and crevices that peppered the canyon walls. They echoed the sound of the rivers as they made their journey south to the Gulf of Mexico.

He exited FM1431 and took Lohmans Ford Road towards Whispering Meadows. According to his GPS he had still another six miles to the golf course. He couldn't help but notice the amount of construction that was taking place in this corner of Travis County. It seemed like around every corner another track of upscale homes was being built. A new high school had just opened and he passed a signed for a new marina planned for construction in 2017.

A couple of miles from the golf course the road took a sharp right-hand turn and for about a mile ran along the edge of a cliff with a sharp drop-off to Lake Travis below. A couple of homes had been built adjacent to the cliff, and one in particular had a stunning cantilever deck that protruded out over the edge. Bill was so taken by the design of the home that he almost lost control of his SUV as the road took a sharp left away from the cliff and dropped down to Whispering Meadows below. He could see the golf course in the distance and he regained his composure and got his mind back focused on the day ahead.

~

It was seven-fifty and the parking lot was already full. There were golf buggies flying around the lot at breakneck speed, their occupants hurrying to get to the tee on time. It was a hive of activity. Sixty-year-olds doing stretching exercises, others cleaning and marking their golf balls. There were more golfers on the putting green than shoppers at a Macy's after-Thanksgiving sale. Wagers were being made and Bud-Lite cans were being popped. This was a typical Saturday morning at any golf course in America.

"Good morning, are you Glenn Stevens?" asked Bill as he approached the man behind the desk in the pro shop.

Glenn Stevens was in complete control of his environment as golfers checked in for the allotted tee time and checked out the latest overpriced golf equipment on offer in the store.

"Yes, I'm Glenn Steven's, what's your tee time?"

"I'm Bill Ross. We talked on the phone a couple of days ago. My tee time is eight forty-seven."

"Yes, I remember the conversation, welcome to Whispering Meadows, Bill, we're glad to have you here. Mr. Stoltz and Mr. Wilson are both checked in and on the practice green, I believe, and here comes your final partner, Mr. Rodriguez."

Bill turned in the direction Glenn Stevens was pointing and saw Jimmy Rodriguez walking toward him, in one hand an unlit cigar and in the other a Bloody Mary. He walked straight past Bill and hollered at Glenn Stevens.

"Are we on time, Glenn, and make sure that cart girl is focused on the job at hand today! Is it the lovely Cindy on the cart this morning?"

Jimmy Rodriguez was larger than life, complete with white golf knickers, plaid socks, matching plaid sweater and white golf cap.

"Bill Ross," said Bill, extending his hand.

"Jimmy Rodriguez, Bill. Good to meet you, hope you're not a sandbagger out here to take our money this morning," laughed Jimmy as he slapped Bill on the back.

Bill was certain that the comment about taking their money was no joke. This was going to be an interesting round.

~

Jimmy Rodriguez led Bill outside to meet the others who would make up their foursome. They were all about the same age, Bill thought, late fifties/early sixties. They all shook hands, swapped handicaps and headed off to the first tee. Bill got on a cart with Bob Wilson. Jimmy Rodriquez rode with Herman Stoltz. They tossed a coin to see who would tee off first.

The game Jimmy Rodriguez chose was left-and-rights, full handicap, with ten dollars a hole. Not a huge amount of money but enough to get serious.

Left-and-rights is a pretty simple game: the two tee balls that are hit right against the two that went left.

Because it's a simple game doesn't mean that you can't manipulate a situation in your favor. After the first tee ball is hit, the order of play from the tee theoretically doesn't matter. However, the person who is last to hit from the tee can see where the others have gone and then choose where best to play his ball to increase the odds of winning by trying to put his ball on the side where the best-positioned shot has landed.

As it unfolded, Jimmy Rodriguez always tried to busy himself with something on the cart or on his bag to ensure that he was last to tee off on every hole.

Golf is perhaps the only game in sport where those who play the game fairly may often call a penalty on themselves, if they did something during the course of play that was against the rules of golf. Calling a penalty on yourself would most times result in losing a hole or even losing the match. Golf is a game for gentleman. It's said that the name came from the first letters of the saying - Gentlemen Only Ladies Forbidden.

It was obvious from the off that Jimmy was no gentleman. In addition to the gamesmanship on each tee, he would improve the lie of his ball by moving it prior to a shot. On two occasions Bill saw him drop a ball out of his pocket while looking for a lost ball in the rough. Jimmy Rodriguez was a cheat. To him it was about winning at all costs.

Bill enjoyed riding in the cart with Bob Wilson.

Bob was a retired dentist from Minnesota and played three times a week. He was an average player, making more bogeys than pars, but didn't much care. He played for the fun of it and for the chance to hang out with the guys and chug a few beers on a Saturday morning.

"So you're originally from Scotland Bill? You Jocks are all good golfers and better drinkers!"

"So you've been around Brits then, Bob. Not everyone calls guys from Scotland Jocks."

"Yes, there were a lot of Brits in Minnesota. I'm half English and half Norwegian. Mostly Scandinavians in Minnesota but lots of other nationalities also. So you're thinking about buying around here, I understand?"

"Yes, we live over by Balcones right now, but we've heard a lot about this area, seems like there's a lot of development going on. On the drive over this morning I must have past hundreds of new homes being built. What's going on. Bob?"

~

Over the next few holes Bob Wilson gave Bill the rundown.

"All started about five years ago. All of this land used to be part of the old McMullen Ranch. Garrison McMullen started to sell it off to developers as part of an overall plan to create a residential and commercial region including a new marina. There is a Chinese consortium involved and they plan to redevelop this course into an upscale country club and we, as founding members, will be grandfathered in. I would suggest that you get in quickly as home prices will skyrocket. We are all pretty excited about what's going on."

"Sounds great! There's been an increase in crime in the Balcones area of late and that's part of the reason my wife and I are looking for somewhere new."

Bill lied, trying to create an opening for Bob Wilson to talk further.

Bob continued on, "Not a lot of crime around here, Bill. We get the occasional fight in some of the bars as the Mexicans get into it after they've had a few beers on a Friday night, a couple of stabbings and fights with broken bottles. Then there are the vagrants and the illegals. One of them set himself on fire about a year ago at Whispering Hollow down by the lake."

"Mexicans and illegals. Don't like the sound of that, Bob, I don't like that lot," said Bill, again lying to get Bob to talk more, which he did.

"A lot of them work on the construction projects; comes with the territory, I guess. They shack up together in some of the condos around here and send money back to Mexico. The guy to get the rundown on them is Jimmy Rodriguez; hell, his construction teams employ most of them. He's got teams working every angle, does Jimmy—electrical, carpentry, concrete, stonework.

"You need a trade; Jimmy will get you the people. He lives in the big house with the deck overlooking the lake; you probably saw it when you drove in."

"I did see it. It's quite an impressive home. He must be making a bundle with all the work going on."

"Yes, he makes a bundle all right, and lets everyone know about it!" responded Bob.

~

They ended the round and, to everyone's surprise (not), Jimmy Rodriguez won most of the money. Later they met in the grill and took a corner table. The bartender, whom Bill guessed rightly was Cheryl Brown, brought them their drinks and they toasted each other.

"Enjoyed the round as usual, guys! Great to have you join us today, Bill!" said Jimmy Rodriguez.

"Yeah, thanks for taking our money again," replied Herman Stoltz.

It was obvious from his demeanor that this was not the first time Herman had lost to Jimmy Rodriguez.

"So you think you'll buy in the neighborhood, Bill? I've got some pull with some of the builders. So if you see a place you like you come see me, okay?" said Jimmy, stressing his importance to the community for anyone within earshot who cared to listen.

"Anyone like a shot? I'm buying since I took all your money!" continued Jimmy, bellowing his laughter around the room.

It was obvious to Bill by the look on some of the faces in the room that Jimmy Rodriguez was not as well liked as he thought he was and that perhaps many thought him a loud-mouth asshole. Bill Ross was one of those people.

They finished their drinks and headed to the parking lot to load up their vehicles and head home.

~

As Jimmy Rodriguez walked out the front door of the golf club he waved to a waiting black Lincoln Town Car parked off to the right of the parking lot. It started up and pulled over to the front of the entrance.

The driver jumped out grabbed Jimmy's clubs and loaded them into the trunk. He then ran around the vehicle and opened the rear door for Jimmy to get in. As he did so his stylish black leather jacket fell open, flashing its Hugo Boss designer label.

Chapter 12

Latisha Williams

ELAINE WAS PREPARING HER FAMOUS chicken chili with homemade cornbread when they all arrived back at Bill and Elaine's home after their day at Whispering Hollow. As they walked in the house was full of the aromas of onions, chili, cumin and cilantro, the perfect meal for a cold November night.

"So how was your day?" said Elaine as she lifted the steaming cornbread out of the oven. "Dinner in half an hour, so get what you need to drink from the fridge."

"Want a beer, Marie? How about you, Shelly, can I get you something?" said Tommy, pulling a couple of Coronas from the fridge.

"I'll have a Corona," said Marie.

"I will too," said Shelly.

Bill emerged from his bedroom. He had discarded his golf cloths and had freshened up. He now wore a pair of dark blue sweats with the Kilmarnock FC logo. He poured himself a glass of Glenmorangie and sat down at the dining room table. Tommy and Marie sat down next to him while Shelly took Claire off to give her a bath before dinner.

"Okay, a few minutes of debrief from our day before we settle down for dinner," said Bill. "Elaine hates me talking shop around the dinner table, so let's make it quick."

"Did you see all the construction going on ever there?" said Marie.

"I did, Marie. There is some serious money being pumped in to those projects. The guys at the golf course today talked about the Chinese but I doubt they are doing this alone. My guess is that Garrison McMullen is in it and there are others for sure. One action item we need to take from today will be to look into the construction projects and the folks involved."

"I agree, Dad," said Tommy. "Marie and I talked to about fifty residents today and over half of them work on those construction projects; that's why they weren't home the other day, they were out on the site. They weren't gone into Austin as the retired folks had said the last time we were there. They are all working right there at Venture Point."

"So what did you find out about the death at Whispering Hollow?" asked Bill.

Marie pulled out her notes and gave him the report.

"Most of the folks we talked with gave us the disinformation story, that a homeless guy had set himself on fire and accidentally burned to death. There were a few who said that something needed to be done about the people who slept in the park. The vagrant problem seems larger than we first thought. I think we need to get down to the park at night and see who sleeps there. There may be homeless people still living there who might have seen something."

"As Tommy said, we talked with over fifty people. The community is split into single-family homes and condos. We talked with three guys in the single-family homes who work as tradesman on the construction sites. Two of them were carpenters and one was an electrician. They saw nothing that night other than the fire trucks when they arrived.

"The person who made the 9-1-1 call was Sally Sessions; she lives on Point View Way overlooking the lake and Whispering Hollow. She and her husband, Jeff, have two young boys— Billy, who is sixteen, and George, who'll soon be eighteen. Sally works in a bank in Lago Vista and Jeff works for a computer software company in Round Rock. Their boys attend the new Leander High School that was just built.

"She said she did hear a lot of men shouting and the sound of trucks revving up their engines, but she assumed it was just kids letting off some steam. Then she saw the flames. She went to get her cell phone to make the call and then returned to the window. She saw two trucks speeding out of the park and, although it was dark, she thought they were white in color. She had thought at the time that they may have been from the power company or one of the construction companies, but she's not sure. That was pretty much it."

"Don't forget about the guys in the condo, Marie," said Tommy, jumping in.

"Oh, yes, sorry I missed that!"

"We talked with a number of folks who lived in the condos. There was one condo in particular that gave Tommy and me the creeps. The guy who answered the door seemed stoned. We couldn't smell anything to suggest that they were smoking weed so we had no reason to ask to enter the property. There seemed to be a lot of people in the house and the guy said that they were just playing cards and that they all lived in the neighborhood. One other guy did come to the door, and he gave his name as Fernando Cazerez and that he lived on Apache Court. He said that they all work for Rodriguez Construction. We checked Cazerez out later and he checked out as legit. We just felt the place was a little strange. They knew nothing and saw nothing the night of the killing, or so they said."

"What did your day on the links reveal, Dad, anything?" asked Tommy.

"I met a guy that we need to check out for sure. His name is Jimmy Rodriguez; he lives in a big house overlooking the lake. This Cazerez guy you mention might work for him. He is a loudmouth, throws his money around and cheats at golf. According to another one of the residents, he employs teams of tradesmen and contracts them out to the developers. When we finished golf he was picked up in a chauffeur-driven black limo. The driver wore a black leather jacket that had a Hugo Boss label. The same make of leather jacket that Raul Hernandez purchased from Martha Goldman."

"Okay, so we need to check out both Rodriguez and his chauffeur," said Tommy.

~

With the police work discussion over, they all sat back as Elaine brought the chili and the cornbread to the table. Shelly had emerged from the guest bathroom with Claire wrapped up in a huge bathrobe. Shelly had her in her arms and dried her off. She then dressed Claire in her Dora the Explorer PJs and sat down beside her at the table.

With their bowls full of chili, and after they had taken a few bites of the cornbread, Bill raised the topic of the late Jack Johnson.

"A few days ago I was telling Marie that Jack's death has had a major effect on my life and that I've still not come to terms with it. I wake up in the night thinking about it and I need to work at putting it behind me."

"Wow, I feel the same, Dad!" said Tommy, taking his father's lead. "We're all in law enforcement and it does come with the territory; however, we are human and we can't just ignore how we feel."

Realizing that Bill had set the scene, Shelly jumped right in.

"Marie needs to find another line of work! I just can't take the stress of worrying about her every minute of the day. I see no other way. She needs to get out of the line of fire and find alternative employment or our relationship is in danger of collapse. I'm sorry to just blurt it out in this way, but we have talked about it. Y'all are a close team working together every day, but I find that it's almost impossible to function in my job worrying about Marie. How is it for you, Elaine? You've been dealing with this with Bill for a lot longer than I have with Marie."

"You just have to get used to it, Shelly. That was the way it was for me at any rate. No, I should say that's the way it *is* for me because it is still the same today! I knew that if I had tried to have Bill leave the police force he would have done it for me, but the Bill that would have been left would not have been the same Bill that I love and married. It would have been like him chopping his right arm off. There would have been a negative lasting effect on him both physically and mentally."

Just as Shelly was about to respond Marie's cell phone rang.

"Marie Mason."

"Detective Mason, this is Latisha Williams of the Austin *Statesman*."

"I know who you are, Latisha. What can I do for you and how did you get my number?"

The name Latisha had an immediate effect on Tommy and Shelly, as they both knew who she was.

Latisha Williams was the chief crime reporter for the Austin *Statesman* and had the reputation of a rabid Rottweiler. When she got her teeth into a story she would not let go and had no concern whatsoever for any collateral damage that her tenacious reporting might cause.

"What's going on over at Whispering Hollow? Are you looking into the death of the homeless guy who torched himself last year? You're asking a lot of questions and costing the taxpayers a lot of money for some guy that no one gives a crap about! So what's the real story? I got a call from an old girlfriend of mine that you were snooping around. I think we should meet."

"Let me talk with my boss, Latisha, and I'll call you back. Don't get your panties in a wad right now; it's not some big conspiracy. The original team asked that we take another look at the evidence, that's it, nothing more sinister than that. Give me a couple of days to get hold of my boss; he's out of town for Thanksgiving. I just need his okay to talk with you."

Marie was just trying to buy some time and it appeared to work.

"Okay, Marie, I'll expect to hear from you Monday, no later, or I'll go with a story to flush out the truth! Have a good Thanksgiving, Marie."

~

"I guess y'all know who that was," said Marie as the others stared at her.

"I don't know how she got my number, but suffice to say Latisha Williams shares the same lifestyle as Shelly and me. An ex-girlfriend of hers, probably Cheryl Brown at the golf club, called her and told her we were snooping around. What do you think we should do, Tommy?"

"We have to meet with her and ask her to work with us on this. She'll want something in return, like exclusivity on the story, but she's a real loose cannon, and if we don't get her in the tent pissing out then she'll piss in all over us."

"Real nice analogy at the dinner table, Tommy Ross, really nice," said Elaine, more than a little upset with her son.

"You know that your daughter is sitting right there!" continued Elaine, pointing to Claire. Then the four-year-old came out with a gem, as she often did these days, that had them almost rolling about the floor with laughter.

"The lady should do pee-pee in the toilet, Mimi, shouldn't she?"

There was nothing more that needed to be said.

They never got back onto the subject of Marie's line of work. It would have to wait for another time. However, the ice had been broken and there were now no secrets. It was out in the open. It would be an issue that would have to be addressed, however, and addressed soon or it would fester and cause an irreparable rift in the team.

Chapter 13

The Spirit Riders

ON MONDAY MORNING BILL ROSS was sitting at the breakfast table sipping on his first cup of coffee of the day and reflecting on the positive progress made over the weekend, when his cell phone rang.

"Good morning, Bill, how's the weather this morning there in Austin?" said Alex Forbes-Hamilton.

"Forty-three degrees and fog, Alex. My guess is it's colder where you are though?"

"It's actually a nice day here, clear skies for a change! The wind and the rain we've had for the past couple of weeks is gone and we have at least one day of respite, thankfully. I have some news, Bill!"

The words had an effect like a triple espresso being injected directly into Bill's brain.

"Let me get to my office, Alex, it's quieter there, and Elaine can continue watching 'Good Morning America.'" Bill ran into his office.

"Okay, Alex, I'm all ears!"

"I talked with two chaps at the Hereford SAS HQ who were both members of my unit back in 2003 and are still active duty today. They agreed to do some digging around for me on the QT and they found some interesting stuff.

"There were six hundred and thirty-six members of the joint Special Forces operation in the Iraqi desert in 2003. Over four hundred were American, one hundred and eighty-two Brits and the remainder were a mix of Australians and Polish. There was one team of six that made a particular name for themselves, taking out eight potential scud site installations and engaging with the enemy in six firefights.

"This team of six was nicknamed *The Spirit Riders*. It was made up of four Americans, a Brit and an Aussie. The Brit's name is Martin Peters and he is now retired from the service and lives in Leeds. The Aussie was Carl Conrad from Ballarat, Victoria in Australia, and the four Americans were Joe Nichol, Jimmy Martinelli, Mike Muguara and Raul Hernandez.

"As it happens there was only one man named Raul Hernandez in the entire operation in the Iraqi desert, so this might be the Raul Hernandez you're looking for, Bill."

Alex Forbes-Hamilton paused to let Bill process all of this. "Incredible!"

This one word was all that Bill could think of, astounded that he might have now actually confirmed the identity of the body found at Whispering Hollow; however, his elation was short lived.

"There is a piece of bad news, however, Bill. Raul Hernandez and Jimmy Martinelli were both killed before the desert operation was concluded. They were exploring a disused culvert when they tripped an IED. They died instantly."

Bill almost threw up. His gut tightened and his head pounded.

"Damn, I thought I had him!"

"Thanks for doing this, Alex, and thank your colleagues for sticking their necks out. I know that they took a risk in getting this info, so I do owe you *and them* on this one. Don't really know where to go from here now. I'll just have to think on it a bit."

"You might want to try Special Operations Command Europe. They're located in Stuttgart, Germany. That was the center of operations for the American contingent that took part in the Iraqi Desert campaign. I can also give you the contact details for Martin Peters. I talked with him and as a favor to me he agreed to talk with you if you wish."

"Thanks, Alex. I wish you and your family a Merry Christmas and a Happy New Year, and the next time I'm back in Scotland I'll give you a head's up and dinner is on me."

~

"Long face, honey," said Elaine as she saw Bill walk into the kitchen after his call with Alex. "A bacon butty will cheer you up!"

Bill couldn't resist, as the entire kitchen smelled of grilled Irish bacon, Bill's favorite. Elaine had found a local source in Austin and it was a breakfast treat for them every so often. It was a godsend that morning, and Bill grabbed another coffee and had his first mouthful of breakfast roll and bacon with HP sauce, the British equivalent of A1 steak sauce. He felt a hundred times better.

He stared out over his backyard as the morning fog was beginning to clear, wishing he could find a way for the fog to clear on the Burning Cross investigation.

~

"Martin Peters."

Bill had sent an email to the retired SAS commando to set up a time for the phone call and referenced the discussion with Alex Forbes-Hamilton. Martin Peters answered in his thick Yorkshire accent.

"Thanks for agreeing to the call, Martin!"

"Aye, that's all right, how do you know Colonel Forbes-Hamilton then?" said Martin.

This was a man who wasn't going to worry too much about the social graces; he was right in Bill's face from the off.

"It's a long story," replied Bill. "I found the two boys who killed his father a few years ago and we've been friends ever since."

"Oh aye, I guess that would do it. Still breathing are they, the two boys?"

"They're locked away for life in Peterhead prison."

"Aye, no doubt they'll get out for good behavior."

It was obvious that Martin didn't approve of Britain's abolishment of the death penalty, and he would have gladly volunteered to save the British taxpayer the cost of keeping the killers incarcerated.

"So what do you want to know about the Iraq stuff then, Bill? It's been a few years ago now and my memories are fading a bit."

"Tell me about *The Spirit Riders*. There were six of you, I understand, four Americans, you and an Aussie. What was it like to be part of that team?"

"Best time o' my life," said Martin and the tone in his voice suggested that he would go back again tomorrow if asked.

"Of all of the operations I was part of over the years, this was by far the best and I was the only Brit. I loved Carl Conrad like a brother, the mad Aussie git. He's back in Ballarat now, retired and taking tourists around the sheep-shearing demonstrations. He's drunk most of the time on Ballarat Bitter, the local beer, and loving life. We keep in contact and send each other a postcard once a year."

"What about the Americans? It must have been devastating when two of them were killed by a land mine."

"Part of the job, mate! We're in the killing business. We want to kill them and they want to kill us. I've seen many boys cop it right there in front of me. If it's your time, then it's your time. Can't let it affect you too much; the job needs to get done, enough said, end of," replied Martin.

"Did you like the Yanks, Martin?"

"They were just like me and Carl. We all were peas from the same pod. We had similar training, almost identical, to be honest. We respected each other, had shared experiences and, most importantly, didn't get in each other's face. Tough to be the big dog in a small group when you know that any one of the other dogs knows just as much as you do and could kill you in an instant. Tends to level the playing field, no egos, no room for them."

"What was Raul Hernandez like?

"Ah, the silent assassin. He was a little pit bull was Raul Hernandez. He was a rich kid, the son of some bigwig banker in Houston, Texas. He reminded me more of a street fighter like that Mexican César Chávez. He was five-seven, hard as nails and never quit. It would have had to be a bomb that would take him out, doubt he would have lost mano-a-mano. He probably never felt a thing!"

"He was only five foot seven?"

"Yes, he was five-seven. We were all pretty stocky. The tallest was Mike Muguara, and he was six-one."

"What happened to him? Is he out of the service now?"

"Don't know, never kept in touch with Buzz. Don't know where he is, if he is alive or dead. Even if he's dead he'll still be with us!" laughed Martin Peters, showing the first bit of genuine emotion since the call started.

"His nickname was Buzz, why was that, Martin?"

"He wanted to be called that, his choice. He told us that he was a Native American Indian and that his tribe was part of the Comanche. They were called the Penateka and he explained that it meant *honeyeaters* in the Comanche language. So he wanted to be called Buzz, like the bees, I guess it was his little joke."

"Why do you say - *Even if he's is dead he'll still be with us*?"

"It's the same reason we were called *Spirit Riders*. Buzz explained that Muguara meant *Spirit Talker* and he would sit off on his own in the desert at night and stare up into the stars and *talk* with his ancestors. Our team got the reputation that our success in engaging with the enemy and finding the scud missile sites was because Buzz talked to the spirits and they guided us in our work. When other teams would try to wind us up with talk of spirit guidance, Buzz would just smile and walk away. Good man, Buzz!"

"I read about the Native Indians in World War II who communicated with each other using a code based on the Navajo language. I also saw the movie that was made about them called *Wind Talkers*," said Bill.

"Buzz was nothing like that. The only conversation he had in his native language was with dead people, the spirits of his ancestors."

"And Joe Nichol ever hear anything about him?"

"Another pit bull was Joe! He was Scots/Irish from Boston. Haven't kept in touch with him either. He's probably breaking heads in some Irish bar in Boston, and good luck to him."

That was all Bill learned from Martin Peters. He ended the call and there were no niceties at the end, no offer to "call again if you need more information."

Bill concluded that Martin would probably not even take another call. He wanted to be left alone with his memories. He had taken this one call because his ex-commanding officer had made a specific request.

Bill sat back in his home office and stared at the ceiling. There were originally six members of the *Spirit Riders* and two were now dead. One lived in Britain, one in Australia and the other two, who knows? They could be living somewhere in the U.S. or elsewhere or they could be dead also. One of them, a First Nation Native Indian, could have met his demise on a cold night at Whispering Hollow on the shores of Lake Travis.

Chapter 14

It's Mike Muguara

"SO WHY WOULD HE use the name Raul Hernandez?" asked Tommy.

They were all back in the conference room for the morning briefing.

"I don't know, Tommy, it might have been the first name that popped into his head when Martha Goldman asked him for his name, or it might have been pre-planned for some reason that he chose to use the name of a fallen comrade as a cover. Don't know, but we need to find out. I think we should write up on the board *RAUL HERNANDEZ - COVER NAME?*"

"So let's hypothesize that the deceased is this Mike Muguara. We still don't know why he bought new clothes in Houston with cash. Who walks around with $4,000 in cash on them? We've also made no progress on the BMW connection. Any ideas?" said Tommy.

"I think we need to check out the bigwig banker connection that Martin Peters made reference to," said Marie. "He could have been saying he was the son of a banker for effect, but as Martin said there was no room for egos on that team, so why say something like that unless it was true? I can take that one if y'all are in agreement. I have friends in Houston and I can go down there and see if I can find a link."

"Sounds like a good plan, Marie," said Tommy. "So let's write on the board *HOUSTON BANKER?*"

"I need to work on the BMW connection," said Bill. "I need to look at other rental companies. He may not have rented it at all, he may have bought it, and if so, we have no idea how old it is, what model, what color, nothing to go on, really. We need to catch a break or this could end up as another dead end."

"Let me split the work with you on the car rental companies. That sounds like a two-man job dad."

~

While Tommy and Bill went off to try and track down the BMW, Marie accessed the LinkedIn business networking service on the Internet. She started with the "Find People" search and then refined that search by using filters. She keyed in Banking, Investment Banking, Houston, and VP and got twenty-three hits. She started calling.

The first three calls were dead ends. The fourth call was to a Yolanda P. Hernandez, vice president and head of commercial operations for Crocker Bank.

"Ms. Hernandez' office."

"This is Detective Marie Mason of the Travis County Police Department. May I speak with Ms. Hernandez, please?"

"She is in a meeting right now with clients. Is it urgent, Detective Mason, or can she return your call later today?"

"Are you her personal assistant?"

"Yes I am, Detective."

"Then yes, please have her call me back when it's convenient on 512-555-2929. What's your name?"

"My name is Sandra Bell."

"Thank you, Sandra, just have Ms. Hernandez call me when she can."

It was less than fifteen minutes later when Yolanda Hernandez called back.

"Yolanda Hernandez here, is this Detective Marie Mason?"

"Yes this is Marie Mason, and thanks for calling back, Ms. Hernandez."

"My pleasure. How can I help you, Detective?"

"I am working a homicide case here in Austin, Ms. Hernandez, and I'm trying to track down information on a person who may have some connection to the case. May I ask, Ms. Hernandez, to your knowledge, is anyone related to you in the U.S. armed forces?"

There were a few seconds' pause as if Yolanda Hernandez was trying to process the question.

"Our son Raul was in the Marine Corps and died in service to his country back in 2003."

Marie had found the mother of Sargent Raul Hernandez, U.S. Marine Corps Force Recon!

~

"I found him!" announced Marie excitedly as she burst into the office where Bill and Tommy were working together trying to track down the BMW. "Well, more accurately, I found his mother," said Marie, regaining her control.

"Whose mother?" said Tommy, genuinely confused about who she was referring to.

"Raul Hernandez' mother, she is the *bigwig banker*, well, they both are, his parents, that is. She is in commercial banking and her husband, Julian Hernandez, is in investment banking. She said that they would be happy to help in any way."

"Okay, now I understand, that's fantastic, Marie. Our first real break," said Tommy. "We should get down to Houston and interview them both and see what we can learn. Let's try and get down there tomorrow. You and I should make the trip and Bill can continue on with the BMW search. Can you call Ms. Hernandez back right away and arrange a place and time to meet?"

"Will do," said Marie, and she left the office to make the call.

"Do you want me to see if I can get you help on this BMW search, Dad?" said Tommy, concerned that he was leaving Bill with a mountain of research to get done.

"No, I can cope. You'll only be gone a day," responded Bill without looking up from his laptop.

~

Tommy and Marie set off for Houston bright and early the following morning. Yolanda Hernandez had invited them to her home and suggested that if they could get there by ten-thirty then she and her husband would work from home in the morning and be there to meet them.

The Houston rush hour traffic is even worse than Austin, and I10 into downtown Houston is a parking lot from six-thirty until late morning. Luckily the Hernandez home was north of the city in the Woodlands residential neighborhood and Tommy and Marie were able to take FM290 to the Sam Houston Tollway and then North on I145, avoiding I10 completely.

They arrived at the Hernandez home right on schedule. It was not a home, more like a palace, with a large circular drive-way and huge bay windows. It was a clear symbol of the opulent lifestyle enjoyed by two successful financial executives. Yolanda had a buffet breakfast prepared by her staff ready for their arrival.

"Please come in," said the maid as she brought them into the marble foyer. "Right this way. Mr. and Mrs. Hernandez have been expecting you."

~

"Julian Hernandez, and this is my wife, Yolanda," said Julian as he shook Tommy's hand, completely ignoring Marie.

Some things never change, thought Marie.

Tommy introduced Marie.

"Pleased to meet you, Marie," said Yolanda. "Your call yesterday came as a bit of a shock. Please help yourselves to coffee or tea, and there are some breakfast eats. I'm sure you must be hungry after your long drive."

They each took some coffee and a plate from the huge buffet and they all sat around the adjoining dining table that had been prepared for the meeting. Julian had already taken his seat at the head of the table.

"So tell us what this is all about, please," said Julian. "We will help as best we can, and you can rely on our complete fidelity in keeping the discussions we have here today in the strictest confidence."

I guess that's banker speak for we'll keep our mouths shut, thought Marie.

Tommy and Marie laid out for Julian and Yolanda Hernandez all they knew.

"As you can see, we know very little," said Tommy, summing up what he and Marie had just shared with them. "Anything you both can share about Raul would go a long way in helping us build out the picture," he said, providing an opening for them to take over the conversation. To their surprise it was Yolanda who led the way.

"We were immensely proud of Raul," said Yolanda as she began to tear up. "He was not academically bright, but he was a great athlete and an even greater person. He had a great soul. We could not have asked for a better son. He was our only child as due to complications during his birth, I was unable to have any more children."

"It was after football practice one day when he came home and told us that he wanted to join the Marine Corps. There was no talk of any other arm of the military; it was the Marine Corps or nothing. He joined and went through basic training at Paris Island and then Camp Lejeune, North Carolina."

"On completion of basic training he joined the 22nd Marine Expeditionary Unit and was deployed to the Balkans and then Somalia. His first sergeant recommended him for Force Recon. The rest of his career, until he was killed in Iraq in 2003, was in Special Forces."

"I am sure that you have kept many photographs of him, Ms. Hernandez. May we see some of them?" asked Marie as she wiped the tears from her face.

"I can do a little better than a few photographs. Why don't you both follow me."

~

Yolanda and her husband led them upstairs and opened the doors to a huge entertainment room. Filling the walls on one side of the room where hundreds of photographs of young men in military fatigues. The photographs had been taken all over the world. The backdrop in some was palm trees and golden sands and in others the snow sparkled on majestic mountains. Finally, there were several photographs of six men in desert fatigues standing beside what looked like military dune buggies.

"I assume that this is Raul?" said Marie pointing to the young man standing closest to the buggy.

"Yes, that's Raul, and to his immediate right is Mike Muguara. Seated in front are Joe Nichol, Martin Peters, Carl Conrad and Jimmy Martinelli. Jimmy and Raul were killed on the same day. The others made it home safely after the operation was completed."

"Do you know much about Mike Muguara?" asked Tommy.

Yolanda immediately shot a glance at her husband and his lips tightened as he caught her look.

"Mike was Raul's best friend in the world; they were inseparable. Mike took Raul's death very badly and he was granted permission by his commanding officer to escort the casket containing Raul's remains back to the U.S. He was there when Raul was put in the ground and he was first to sprinkle earth over the casket. He asked that he be allowed to stand over the grave for a few minutes before the final blessing from the priest. He said that he wanted to speak to the spirits to ask them to help Raul find his way home. Knowing his devout Indian beliefs, we allowed him to do that."

"Why do you ask about Mike?" said Julian.

"Based on the evidence to date we have a strong suspicion that he is the victim of this horrendous crime, Mr. Hernandez, and having seen the photographs of him here today, I am now convinced that he *is* the deceased," said Tommy.

The look on Julian Hernandez' face suddenly changed. Tommy could feel the anger radiating from the man.

"Detective Ross, I tell you now, do not leave any stone unturned to find the murdering swine who did this! If there is any shortfall in budget to get the needed resources, you can count on me to personally fund that shortfall, you have my word on that. You get these people! You get them, please, detectives, and bring them to justice!"

As they drove back to Austin, Tommy turned to Marie and said, "We're making progress, Marie. It's one step at a time but we're getting there."

Chapter 15

Let's get our ducks in a row

"SOUNDS LIKE YOU HAD a very successful trip to Houston," said Bill as he put down his morning coffee on the desk and hung up his coat in the corner of the office to dry. "It's raining cats and dogs out there. I guess we're lucky though. I saw in the news this morning that Buffalo is expecting seventy inches of snow in the next twenty-four hours. Those cold fronts come straight down from Canada, hit Lake Erie and then dump lake-effect snow everywhere. I was up there a few years ago and got caught in one of those things. Talk about whiteout, it was unbelievable."

"I think we need to get back into the conference room and update the whiteboard with where we're at, what we know and what we suspect. I think there are now multiple parallel lines of inquiry that we need to be running," said Tommy as they headed off to the conference room.

~

"Okay, I'll lead this exercise," said Tommy. "We go through what we have already up on the board and we add other stuff as we go."

1. Motive - No further forward in this.

2. Location - Doesn't make sense. We feel that if we can discover the motive then the location might make sense, but right now the location seems really odd.

3. Identity - We now have a strong suspicion now that the victim is Mike Muguara.

4. Raul Hernandez - We now know for sure that he was not the victim. Why did the person buying the clothes (we are assuming Mike Muguara) use the name of his dead comrade and best friend?

5. The Spirit Riders - We know that two are dead, one lives in the UK, one lives in Australia, and we believe that Mike Muguara is now dead. That leaves one - Joe Nichol. We need to track him down and talk with him to close the loop and to see if he knows anything.

6. Follow the Money - This could be about the development around Whispering Hollow. We have no evidence to suggest this yet, but we should make inquiries to rule this in as motive or rule it out. Check out who is investing, including the Chinese. Let's look for connections.

7. Check out Jimmy Rodriguez and his driver - The leather jacket!

8. Homeless in the Park - We need to visit the Whispering Hollow Park at night and see who is sleeping there and if they saw anything or heard anything.

9. White trucks seen by the Sessions couple leaving the scene.

10. The message found by the body - is there a handwriting clue?

11. The BMW - Still no progress here, we need to close the loop on this.

When they were done with the list Tommy led them through a list of actions and assigned responsibility:

1. Tommy to ask Chief Dunwoody to approach Special Forces Command and see if we can get information on Joe Nichol and Mike Muguara. We need social security numbers, last known address, etc. Suggest to the chief that he might enlist the help of the governor to get this information.

2. Marie will take the "Follow the Money" action. We might be able to get the help of Julian Hernandez on this given his investment banking connections, and/or his wife Yolanda.

3. Bill will take the BMW and the Whispering Hollow park site. Go out there at night and see if there are any homeless people who saw anything.

4. Bill and Tommy will pick up on the information from Special Forces Command if we get it and try to track down Joe Nichol.

5. The Victim - We are assuming that it's Mike Muguara. We are also speculating that he perhaps came into Houston from Europe or Canada given his slip in the clothing store when he ordered in metric sizes. Where did he live? If we find out, we may need to go there and look at his accommodation; there may be clues there. We may get some help in this from Special Forces Command also.

"We also need to deal with Latisha Williams from the Austin *Statesman*. Marie, you get back to her on Monday as promised and set up a meeting for next week. I will come to that meeting with you and ask her for help in working through the lines of inquiry we have in return for her getting an exclusive when we eventually solve this thing," said Tommy.

"For example she may also be helpful in getting us information on the investors behind the development. I would be surprise if she hasn't been digging around in that. I did see an article written by her a few months ago about the Marina project, but I'm sure she's been try to dig up mud to build a story about the other development in addition to the Marina.

"I'm pinning up on the wall beside the whiteboard several photographs that we were given by Yolanda Hernandez to help in our investigation.

"The *Spirit Riders* did great service for our country; let's return the favor. We need to find out who killed one of their own and why.

"Let's get to it!"

Chapter 16

Sixt Car Rental

THE THANKSGIVING HOLIDAY SEASON WAS getting into full swing; most of the people the team needed to talk to were already off to spend time with family or using the holiday to get in a mini-vacation before the madness of Christmas.

Julian and Yolanda were off in the Caribbean somewhere. Governor Shaw was unavailable, although his aides would not share where he was exactly and the Special Forces Command were awaiting confirmation from the governor that the request for personal details of former Special Forces members being made by the Travis County Police Department was indeed crucial to a murder investigation.

Bill and Elaine were looking forward to having Tommy and Claire for Thanksgiving dinner. They had extended an invitation to Marie and Shelly, but they had made previous plans to spend the holiday with Shelly's folks in Corpus Christi. Shelly's mother was still quite frail following her illness earlier in the year, so Shelly decided that the best plan was that she and Marie would travel to Corpus and cook Thanksgiving dinner for Shelly's parents.

~

It was the night before Thanksgiving and Bill had the Thanksgiving turkey all prepared, ready to be smoked in the Green Egg the following day. He had it in a brine mixture ready for its overnight soaking. He would dry it off in the morning and give it a dry rub of spice mixture before smoking it with pecan chips. He had tried different types of wood for smoking the turkey over the years, cherry, apple, mesquite and oak—but he had settled on pecan as the sweetness of the pecan gave the turkey such a great flavor.

With everything prepared, he sat at his home office desk, which was covered with the paperwork from his research on the BMW. He had determined that there were fourteen car rental companies that served the needs of the travelers coming into George Bush International Airport. He had talked with all of them, including Sindhur at Hertz, and had come up empty. Maybe his hunch was wrong and Mike Muguara aka Raul Hernandez had not flown into George Bush and had not rented a BMW from there.

The last rental company he spoke with was SIXT. SIXT is a huge rental car company headquartered in Germany and has been in business since 1911. It's not that well known in the U.S. and expanded into the U.S. market fairly recently, in 2011 to be exact. Their operation in the U.S. is conducted through regional franchises, so when Bill spoke with the management at the George Bush airport location they said they would have to get back to the corporate office in Germany before they could release specific rental contract details.

~

Bill's cell phone rang at seven-thirty on Thanksgiving morning.

"Hello?" said Bill, trying focus and clear his mind from a deep sleep. Who could this possibly be this early?

"Am I speaking with Bill Ross of the Travis County Police Department?" said the man on the line.

Bill detected immediately from the heavily accented but impeccable English that the caller was German, and he put two-and-two together.

"Yes, this is Special Officer Bill Ross."

"Yes, good morning, Officer Ross. Sorry for not addressing you in the proper manner, my error. I am Wolfgang Meier, director in charge of U.S. operations for SIXT Car Rental Company. I am calling you today from our Pullach headquarters in Munich. Is this a good time to talk? I hope it's not too early for you."

Bill wanted to strangle Herr Meier for calling so early on a holiday and also for the little dig at the end *I hope it's not too early for you.* This German knew exactly what time it was. He respected German efficiency, but sometimes they could be a right pain in the ass!

"This is a perfect time, Herr Meier, I am already well into my work for the day. Even if it *is a holiday* here police work must still get done!" Bill lied for effect and wanted to gain some kind of control of the conversation.

"Great, but do please call me Wolfgang, and may I call you Bill? I find it much easier to dispense with these types of formalities and get to the subject at hand."

"That would be fine, Wolfgang. I take it that your employees at the George Bush Airport briefed you on our investigation?"

"They are not our employees, Bill, they are employees of the franchise there. They did brief me, yes, but unfortunately, due to our corporate governance procedure, I need your request in writing and on Travis County Police Department letterhead. In the written document you must have the following information:

1. Your name and rank.

2. The name and rank of your immediate superior.

3. The nature of your investigation, including relevant case number identifiers.

4. The level of urgency of your request.

5. The name of the person you believed rented our vehicle.

6. The date you believe that the rental was made - the date of pickup.

7. You must sign the document.

8. Your superior must countersign the document.

"You can fax this to my attention. I will give you my contact details at the end of the call. Or you can send the document as an email attachment. Either way you must mail the original to me and I will countersign and send it back to you for your records and I will retain a copy for our records. I will provide you with a written response that will detail the results of our search. I will be happy to email that as an attachment, but we must exchange originals in the same manner as we have just discussed. Is this satisfactory to you, Bill?"

Bill could see a mental picture of Wolfgang Meier sitting back in his chair with a smile, fully expecting that Bill was impressed by his efficiency. It *was* efficient and Bill *was* impressed but he was always frustrated by the lack of flexibility in process when dealing with the Germans. They always got the job done and it was always done well, it just took *so* long.

"Yes, that's satisfactory, Wolfgang, I will get right on it and get you the document you need. Thanks so much for your help!"

They exchanged contact details and the conversation ended.

~

Well, that was an interesting wake-up call, thought Bill as he brewed a fresh pot of coffee and looked out his kitchen window over the greenbelt.

He sat down at the breakfast table and started to surf the web to see what was going on in the world. The CNN, Fox News and USA Today websites were still dominated by the immigration discussion. The battle lines were now clearly drawn between the president and the legislature on the topic. There was complete polarization in opinion on both sides, and from Bill's point of view both sides of the political divide were making good arguments. Bill likened the situation to the war on drugs. To really change what was happening, the demand side had to be dealt with. If employers continued to hire illegal immigrants, then they would continue to come over the border in great numbers. Yes, we needed to secure our borders—he agreed with the argument on that—but human beings are very creative and if the attraction of a better life for their family is there and employers continue to hire, the illegals will find a way to get here.

He wasn't going to solve the immigration problem on Thanksgiving morning; there were more important issues to be dealt with. He needed to get the charcoal fired up in the Green Egg and he needed to rinse the turkey after its overnight bath in the brine mixture and get the dry rub massaged into the bird. It was a beautiful crisp morning in Austin as he walked out onto his deck.

~

As is the custom every year, on Thanksgiving there was a full schedule of football. Bill was looking forward to putting his feet up later in the day with Tommy and drinking a few beers while enjoying the games. He had found Belhaven beer at World Market in Austin and bought a six-pack. Tommy would drink Corona and probably bring over a bottle of the Del Maguey Single Village Mezcal that he had developed a taste for. There would be no concern about Tommy driving home under the influence, which he never did anyway; Tommy had decided that he and Claire would spend the night. It would be a great day.

When Tommy and Claire arrived, the Bears/Detroit game was already underway and the house smelled of the smoke from the pecan wood combined with the scent of sweet potato roasting in the oven. Elaine had already set the table in readiness for the feast and was busy preparing the sticky toffee pudding that she planned to serve for dessert.

Bill pulled Tommy aside as Claire ran to Elaine to give Mimi a hug.

"I got an interesting wake-up call this morning. The corporate guy from SIXT car rental called me from Germany, and I have to get him the information we need in writing before he will make a search in their database to see if Raul Hernandez rented a BMW from them. As my immediate boss, you need to sign the document, Tommy, and I thought that while Mom sat with Claire after dinner today we might go into my office and get the document completed and emailed to SIXT."

"We can do that, Dad, but we better get it done before we settle down with a few beers!" laughed Tommy.

~

The day turned out as planned. The turkey was fabulous. The fixings included—sweet potatoes, roast potatoes, Brussels sprouts and carrots—were delicious. It was a meal fit for a king. Sticky toffee pudding with ice cream followed, and after they had eaten their fill and the dirty dishes were cleared and loaded into the dishwasher, everyone collapsed on the couch.

While Elaine sat with Claire, showing her how to make little miniature candy canes using red and white beads and wire to hang on the Christmas tree, Tommy and Bill went off to the office to get the document prepared and sent to Wolfgang Meier at SIXT.

With mission accomplished and the document on its way, the Ross family enjoyed the remainder of the day.

While Claire slept, Tommy talked about his plans for Christmas. It was tough being a single parent balancing work demands and the needs of a four-year-old. Elaine helped out, of course, picking Claire up from daycare in the evening and feeding her dinner if Tommy was delayed at the office. Without the help from his mother it would have been impossible for Tommy to have a job with such long hours.

"I plan to order all of the Christmas presents for Claire online from Amazon," said Tommy. "Can I have them delivered here? I can wrap them and get them hidden in our house for her to open on Christmas morning."

"Of course you can," said Elaine. "I can help you with the wrapping; you can just pick the Christmas paper you want and I can help you get it done."

Elaine and Bill planned to be at Tommy's house on Christmas Eve and to bring all of the wrapped presents. In the Ross family tradition, they planned to open one present each before Santa arrived. It was a good plan and everyone in the family needed to play their part. This year was to see a change in the process, however.

"Dad has probably told you by now, Mom, that I have been taking Claire to church. I decided to do that a few months ago as I needed to get out and meet new people, and I thought church would be a good place to start and that Claire might enjoy the experience. We are attending the Cedar Park Methodist Church that is just a few blocks from where we live. They are great people. I plan to take Claire to church on Christmas Eve and then be home and let her open one present before she goes to bed. I know it is a little change in the family Christmas routine."

"I think this is great, Tommy. It will be good for you and for Claire. Dad and I will bring the presents over to your place while you're at church, hide them and then wait for you and Claire to come back from church."

"Thanks, Mom, that sounds like a great plan."

Later that night as he lay in bed, Bill Ross, reflected that life couldn't get much better, and sleep came fast, as did the Glenmorangie fuelled dreams.

He was there in the Iraqi desert riding in a dune buggy looking for scud missile sites. He had on his blue and white Kilmarnock FC soccer shirt. Mike Muguara and Raul Hernandez walked over to him and said, "Glad to have you on our team Bill." He was part of the *Spirit Riders,* and they drove off into the desert as the sun sank over the horizon.

Chapter 17

Geist Reiter GmbH

MARIE MASON CALLED LATISHA WILLIAMS on Monday morning as agreed. Latisha suggested that they meet at Oil Can Harry's, a bar on 4th Street in Austin, on Monday night after work. The bar is known by locals to be friendly to those with an alternative lifestyle, and Marie was a little concerned that Tommy might be less than comfortable in this setting; however, she agreed to the meeting location that Latisha suggested.

Wolfgang Meier of SIXT sent an email to Bill, acknowledging receipt of the document and that it was satisfactory to allow him to instruct his team to carry out the search on the rental records. He hoped that he could have the results of the search emailed to Bill by end of the business day on Monday.

Germany is seven hours ahead of U.S. Central Time. On Monday morning, as if on cue, an email with a pdf attachment popped up on the screen of Bill's laptop at precisely 10 a.m. Central. It was the end of the business day in Germany.

~

For a few seconds Bill just stared at the email.

"Please let this be the breakthrough we need," he said to himself, and then he clicked on the pdf file attachment and it popped open on his screen. He read the first few sentences and his mouth fell open in total amazement. This was not just a breakthrough; this was a megalithic explosion. The information contained in the email could blow the case wide open!

Dear Bill,

My team has determined the following information from our database and I hope that it will be helpful to you in your investigations.

A Raul Hernandez did rent a BMW 3 Series from our location at George Bush International Airport at three-thirty pm on the afternoon of October 22nd 2013. It was a black vehicle with black interior and representatives of our franchise recovered it January 21st 2014, after an alert was received from the Travis County Police Department's office that it had been abandoned in a parking lot at 6047 North Lamar Boulevard, Austin, Texas.

According to our records Raul Hernandez rented a BMW from this location three times in the previous twelve months, this being the third time, and that on the two previous occasions he had the vehicle for a three-week rental period. Also in the most recent rental, prior to the car being discovered abandoned, the odometer indicated that the car had been driven an average of 164 miles per day for a total of 3444 miles, somewhat excessive for our typical rentals.

We chose to ignore this excessive mileage in this case as the renter is employed by a corporate client and the average of all rentals over the four years that the SIXT company has supplied this client with cars is well within the average miles per day we contracted for.

The name of the corporate client is Geist Reiter GmbH, PO Box 1274, Ladenburger Strasse 17, 69116 Heidelberg, Germany. There are five registered employees who can rent vehicles under the contract:

Mike Muguara, President and CEO
Raul Hernandez
James Martinelli
Joe Nichol
Claudette Weiss

I trust that this is the information you need and as we discussed please sign and send back to my attention, formal acknowledgement of receipt.

If I can help further, I am at your service.

Sincerely,

85

Wolfgang F Meier
Senior Vice President North America Operations
SIXT Car Rental

~

"Tommy, Marie, we need to meet in the conference room right now!" Bill yelled across the room like someone who had just won the Texas Lottery.

~

Bill raced ahead of them, a copy of the pdf attachment in his hand. He threw open the conference room door and stood at the end of the table as Marie and Tommy sat down and stared up at him.

"Okay, Dad, tell us what you have!" said Tommy.

"Geist Reiter!" said Bill Ross, hardly able to contain himself and shaking the copy of the pdf in his hand.

"Geist Reiter is German for *Spirit Rider*! Raul Hernandez rented the BMW from SIXT Car Rental and, not only that, Geist Reiter GmbH, the company that paid for the rental, employs him.

"And there's more. SIXT has five approved drivers as part of their contract with Geist Reiter. One is an unknown woman by the name of Claudette Weiss, and then they list Joe Nichol, another member of the *Spirit Riders,* who, according to Martin Peters, is 'busting heads in Boston'!

"We need to track down Joe Nichol and we need to get the information from Special Forces Command to help us do that. Tommy, can you speak with the chief, bring him up to speed on what we now know and have him brief Governor Shaw on the need for us to get this information as soon as possible?

"We also need to get over to Heidelberg and, of course, we need to get the chief to approve that. My guess is that if we can get access to the Geist Reiter offices or, even better, to Mike Muguara's residence, wherever that is, we may find additional valuable information. We can now work on the hypothesis that Mike Muguara used the Raul Hernandez name to rent the car and he has been to the U.S. three times in the last year. Why? Also, Jimmy Martinelli is listed as an employee. Why?"

Tommy jumped in, "Okay, Dad. This is the breakthrough we have been looking for, but we need to slow down. The chief will have a tough time approving a trip to Germany, I know that for sure. So we need to step him through the evidence we now have and let him conclude for himself that a trip is necessary. You and I will work these lines of inquiry while Marie continues with her research into the funding behind the construction going on around Whispering Hollow. She and I are scheduled to meet with Latisha Williams tonight, and we need to keep her under control. I will go and brief the chief now. I will also ask that he follows up with the governor regarding the information we need from Special Forces Command. This is fabulous dad; I'll get back ASAP after I speak with the chief."

Tommy left to go off and speak with Bill Dunwoody.

~

"Wolfgang, Bill Ross here!"

"Good day, Bill, I trust that the information I sent was helpful," said Wolfgang.

He knew full well that the probability was that the information was indeed helpful. He was asking the question in this way so that he might enjoy accolades from the recipient, and he was not disappointed.

"It was incredibly helpful, Wolfgang, please thank your team from me for their diligent efforts—most efficient!" said Bill, knowing that Wolfgang would be positively glowing at this endorsement.

"Would it be possible to get some additional information regarding the rental history for the employees of Geist Reiter?" asked Bill.

"Of course, Bill, it was Horst Fleischer who did the research and he happens to be in the conference room next to my office here with some other colleagues. Let me ask him to join us and to bring his laptop."

Wolfgang went off to get Horst.

"Bill, I have my colleague Horst Fleischer with me here in my room, please ask what you need and we will do our best to answer."

"Good to meet you, Horst and thank you for your help in this investigation. What I need is a list of the rental activity for the five employees of Geist Reiter over the past twelve months."

"I can pull that up here from our database, Herr Ross, and I can give you some information verbally and then send you an excerpt report. Would that be satisfactory?"

"Perfect!"

"Yes, I have it here, Herr Ross."

"Claudette Weiss - She has a car rented from SIXT on a monthly recurring rental here in Germany. She is obligated to bring it in each month and exchange for a new vehicle so we can control the mileage. She only rents in Germany.

"Mike Muguara - He rents only in Germany. His preferred automobile is the BMW, but he does exchange for less-expensive vehicles when he travels to certain eastern European countries where BMW models are frequently stolen.

"Joe Nichol - Very little rental activity, nothing in Germany, one rental in the U.S. in the past twelve months.

"Raul Hernandez - No rentals in Germany, all rentals in the U.S. You have the list of his rentals that I provided in my previous report.

"James Martinelli - No rentals in Germany. Many rentals in the last twelve months in the U.S. I list here sixteen rentals.

"As I said, Herr Ross, I can send you the report extract in the next hour. Is there anything else I can help with at this time? The colleagues are waiting for me in my previous meeting," said Horst, concerned that his colleagues would now be agitated at the unplanned delay in their meeting.

"This again is incredibly helpful, Horst. Just two additional questions, if I may, and then you must get back to your previous meeting. The Raul Hernandez rentals, were they all from the Houston location? And the James Martinelli rentals, were they all from the same location, and if so where?"

"Yes, Raul Hernandez rented BMW 3 Series and only from the George Bush International Airport. James Martinelli always rented Cadillac SUVs. He had six rentals from Logan Airport in Boston, four from Chicago O'Hare Airport, two from Los Angeles Airport LAX, two from San Francisco Airport and two from New York JFK. All of the rentals were short duration and not flagged in our system as excessive, with one exception. There was a rental from our Boston Logan Airport location on October 18th 2013, returned October 26th with a total of 4010 miles driven."

"That's super, Horst, this is all I need. Please do send me the report and, again, thanks for your help."

Horst Fleischer returned to his meeting.

"Please acknowledge receipt of the report, Bill, by signing it and sending a copy back to us," said Wolfgang Meier, ensuring that proper standard governance procedure was followed.

"Will do, Wolfgang, and many thanks," said Bill as he hung up the phone.

~

We have two dead men driving rental cars all over the USA, thought Bill as he sat at his desk digesting all that he had learned in the past few hours.

"What is going on here?" he mumbled. He remembered what Horst had said about the Jimmy Martinelli rentals; almost half were from Logan Airport in Boston. *Joe Nichol is busting heads in Boston. I wonder if that's all he's doing,* thought Bill.

~

Tommy arrived back from his meeting with the chief, interrupting Bill and his thoughts.

"It's a no-go on Heidelberg, Dad. The chief is very impressed with our progress, but he doesn't have budget for a jaunt to Deutschland. I told him about Julian Hernandez's offer to fund any budget shortfall and he said that if we could get Julian to pick up the tab for the trip then it was okay by him. We would need to understand the protocol for working with

German law enforcement, but let's take one step at a time and get the green light from Julian Hernandez first.

"I'll go check with Marie and see where she is on the research on the investment behind the Whispering Hollow construction program. I think she was reaching out to Julian for help on that so she could ask him about funding the trip."

~

Marie was busy at her desktop computer, making notes furiously as she went.

"This is a real can of worms!" said Marie, looking up as Tommy walked up to her desk. "I don't know where I would have been without the help of Julian and Yolanda. They are both in the financial business sector and Julian is an expert in corporate investment, but even he is struggling with the complexities of this investment consortium."

"We have the meeting with Latisha Williams tonight, "said Tommy. Let's see what she can bring to the table. We can compare notes and see what she discovered when she did the editorial piece on the marina some months back. We don't need to tell her about everything we have, but tell her just enough to wet her appetite and see what she knows and, more importantly, what she could go find out for us. All of this construction and development must have gotten approvals through the various planning authorities. I'm sure that they must have been salivating about the revenue potential. There must be records on all of this at the local and regional level. This is a huge project and some politicians must be taking the credit for making all of this happen. Let's look under all of the rocks.

"I need you to call Julian Hernandez and ask if he was serious about funding budget shortfall. The chief doesn't have budget to fund a trip to Germany for Bill, so let's see if Julian will help."

Marie agreed that she would make the call.

Chapter 18

Venture Point Holdings

LATISHA WILLIAMS WAS STANDING AT the bar ordering a drink when Marie and Tommy walked into Oil Can Harry's. A Monday is generally a quiet night in this Austin icon for those with an alternative lifestyle, and the Monday after the Thanksgiving weekend was even quieter than normal. This was perhaps why Latisha had suggested that they meet there, or perhaps she just liked the décor.

There was a poster adjacent to the bar advertising "Drag Survivor" every Wednesday and another pitching "Stripper Circus - The Dirtiest Show on Earth" on Thursdays. Tommy was really glad it was Monday.

The Williams family was from Mississippi. Latisha had grown up in Jackson, the state capitol, and she had attended Mississippi University. She graduated with honors from the Meek School of Journalism and was now a nationally renowned crime reporter with the Austin *Statesman* newspaper. Her father and mother lived in New Orleans, where her father Leroy H. Williams sat on the city council.

~

"Hi, Marie, haven't seen you in quite some time, how's Shelly?" said Latisha in her dark, sultry southern voice.

"She's good, Latisha, how've you been? I see you still get enjoyment poking the badger. Someday you'll upset the wrong people, or perhaps that's what really turns you on," replied Marie.

"Good to see you too, Marie, you haven't changed a bit," laughed Latisha. "I take it this this is the great Detective Tommy Ross that I've been hearing so much about. Good to meet you, Tommy."

Tommy and Marie ordered a couple of Lone Star long necks and followed Latisha to a table in a quiet corner that she had obviously chosen in advance of their arrival.

"So you suggested that we meet, so here I am and I'm all ears. So what's really going on over at Whispering Hollow," said Latisha not wasting any time.

Tommy took it from there.

"I am sure that you've done your homework, Latisha, and you know that earlier this year there was a body of a man found at Whispering Hollow. It was reported that it was a homeless person who had accidently burned to death when setting a fire to keep warm."

"Yes, I remember that, not exactly going to make CNN. Wolf Blitzer is not flying into Bergstrom any time soon," said Latisha, getting a little bored with the preamble.

"So as you guessed it there is more to this story than meets the eye, but we're not going to share it all with you unless we get your agreement to stay quiet for now. If you do, we would also like to enlist your help as we think that you may have information that could be useful. We also think that you're good at what you do, and working together we might be able to solve this. If you do this and give us your word to stay quiet for now, then we'll give you the exclusive when we eventually get all the pieces of the puzzle to fit. It could be big, Latisha, and you would have it all to yourself."

Tommy paused to allow Latisha to take it all in.

"What if I just say yes and then go run with the story to-morrow anyway?" said Latisha with a grin.

"Then I would spread the word on what you did and you would be finished in Austin. I would make sure that everyone was told and your sources in the Austin Police Department and elsewhere would dry up," said Tommy.

The grin was suddenly gone from Latisha's face.

"Well, I guess I have no choice then. You have my word. *Now spill the beans!* What's going on, what do you think I know and how do you think I can help?

~

Latisha was on board! Tommy brought her up to speed on where they were in the investigation and the fact that they thought it might be linked to the huge construction project in some way.

Latisha sat for a few minutes digesting all that she had heard. Her brain was wired to look for conspiracy in almost everything. That's what made her such a good reporter and helped to earn her the Rottweiler reputation and be voted as one of the most influential black female voices in America. She was not about to share completely what she knew about the marina project; she needed these two detectives to talk more, so she started a conversation to dig into the detail a little more.

"It's a big leap from a dead homeless guy to a murder connected to a regional development project. What evidence do you have to suggest that there might be a connection?" Latisha had stuck the shovel in the ground, now she wanted to see if they started digging. Tommy picked up the shovel.

"You are right, Latisha; however, good detective work starts with gathering facts and then trying to organize them into an overall pattern. Most times it involves looking for the parts that don't fit a given situation and asking the question, why? We are not saying that it's linked to the construction project. However, the killing did take place right in the center of everything that is going on over there at Whispering Hollow. We have many whys here that need to be examined:

1. Why try to make the murder looking like a lynching?

2. Why choose that spot miles from main highways?

3. Why cut the dead man's hands off?

These whys then lead us to speculation:

1. The "lynching" plot was designed to set us off in the wrong direction right from the start.

2. The wording on the "message" was not written by rednecks looking to kill wetbacks.

3. Eyewitnesses had suggested that white trucks were seen leaving the scene after the fire was set.

4. We have seen lots of white trucks in the area involved with the construction work.

"Marie and I discussed this with the third member of our team, my father, Bill Ross, who has had many years of experience working homicides in the UK. He was instrumental in helping us solve the Luther Fisher case a few months back. His speculation is that this might be another example of "hiding in plain sight."

The murder took place in such a remote area as Whispering Hollow for a reason, and that reason was not a lynching of some poor vagrant or wetback. It was because the killers *lived in the neighborhood.* They drove white trucks around all the time. No one would think anything suspicious, and when the deed was done they would simply fade into the background and return home at the end of another day's work."

"I see," said Latisha, leaning back in her chair, feeling rather proud of her plan. She had let them tell her perhaps more than they wanted to tell her at this stage.

This could be something big! she thought to herself. She needed to decide if she wanted to go all in with these detectives, tell them what she knew and then continue to work with them as they had suggested, and see if this did lead to something big. She decided to go all in.

~

"I wrote an editorial piece a couple of months ago around the plan for a new marina in the Whispering Hollow area. The marina is actually planned in the Venture Point neighborhood that is adjacent to Whispering Hollow. The reason I wrote the piece was not about the marina per se; it was about the rapid transit rail link extension that's planned as part of the marina development. What was planned did not make a lot of sense to me and the proposal was that it would be a private development not funded by issuing a bond that taxpayers would have to fund. That made me even more suspicious."

"Austin is exploding as *the* place to be in the U.S. There has always been a great music scene here and the South by Southwest annual music and film event is now huge and has been expanded to include a Technology Summit with VCs with deep pockets coming in to town looking for the next big thing.

Then there is the Circuit of the Americas. This world-class racing circuit is now the home of the U.S. Formula One Grand Prix. A once-a-year event that attracts some of the richest people in the world to flock to the city.

"As you can imagine, in the years ahead the entire infrastructure of the city and the surrounding area will be stretched to breaking point by this explosion of activity. There are major opportunities for private companies to invest and the profit potential is off the charts. Where there is money to be made in this type of scale there is always the opportunity for corruption. I smelled a rat with the proposal for a private rail line to a new marina out in the middle of nowhere. That was the starting point for my editorial piece."

There was more she could share with them on the work she had done but she chose to hold that back until she understood what "working together" meant.

~

"So how do you propose that we work together, Tommy?"

"I propose that you and Marie work on building on what you have uncovered about the rail link and the marina. Marie can share with you what she has done in trying to get to the bottom of the funding for all of this development work, including the marina and the rail link. We can then see where all of this might lead," replied Tommy.

Working closely with Marie, now that sounds good, thought Latisha. *Not sure that Shelly will be thrilled about that!*

"Marie, why don't you bring Latisha up to speed on the work you have done on this to date."

"I have enlisted the help of an investment banker from Houston. No need to go into why he is assisting us right now—I can share that with you later. But suffice to say he has been a great help."

"All of the land in the area of Whispering Hollow and Venture Point plus the surrounding area to Cedar Park in the south and to Lago Vista to the north was originally part of the huge McMullen ranch. Garrison McMullen started selling off pieces for residential and commercial development some years ago, but he still owns the majority of what was the original ranch land and he also retains mineral rights for the pieces he sold off.

"Venture Point Holdings (VPH) was formed in 2008. VPH consists of several components: The Venture Point Investment Fund, Deng Tang Corporation, Robertson Richards LLC and Rodriguez Holdings. The chairman and largest stockholder of VPH is Garrison McMullen, and the vice-chairman and second largest stockholder is Enrique Escobar Rodriguez, owner of the third largest ranch in Texas, the Colinas Verde ranch on the Mexican border just north of Laredo.

"We have discovered in our research that VPH operates like a closed cartel. VPH owns smaller so-called independent contracting companies. These companies provide products and services for all of the construction and development work being undertaken by VPH. These products and services include electrical trades, plumbing trades, timber supplies, cement, roofing materials, and everything needed for internal finishing, including appliances, kitchen and bathroom fixtures, lighting and all painting and decorating trades. These firms "compete" for contract awards with other firms not owned by VPH, but eighty percent of the time the winning bid is a VPH-owned company.

"Rodriguez Trucking provides all transportation in the U.S. International shipping of appliances and other products from China is provided by Deng Tang Shipping Lines. Deng

Tang is a huge conglomerate in China; they not only own ocean freight operations, they also manufacture the products they ship to the U.S., and they own and operate residential complexes, casinos and golf courses to cater to the needs of a rapidly growing middle class in Asia."

"So you can see, Latisha, there could be a huge story here, and my guess is that we haven't even scratched the surface yet," said Tommy. "Our interest is finding the killer or killers. You can have the story to take in whatever direction you see fit. You and Marie working together could get to the bottom of this, I feel sure! "Do we have a deal?" said Tommy, making sure that he kept solid eye contact with Latisha till she gave her answer.

"Deal!" said Latisha.

Chapter 19

Heidelberg

WITHOUT HESITATION, JULIAN HERNANDEZ agreed to pay for Bill's trip to Germany. "Call my assistant and tell her what you need. She can help make your travel arrangements and charge it to my personal account."

Before any travel arrangements could be made, they needed to reach out to the relevant German law enforcement agencies and brief them on the case and the need to be on their turf to further the investigation.

Located in the southwest of Germany, east of the Upper Rhine, Baden-Württemberg is Germany's third largest state with 10.7 million inhabitants. Most of the major cities of Baden-Württemberg straddle the banks of the Neckar River, which runs through the state. These cities include Stuttgart (the capital), Heilbronn, Heidelberg, Mannheim and Karlsruhe.

The Baden-Württemberg Police is the state law enforcement agency with approximately 25,000 officers and 7,000 civilian employees. The responsibility for law enforcement in Heidelberg falls under the regional command located in Karlsruhe.

To get permission to pursue the case and to interview German citizens, proper permissions had to be received via the office of Herr Gunter Fassbinder, the Regional Police Commissioner in Karlsruhe.

It took Bill Ross a week to get these permissions in place and to coordinate with the Karlsruhe and Heidelberg police and to make arrangements to meet with Claudette Weiss in Heidelberg. It was made clear that Miss Weiss was not a suspect and that the reason for the trip was simply to gather as much background as possible on Mike Muguara and his company, Geist Reiter GmbH.

With all the needed authorizations and paperwork in place, Bill flew out of Houston to Frankfurt on United Airlines flight UA8867. Julian Hernandez had approved a business class ticket, so Bill was able to stretch out on the sleeper seat and get some shuteye for the ten-hour flight.

The Airbus touched down in Frankfurt thirty minutes ahead of schedule at 8 a.m. local time. Bill could see the snow being blown across the runway as the wide-body jet negotiated its way to Gate16A at terminal one. He shivered in anticipation of the cold weather he knew he would have to endure in his few days in Germany, but also with the excitement of the chase. What mysteries would he uncover about the life of Mike Muguara, and would it bring him any closer to finding his killers? Only time would tell.

For even the most seasoned traveler, a ten-hour overnight international flight is exhausting. Bill navigated his way through the river of humanity in the airport terminal as multiple wide-bodies disgorged their contents in the early hours of the morning. It got worse when he hit the lines for immigration control. What appeared to be thousands of people were moving through the control barriers left and then right, single file, weaving their way ever closer to the uniformed border control agent to present their paperwork and hopefully gain entry to the country without further delay.

Bill had some advantage over most others that morning; he was a business class traveler and could therefore access the shorter lines for preferred travelers. He looked on with genuine pity at the families with young children enduring the economy class lines. He guessed that they could be in line for hours, their kids tired and hungry, with no understanding or appreciation for the delay.

And then it was over. He emerged from the customs hall with his luggage and he saw the sign immediately: "HERR ROSS," held high by a young police officer in his light blue uniform and white-topped hat. He had obviously drawn the short straw to be the one to drive to Frankfurt that cold December morning to pick up a Texas police officer. Who knows what this young man expected to see, and Bill was tempted to joke about needing to pick up his horse and saddle from the oversized luggage area, but thought better of it.

"Herr Ross, my name is Officer Hartmann, pleased to meet you. Is this all of your luggage? We have a short walk to the car. Would you like to take a coffee and perhaps a croissant to enjoy on the drive to Heidelberg? It should only take 30-40 minutes," said the young, nervous officer.

Bill declined the kind offer of coffee and climbed into the back of the Mercedes police car with its light blue and silver livery. A few minutes later on the 5 Autobahn South to Heidelberg, Bill was glad he had made the decision to pass on the coffee. The young officer was in the fast lane doing 160 kilometers per hour. Bill's knuckles were the color of the falling snow as he hung on for dear life in the backseat, squeezing his eyes closed for extended periods, almost terrified to open them again.

~

They made it safely to Heidelberg and Officer Hartmann helped Bill get checked into the Crown Plaza in the center of the city. Bill's legs were still shaking from the terror of the high-speed drive as he provided the young desk clerk with his identification. On completion of the check-in process, Officer Hartmann considered his duties to be successfully completed. He shook Bill's hand, wished him a pleasant stay and clicked his heels. He then saluted and was gone in an instant.

The Crown Plaza is the best "American" hotel in the center of Heidelberg. The Old Town is a short walk away as is the main bridge over the river Neckar to the Neuenheim area of the city. Bill would need to take that bridge to get to Ladenburger Strasse where the offices of Geist Reiter GbmH were located and where he had scheduled to meet Claudette Weiss the following morning.

He had a short nap to recover from his travels. Around three in the afternoon he got up, showered and wrapped himself up in coat, scarf and hat and went out for a walk to the old city. He walked along Bismarkplatz and then turned onto Hauptstrasse toward the old town.

~

In December the old town of Heidelberg transforms into a winter wonderland of outdoor markets. It was getting dark and the snow was beginning to fall when Bill reached the main section of the market. There were traders as far as the eye could see lined up one after the other, selling their wares in stalls set up for the season. Each stall was festooned with Christmas lights twinkling in the night sky.

There was every conceivable Christmas ornament and traditional German gingerbread baked goods on sale. The food and drink stalls were packed to overflowing with market-goers having their fill of Gluhwien, a local hot-spiced wine, to keep out the cold and add to the Christmas cheer. Hot steam rose from the cooking and the air was heavy with the smell of grilled bratwurst, onions, hot chocolate and roasted nuts. Children were yelling and carolers were singing. Bill tried to take it all in and he let it engulf him like the warmth from a raging log fire on a cold winter's night. It was perfect. *Welcome to Germany,* he muttered to himself as he smiled and sipped on his Gluhwien.

~

Bill slept well after his Christmas market experience, and he rose early to have breakfast with Erwin Gunst, whose title was Polizeioberkommissar, which roughly translated was a senior inspector role, and Markus Schweible, Kriminalkommissar, a plainclothes detective, similar in rank to Tommy.

After the initial exchange of pleasantries, the three got down to discussing the case and the planned meeting with Claudette Weiss later that morning. Markus was able to bring Bill up to speed on what he knew about Geist Reiter GbmH.

Marcus had done considerable research since his preliminary telephone discussion with Bill the week before.

Mike Muguara had established Geist Reiter five years earlier after leaving the U.S. military. He had been stationed in Stuttgart and had fallen in love with Germany and decided to stay there. He formed a partnership with a German national, Saul Weiss, and his partner, Henri Hoffman. They were joint owners of a company that traded in diamonds. Mike provided security services to Saul and Henri and to other rich business executives who traveled internationally. Saul and Henri had both invested in Geist Reiter, giving Mike the working capital he needed to get his security business rolling. Claudette Weiss was Saul Weiss's granddaughter.

As far as Markus could tell, Mike Muguara would do all the security work personally for executives traveling in Europe. For those traveling to the U.S. he would travel there with them or hand off the assignment to one of his three associates in the U.S. They would be able to find out more when they met with Claudette.

~

When they arrived at the office of Geist Reiter, they found that it shared the same building as the Weiss & Hoffman diamond business. Security to gain access to the building was only marginally easier than getting into the vault at Fort Knox.

It was a four story grey stone building in the oldest part of the town. Bill speculated that it probably had not changed much since WWII. Claudette greeted them as they exited the 1920s era elevator with its metal expanding safety door. She led them into a small conference room where coffee and water awaited their arrival, as did Saul Weiss.

They all shook hands and sat down. Bill felt the tension in the room. Saul Weiss was not a happy camper and it was obvious that he was uncomfortable that there were strangers in his inner sanctum, let alone German and U.S. law enforcement.

"Before we start, may I look at everyone's official credentials. please," said Saul Weiss with a fair degree of controlled aggression in his demeanor.

With their credentials reviewed. Saul continued on. "Do you have positive identification that the deceased is Mike Muguara?"

"We are not one hundred percent," said Bill and it was obvious that this answer did not sit well with Saul. Before Saul could further vent his obvious anger Bill continued, "However, we are better than ninety percent. I would say that only when we can match DNA will we be one hundred percent." This seemed to calm Saul down a bit.

"So, you have come a long way, Officer Ross. How can we be of assistance?"

"We need to try to find out why Mike Muguara was in the USA and why he was using the name of a long-dead military colleague," said Bill.

At that Claudette and Saul Weiss looked at each other, Claudette obviously waiting for her grandfather to give her the okay to talk. Before he did that, the old man looked at the two German police officers and made an opening statement.

"For the benefit of Detective Ross, I will continue to speak in English. Polizeioberkommissar Gunst, this is a murder enquiry, yes? To answer the questions that this U.S. officer may have, I need your assurances that anything we say about our business here today is private and only for the purposes of helping the officer find the killer or killers of my friend and colleague Mike Muguara. You have my assurance that there is nothing we are doing in our business operations that is illegal, but others could construe our processes as being so if they twisted the facts to fit their own ends. Do I have your word that what we discuss here today will be held private between us and not used to prosecute us in any way later?"

There was a long pregnant pause and Bill felt for a moment that no such agreement would be reached. He was both amazed and relieved when Ernie Gunst responded.

"You have my word."

"Good, then let's move on. Go ahead, Claudette, and answer Officer Ross's question," said Saul, now beginning to look a little less agitated.

"The answer to the first part of your question, Officer Ross, is that Mike used the name of Raul Hernandez for two reasons," said Claudette. "One was to stay under the radar in the security work he undertook and the second was for tax purposes that we need not go into here. He would occasionally employ his friend Joe Nichol to help him in larger jobs in the U.S. and Joe would use the alias of Jimmy Martinelli.

"To the second part of your question, why was he in the U.S.? I am not completely sure, as I was not fully informed as to the details of each assignment. Earlier in 2013, after he completed another corporate assignment, Mike had taken a few days off to try to track down his birth parents. His grandparents in Oklahoma had raised him but he promised himself that after leaving the military he would try to find out who he really was.

He had made some progress in the search for his birth parents' identity when he had to return to Germany for another European assignment. A couple of months later he went back to the U.S. to continue his search, and this time when he returned he became very secretive, very distant. Something had changed him. I could tell, Detective, because Mike was not just my employer, he was my lover."

"Oh, I'm so sorry for your loss, Miss Weiss, condolences," said Bill with respect, and his words were not lost on Saul Weiss, who silently nodded his thanks.

"He seemed to be carrying a lot of cash, Claudette, was that usual?"

Again Claudette glanced over at her grandfather and it was he who now spoke.

"He did this, of course, to avoid being traced through credit card transactions. He flew back and forth from here to the U.S. using his own identity and then once in the U.S. he became Raul Hernandez. His role in my business was not only security; he was also a courier for my diamonds, taking them to my brother's operation in Houston. My brother would give him cash that he would then use for his expenses, allowing him to become Raul Hernandez," said Saul.

Bill Ross shot a quick look at the two German policemen and they rolled their eyes, now realizing why Saul Weiss had asked them for the earlier commitment to secrecy.

"Would it be possible to get access to his apartment, Claudette? I'd like to take a look around and see if there is anything that might help with our investigation."

"We lived together in the apartment upstairs, Detective Ross. There is nothing related to the business there. I keep personal items Mike and I bought together, but there is nothing related to the business in the apartment. We were very diligent in keeping the activities of the business out of our personal life.

"Everything related to the business is either on my laptop or his. We were very concerned about data security in our line of work. He used a laptop with a separate removable hard drive for external data storage. We kept nothing on the Cloud, everything on removable hard drives, so if someone stole the laptop there would be nothing on it of any significance. I am happy to take you through my files, but I dealt mostly with finance, not operational matters."

"There is one place that you might want to check out, Officer Ross, and that's a storage unit that Mike kept in Houston. I can give you the address and send an email to the management there that you are authorized for access."

"That would be *very* helpful, Claudette. What did he keep there?"

"Not sure, I didn't ask. I didn't interfere with operational issues and that's why even though I had not heard from him for almost a year, I didn't get too alarmed. He had done this before, being gone without contact for over six months or more at a stretch, and then he would email to tell me he was coming home."

"So what happens to Geist Reiter now?" asked Bill.

It was again Saul who provided the answer.

"The business will be closed down. Mike left very explicit written instructions with me in the event of his death. The business has a little over five million euro in cash and other assets. Twenty percent is to be given to Claudette and the balance is to be paid to a law firm in Oklahoma as a donation to the Penateka tribe. As you probably already know, Detective, Mike Muguara was Comanche Indian.

"One final question for Claudette, if I may," said Bill.

"Do you have the contact details for Joe Nichol?"

"The only way they communicated was via text, email and instant messenger. I can give you that information. I have no phone numbers or a mailing address," said Claudette.

"That will be good, Claudette. Oh, I almost forgot, could I have the name of the law firm in Oklahoma, please? I don't know if it might help but it's another piece of the jigsaw puzzle."

Saul agreed and gave Bill the information he requested. They all shook hands and the meeting ended. Markus and Ernie drove Bill to the Holiday Inn at Frankfurt airport. The following morning Bill flew back to the U.S.

Chapter 20

Joe Nichol

BILL ROSS WAS STILL SUFFERING from jet lag the following morning when they all met again in the conference room to update the white board on what they now knew and to agree on next steps.

"Very successful trip to Heidelberg," said Bill, kicking the meeting off and providing a written report on his trip to Germany.

"Some of the smoke is now clearing on this. We now know that Mike Muguara used the name Raul Hernandez when engaged in security assignments in the U.S. We can say with a fair degree of certainty that the person who bought the clothes from Martha Goldman was Mike Muguara and that he is our victim. We'll not be able to be one hundred percent certain on this until we can match DNA.

"A storage unit was opened a couple of years ago in the name of Raul Hernandez at the U-Haul center by the Greenspoint Mall close by the Houston Airport. Claudette Weiss will contact them and get us clearance to open this unit. She has no idea what the contents might be, as she consistently stressed that she was never involved in operational matters. It will be interesting to see what that storage unit might contain.

"We also have new information that Mike employed his friend and ex-member of the *Spirit Riders*, Joe Nichol, to do occasional security work for him in the U.S. and that when Joe engaged in this work he used the alias of Jimmy Martinelli. We need to track down Joe Nichol and see what he knows, if anything. We have email info for him but nothing else.

"The final piece of information that I found out in Germany and could be relevant is that upon his death he stipulated that most of his financial assets were to go to the Penateka Indian tribe. The financial transaction was to be managed by a law firm in Lawton, Oklahoma named Corbin, Clayton and Anderson. We need to talk with them.

"One other thing. We need to do more work on the BMW; it could still be helpful in providing clues if we could track its movements from the time it was rented from the George Bush Airport until the time it was discovered in a parking lot on Lamar Boulevard.

"That's it from me," said Bill.

"Marie and I met with Latisha Williams. We have her agreement to work with us in return for getting an exclusive to the story when we fit this all together," said Tommy.

"I have contacted Julian Hernandez and he has agreed to help in the research on Venture Point Holdings, the conglomerate behind the development at Whispering Hollow and Venture Point," continued Marie.

"Then there is Jimmy Rodriguez," said Bill. "Let's not forget that piece of work. We need to learn more about his activities and his limo driver, the guy with the Hugo Boss leather jacket."

"I also need to get back to Chief Dunwoody. We still have nothing from Special Forces Command on the service records of Mike Muguara and Joe Nichol. Some of the information might not be needed now, but we still need to track down Joe. We have the email info you brought back from Germany, so I guess that's where we should start."

"Okay, action items," said Tommy getting everyone's attention.

"Dad, you take the Joe Nichol connection and the storage unit in Houston. You can stop by M & J Fine Clothing when you're there and thank Martha from all of us as it was her clue about the shoes and the BMW that really got us rolling on this.

"Marie, you continue your work with Julian Hernandez and ensure that Latisha is focused and is not tempted to do anything dumb.

"I will see if I can get more information on the movements of the BMW and get back out to Whispering Hollow and meet with Jimmy Rodriguez and his driver. He doesn't know me, and I can keep quiet on what we know based on your day of golf with him, Dad. I'll use the 'routine inquiries' mode to try to put him at ease."

"We all have work to do, so let's get to it."

~

Bill Ross was back at his desk and still fighting the jet lag. It was just after lunchtime as he fought to keep his eyes open. He launched an email to Joe Nichol using the information provided by Claudette.

Bill's email read, "My name is Bill Ross. I am an officer with the Travis County Police Department and would like to speak with you about Mike Muguara. I was recently at the Geist Reiter offices in Heidelberg visiting with Claudette Weiss and she gave me your contact info. We believe that Mike Muguara was murdered in Travis County some months ago. Given your relationship with the deceased, we would like to talk with you as soon as possible. Can you provide a telephone number that I can call?"

The reply to the email arrived less than an hour later and it was short and to the point.

"No telephone. You want to talk, come to Boston. The Bootsy Brogan's pub on Kingston Street and ask for Sean O'Driscoll at the bar. He will check your credentials and if it's you, he'll tell you where you can find me."

"I guess I'm off on another road trip," mumbled Bill.

~

Based on the progress being made on the case, Bill Dunwoody approved the trip to Boston, and the following night Bill was on Jet Blue flight 1038 leaving Austin at 6:45 p.m. and arriving at Boston Logan just before midnight. He grabbed a cab and got to his hotel in South Boston about 1 a.m. He was exhausted and fell asleep fully clothed on the top of the bed.

Bootsy Brogan's pub smelled like a mixture of Pine-Sol disinfectant and Pledge wood polish. It had just turned 11 a.m. and the pub had just opened its doors. It was a U.S. version of an Irish bar with dark wood and gleaming brass. Signs for Guinness and Jameson Irish whiskey dominated the walls, and the chalkboard by the bar listed the lunch specials, fish and chips, Irish stew and all-day Irish breakfast. It reminded Bill just a little of the pubs in Scotland and, in particular, a certain area of Glasgow within a stone's throw of Celtic Park—watering holes for the faithful, where tall tales are told and ballads sung.

"Is Sean O'Driscoll around?" said Bill to the attractive young girl behind the bar already pulling pints of Guinness for the regulars.

"Gets in about noon, you'll have a pint while you're waiting, will you?"

Bill guessed that the accent was County Cork but, if not, certainly from south of Dublin.

"Are you from Cork then, Miss?"

"No, I'm from Waterford me'self, and you're not from Boston. My name's Kathleen and your name?"

"My name's Bill Ross and yes I'm not from Boston. I'm originally from Scotland, a town called Kilmarnock on the west coast, just south of Glasgow."

"I know Kilmarnock, I've actually been there once. My sister lives in Ayr and her husband is an Ayr United supporter. We went up to Kilmarnock when Ayr played them in some cup game. What a laugh we had. Great place Kilmarnock."

"Well I never, you've been to Killie. I *will* have that pint, thanks, Kathleen. I'll sit right over there and perhaps you can ask Sean to come join me when he gets in?"

"I'll bring your pint over and tell Sean what you ask. Go sit yourself down," said Kathleen with a smile.

Bill was drawing on the last few drops of his Guinness when Sean O'Driscoll sat down beside him. He had a big round face and red cheeks and looked like he was born to be a bartender in an Irish bar.

"Bill Ross I understand? Do you have something on you that will confirm that?" Bill gave him his ID and he looked at it purposefully before handing it back.

"Pretty good likeness. The guy in the picture is a little younger, but I guess you're him," laughed Sean. "The guy you're looking for is sitting by the bar over there in the corner. We both saw you arrive and we've been watching you for the past hour. Good wee liar is our Kathleen." Again the bartender laughed, got to his feet and walked past the bar to the office beyond.

Bill walked over to the man seated at the bar. He pulled up a stool and sat down next to Joe Nichol. He looked like Billy Connolly in his role as Il Duce in *Boondock Saints*. In front of him was a half-drunk pint of Guinness, standing guard over a smaller glass that Bill guessed contained Jameson.

"Ever try Glenmorangie?" said Bill, looking straight ahead with not even a glance in Joe's direction.

"And why the feck would I do that?" replied Joe Nichol.

Their conversation was off to a good start.

"You sure it's Mike?" said Joe.

"Afraid so."

"How'd he die?"

Bill explained the circumstances as he knew them surrounding the death of Mike Muguara.

"We all have to go sometime, I guess, but that's one hell of a fucked-up way to check out," said Joe.

"You know anything that might help us?"

"Something happened last year when he was over here. He'd been trying to track down his birth parents and he stumbled onto something. He wouldn't tell me about it, just said that he might need my help and that he would be in touch in the normal way if that need arose."

"One question, Joe. On October 18, 2013, you rented a Cadillac SUV using the alias James Martinelli and returned it on October 26th with a total of 4,010 miles driven. What was that all about?"

"Mike wanted me to drop off a package for him at his storage locker in Houston,"

"What was in the package?"

"Certain items that we use in our profession, and I won't talk about any of that. You might want to check out the storage facility; my guess is that you already know where it is. I would like to be kept in the loop regarding your investigation. You can text or email me, now that we've met. If you are open and honest with me then I will help in any way I can. I would like that the killers get what's coming to them sooner rather than later. No need to shake hands or any of that shit. That's all I have for you. If you want to stay and have a few pops that's fine, but no further talk about this."

Joe Nichol had ended the conversation. After a few additional "pops," Bill Ross caught a cab back to Logan Airport for his flight home.

~

While Bill was in Boston, Tommy was on the trail of the BMW. He visited the car park on Lamar Boulevard where the SIXT Car Rental team had picked up the abandoned vehicle. Tommy looked around the parking lot, wondering why Mike Muguara might have been in this vicinity, and saw the Gold's Gym.

"Hi, I'm Detective Tommy Ross with Travis County Police Department. Is the manager around?" said Tommy.

"Let me get him for you."

"Hi, Detective, I'm Alan Archer. How can I help?"

"How long have you been a manager here, Mr. Archer?"

"Almost five years now."

"Do you recognize this man? He may have worked out here, perhaps paid for a short-term membership in cash a year or so ago?"

Alan Archer studied the photograph of Mike Muguara.

"Yes, I believe I do recognize him, Detective Ross, for two reasons. One, he paid three months' cash up front, and also his workout routine. Not many people can run flat out on a treadmill for an hour and then go through a weight routine that some NFL players would have had a tough time with!"

"Would you have any paperwork for him?" asked Bill.

"Give me a name and I'll look and see,"

"Raul Hernandez."

"Raul Hernandez, you say, yes, here it is. He gave an address as the Extended Stay Hotel on Braker Lane by the Capital of Texas Highway."

"His BMW was recovered in the parking lot in January. Do you remember seeing that?" asked Tommy.

"Yes, I do, Detective. Was that Raul Hernandez car? I always wondered who it might have belonged to."

"You've been very helpful, Mr. Archer., Is there anything else you remember, anything at all?"

"Sometimes we get some altercations in the parking lot, Detective. Adrenalin and testosterone is flowing when some of the guys leave the gym. We watch for it since we know it happens a lot. I remember a couple of times some guys got in his face, but he would always completely ignore them except for one night."

"What happened this particular night?" asked Tommy, his sixth sense sending signals that something of significance might be about to appear.

"This black limo was parked in the corner of the lot next to a white pickup and another Ford of some type, I think it might have been a Taurus. There were several guys all talking together and every so often looking over here at folks entering and leaving the gym. When Raul walked out they approached him and a big argument ensued. Right at that moment I was distracted by a problem in the gym. A few minutes later when I got back to the window they were all gone. I never thought any more about it until now."

"I don't suppose you could recognize any of the men again or the license plate of any of the vehicles, including the limo?" asked Tommy, knowing what the answer would be.

"Afraid not, Detective. Now I think of it, the white pickup had a logo on the side of the door. I don't remember what it said but the colors were red and blue. It was the name of some contractor, like electrical or plumbing, I think. If I saw it again, I might recognize it."

"This has been very helpful, Mr. Archer. Here is my business card; if you think of anything else, please call."

~

Tommy left the gym and headed over to the Extended Stay Hotel on Braker Lane. The duty manager was busying himself on the desktop computer when Tommy walked in.

"Detective Tommy Ross, Travis County Police Department. Did you have a guy stay here a year or so ago, name of Raul Hernandez?

"Let me look on the database, Detective," said the tall, black duty manager. "Can you be a little more specific than a year ago, the month perhaps?"

"Try December 2013," said Tommy.

"Yes, we had a Raul Hernandez stayed with us then, paid three months' rent cash up front. Do you have a photograph?"

Tommy gave him the photograph.

"Yes, I recognize him, real nice guy. Military type, I would say, no small talk, all very yes sir, no sir. Toward the end of the three months he never slept here. I tried to call him on the cell number he had given me but the number was no longer in service. When we couldn't locate him we entered the room and looked in the closet. Everything was very orderly, all clothes folded, everything in place. We stored it all for six months in case he came back and then we gave it all to Goodwill."

"Okay thanks, this has been very helpful. Sorry, I didn't get your name."

"My name's Nate Brown," said the young manager, stepping around the desk to shake Tommy's hand.

Tommy happened to glance down at the young man's shoes. "Real nice shoes, Nate, what make are they?"

"Oh, they're Hugo Boss," replied Nate proudly.

"Looks like you take about size ten or eleven, same as me," said Tommy.

"Yes, size ten, Detective."

"I guess not everything went to Goodwill," mumbled Tommy as he walked to his car.

~

When Tommy arrived back in his office there was a note on his desk that Bill Dunwoody wanted to see him as soon as possible. When he arrived at the chief's office he was told to go right on in.

"Special Forces Command has sent over the service records for Mike Muguara and Joe Nichol as we requested," said the chief.

Tommy and the chief looked over the information, and a lot of the content had been blanked out with black marker as the information was considered to be too sensitive to national security. The main information was all there, including initial training and qualification for Special Forces. The teams in the Iraqi desert had been selected based on their complementary skills. Mike Muguara was an explosives expert and Joe Nichol a sniper. Other than that there was little in the records that the team didn't already know.

Chapter 21

U-Haul Storage

IT WAS MONDAY MORNING AND Bill Ross arrived in the office with his customary coffee in hand in a brand new mug. Elaine had sent off to Scotland for a set of four mugs with the Kilmarnock FC logo and surprised Bill that morning with one of them when he went to pour his coffee. He was ecstatic about the gift and it helped to dull the pain of the Killie loss to Glasgow Rangers in the Scottish Cup on the weekend. Tommy's Oakland Raiders had not faired any better, and he sat at his desk head in hands as he had done on many Monday mornings over the past few years.

"Why are you so bright and cheerful this morning?" said Tommy, his mood as black as a Raiders player's jersey.

"New mug, Tommy, you know me, KTID - Killie Till I Die," replied his dad.

"I was thinking over the weekend that you should hold off going back to Whispering Hollow to interview Jimmy Rodriguez and his limo driver. If the leather jacket that I saw the driver wearing was the one that Mike Muguara bought in Houston, he might try to dump it if he thinks we suspect him. Let me get down to Houston tomorrow and see what's in the U-Haul storage locker first and then we can regroup." said Bill.

"Makes sense, Dad. I interviewed the desk manager at the Extended Stay Hotel the other day and he was wearing Hugo

Boss shoes that I have no doubt belonged to Mike. Seems like most of Austin is wearing dead man's clothes," replied Tommy.

"Marie is over at the *Statesman* today working with Latisha Williams and making good progress on the financial network behind Venture Point Holdings. What did you learn from your trip to Boston? I guessed that given that you didn't call me over the weekend that it wasn't any great breakthrough," continued Tommy.

"Interesting guy Joe Nichol. I wouldn't like to cross him. He could probably kill me with the little finger of his right hand. He was very careful with everything he said, and the reason for the extended rental of the Cadillac SUV back in October of 2013 was to deliver a *package* for Mike Muguara to the storage locker in Houston. He wouldn't tell me what it contained, but suggested that I go and look for myself. That is the reason I want to get down to Houston tomorrow.

"He did confirm that Mike was disturbed about something he had uncovered in his search for his birth parents, and this gelled with what Claudette Weiss had said to me on my trip to Germany."

"If I'm not going to go visit Jimmy Rodriguez right now, why don't I drive down with you to Houston tomorrow?" said Tommy.

"Sounds like a plan," replied Bill.

~

They called the Harris County Sheriff to give them a head's up that they were coming into the Houston area. Harris County offered their assistance and just to call them if the need arose. With this green light in place, the following morning they set off down FM290, passing through Elgin on the way.

"We need to stop at Southside Market on the way back and pick up some brisket and sausage," said Tommy as they drove past this bastion of barbeque perfection. The smoke from the meat slowly roasting in their oak barbeque pits was drifting across the highway, filling their car with an aroma that made their mouths water.

It was almost eleven when they arrived at the outskirts of Houston. They decided to surprise Martha and Jacob Goldman at M & J Fine Clothing before visiting the storage facility out by the airport.

The bell tinkled as they pushed open the door to the clothing emporium. It was like being transported back in time; it looked like a real tailor and smelled like one. The finest worsteds hung from rails for the welcomed inspection of potential customers. There was no background music or loss-leader sale item displayed to entice the spur-of-the-moment shopper as they entered the store. No prices could be seen displayed anywhere. If you couldn't afford the merchandise you shouldn't be in the store.

"Good morning, gentlemen, and welcome to M & J Fine Clothing, how might I be of assistance today?" said Martha as she emerged from the back of the store.

"Good morning to you, Martha!" said Bill, and the woman recognized the accent right away.

"Officer Ross, how wonderful. Jacob, it's, Officer Ross come to visit with us." Martha could not hide her excitement as she called her husband to come meet the Scottish detective she had told him so much about, as she stepped forward and gave Bill a huge hug.

Jacob Goldman appeared from behind the curtain that led to the tailor's workshop at the rear of the store. The years of tailoring had caused him to walk a little stooped over and he looked up over the top of his gold-rimmed spectacles.

"Welcome. My name is Jacob Goldman."

"Very pleased to meet you, Jacob, and you also, Martha. We have business here in Houston today as we continue to work the case, and we both decided that we should come visit with you first. This is Tommy Ross, the lead detective on the case. Tommy is also my son."

"We are so glad you came, and I can see the resemblance. You both must have some refreshment after your journey. May we offer you coffee or tea or some water perhaps?" said Martha.

"Coffee would be great," said Tommy.

Martha invited them into the back of the store to a little sitting area adjacent the workshop.

"We want to thank you for helping us make the breakthrough on this case," began Bill. "The BMW clue and the name Raul Hernandez helped us immensely. Thank you so much, Martha."

"Ever since the call we had together, Officer Ross, I have been racking my brain to think if there was anything else that I could remember that might help you in your investigation, but alas not," said Martha apologetically.

"You gave us what we needed, Martha, and thank you for that. We have made really solid progress and we think we might be on the verge of another breakthrough," said Tommy, wanting to put Martha at ease and to reinforce the genuine gratitude they had for her help.

"You offer your customers a level of personal service that they can't get from the big chains. Is that what allows you to remain competitive? It must be a hard life," said Bill.

"It's not a hard life, Officer Ross," said Jacob taking the opportunity to engage in the conversation. "Both of our parents and their extended families had to endure hardships beyond our comprehension during the war, Deputy Ross. Our life is full of riches today because of their sacrifice. Whither it's bespoke tailoring services or off-the-shelf merchandise, we put our signature on every product and they walk out of our store knowing that they have a lifetime commitment of service from Martha and me. That's all we can do, ensure that our customers know that we want them to look good in our clothing and feel good about life."

The depth of passion in Jacob Goldman's response almost took Bill's breath away. *This is what it meant to be Jewish*, thought Bill. *A lifetime of commitment to their faith, their family, their lineage and their chosen profession. No matter your political views you couldn't help but admire that.*

"You said *put your signature on every product*. Did you mean that literally or was it just a figure of speech?" said Tommy, his sixth sense again kicking in that the comment may have real significance.

"We do *sign everything,* Detective Ross, it's not a figure of speech. We have a patch with a replica of my signature and the telephone number of our store. It's stitched on every item we sell. We have different styles of patch based on the particular item of merchandise. It is our commitment to lifetime warranty," said Jacob proudly.

"So the leather Hugo Boss jacket that you sold to Raul Hernandez, there would be a patch with you signature on the jacket, yes? Where on the jacket would you typically attach this patch?"

"It's always in the same location on a man's jacket, Officer Ross. It's on the inside of the right sleeve two inches up from the end of the sleeve. It would not be seen, but the customer would know where it was located and he could simply turn the end of the sleeve inside out and retrieve the store telephone number."

"This will be extremely helpful to us in our inquiries," said Tommy, looking over at his father, and they both knew what this meant. They had now a hook to bait the limo driver.

~

They said their goodbyes to Martha and Jacob and headed to the U-Haul storage facility at the Houston airport.

Given its location, the U-Haul facility was huge. It offered mostly large air-conditioned units, although there were smaller storage lockers that could also be rented on a daily basis by travelers from the airport.

They checked with the manager and showed their IDs. Claudette had been as good as her word and had advised the manager that it was likely that detectives from Austin would want access to the unit. Each renter fit their storage unit with their personal lock of choice; the manager cut off the lock on Raul Hernandez' unit with a huge pair of shears. It was obvious that this manner of entry was a regular occurrence, as he completed the task with ease and, when complete, left the detectives to inspect the contents.

Bill had speculated on what they might find in the locker, and when they lifted up the heavy metal roller door, Bill's speculation had been right - weapons, lots of weapons, not only guns and ammo, but surveillance equipment, explosives and timers - Semtex. They needed to call the Harris County Sheriff and get the area secured.

In the corner of the unit there was a desk-come-workbench and a chair. On the desk was a laptop, a high intensity lamp on an extending arm and a similar extending arm with a lighted magnifying glass. Mike Muguara could sit in this air-conditioned locker, completely unseen, conduct his research on his laptop, and assemble whatever he needed for any security job he had contracted for.

While they waited for the local sheriffs to arrive they conducted a detailed search of the locker and an inventory of the ordnance.

1. SR 25 Sniper rifle with night force scope and Harris bi-pod.

2. FN MK20 Sniper Support Rifle (SSR).

3. FN SCAR STD Assault Rifle.

4. FN SCAR CQC with Grenade Launcher.

5. HK MP5N (9mm) Sub Machine Gun.

6. HK MK 23 SOCOM 45mm Handgun.

7. Smith & Wesson 686 .357 Revolver.

8. Sig Sauer P226 Handgun.

9. 2 pairs Armasight PVS7-3 Alpha Gen 3 Night Vision Goggles.

10. Ultra Long Range HD IP PTZ Surveillance Camera with IR Laser Illumination.

11. About 18 pounds of Semtex and detonators.

They booted up the laptop and it was obvious that it had been cleaned using some sophisticated software. Bill remembered what Claudette had said:

"We were very concerned about data security in our line of work. Mike used a Mac Air with a separate removable hard drive for external

data storage. We kept nothing on the Cloud, everything on removable hard drives, so if someone stole the laptop, there would be nothing on it of any significance."

There was no removable hard drive or external data storage device anywhere in the storage unit.

~

The Harris County Sheriff's officers arrived. Bill and Tommy briefed them on the investigation and that the Raul Hernandez who had rented the unit, alias Mike Muguara, was now deceased. The team secured the area and removed the entire ordnance.

Bill and Tommy asked that they not touch the desk and the laptop as they still wanted to try to access information from the computer. The Harris County team agreed. By early evening they had gone and Bill and Tommy stared at the empty storage unit containing only the desk and a laptop. There was something really eerie about the scene.

The desk drawers were empty and Tommy removed each of them so he could look into the back of the desk to see if any papers or other stuff had perhaps fallen down the back. He saw a crumpled piece of yellow notepad paper immediately and stuck his hand in the back of the desk and pulled it out. It looked like it had been in there for some time, and he uncrumpled it and laid it flat on the desk.

It was a random list of words and names.

Venture Point Holdings

Enrique Escobar Rodriguez

Pablo Zambrano

Jimmy Rodriguez

Pepe Vivar

Garrison McMullen

Alyana McMullen (Reyes)

Achak Muguara

Gavin McMullen

Antonella Aguilar

McMullen riding accident?

Merry Christmas -Feliz Navidad in Colinas Verde?

US-China supply line?

"So what do you make of it, Dad?" said Tommy.

"Strange. It's very strange that we should find it like this. Strange list. There are questions interspersed with people's names, so what questions belong to which names and why write the list this way?

"It's like a random word cloud, and all of the words in the cloud are connected to some overall theme. Sorry to keep saying this, but it's like a jigsaw puzzle when you first dump all the pieces out of the box onto the table. You know they are all connected, but you first need a place to start and you always start with taking two separate pieces and putting them together, then a third and a fourth. The other thing you do with a jigsaw puzzle is that you begin to assemble different groups of parts in separate sections and then bring these sections together to complete the overall picture."

"The advantage you have with a jigsaw is that when you dump all of the parts on the table you know for sure that somehow they all fit. Every single part on the table fits together into an overall picture. In our world we don't have that luxury. We need to find the parts that absolutely don't fit, that don't belong, and when we find these parts we eliminate them— throw them away so they don't distort the overall picture that we are trying to see. It's what Sherlock Homes said:

"When you have eliminated the impossible, whatever remains, however improbable, must be the truth!'

"There are perhaps items on this list that don't help us find the truth and they don't belong in the overall big picture. We need to investigate them, recognize them for what they are— dead ends or deliberate attempts to deceive—and throw them away. To say what Holmes said a different way, what we will have left after we eliminate the items that don't belong will be the right answer - what's left *is* right!"

"Interesting, Dad. We are pretty sure now that one part that doesn't fit in all of this is that Mike Muguara was killed for racial reasons. The *kill the wetbacks* message was an attempt to deceive, it doesn't belong and we need to throw it out," said Tommy.

"Correct! Now if he was not killed for racial reasons, why was he killed? We still have no motive, and although we suspect that the limo driver was involved in some way and that Jimmy Rodriguez might also be involved, we have no motive. If we show our hand too soon and use the leather jacket connection to sweat the limo driver, they could just lawyer up and they would argue that we have no connection to the dead man and no motive.

"The key to this case is to start at the beginning and follow the road that Mike Muguara walked. While walking that road he uncovered something that caused him to change. Claudette saw the change in him and so did Joe Nichol. Why did Mike ask Joe to get this entire ordnance for him—guns, ammo, explosives and very sophisticated surveillance equipment? Something he discovered scared him!"

Tommy was digesting everything his father was describing and trying to put himself in Mike Muguara's shoes. Mike was a trained fighter, Marine Corps and Special Forces, perhaps one of the best in the world at what he did. Why would he ask his trusted colleague to get him weapons?

"There are two main reasons that you obtain this type of weapons stash: offensive or defensive. If it had been for offensive purposes, being the good soldier he was, he wouldn't have taken on whatever scared him on his own, he would have asked Joe Nichol to join him in the fight and Joe would have been there in an instant, standing shoulder to shoulder with him. No, this stash was for defensive reasons.

"The other clue here is the surveillance equipment. That was real high-end stuff and designed for medium to long-range surveillance, not up close and personal. I think that he was scared of what he had *possibly* stumbled upon and was still collecting intelligence. The weapons were not for immediate use, they were for future use, once he had a complete picture."

Tommy could see that his father was nodding in violent agreement.

"Right on, Tommy. Mike made the discovery when searching for his birth parents. We need to get on that trail. We need to get to Oklahoma and meet with the attorneys Mike entrusted with the disposition of his assets after his death. They may be able to shed some light on this. We get on the right path and follow in his footsteps."

~

It was almost eight and they had been in the storage locker for six hours. They needed to get on their way back to Austin.

With Tommy driving, Bill Ross sat back in the passenger seat and closed his eyes.

For some reason, he thought of Little Red Riding Hood. He imagined Mike Muguara walking a path through a deep and dark forest looking for his mommy and daddy. The entrance to the forest was a place called Houston, and he walked and walked and looked for clues, and then he came by a clearing called Austin where he met a woodsman who suggested that he try walking down the path by the river. He saw signs that he was not alone in this deep dark wood and that there might be a big bad wolf watching him and ready to gobble him up. He got really frightened.

Bill Ross woke up with a start. He had nodded off.

"Why Austin?" said Bill out loud. "Does the big bad wolf live in Austin?"

"The big bad wolf, Dad? I think you need some Glenmorangie and then bed!"

"I think you're right, son. I think you're right."

Chapter 22

A nest of vipers

THE FOLLOWING MORNING MARIE WAS in the office early. She had laid everything out on the conference room table and had charts on the walls. All of this was the work in progress for the research into Venture Point Holdings. She had arranged that Latisha and Julian to be on standby to link into the videoconference facilities in the room. She planned to have them be part of a briefing with Tommy and Bill when they arrived in the office later that morning.

Tommy arrived first and Bill a few minutes later. It was now gone nine and they had each slept late after their long day in Houston. Before they could get settled in at their desks Marie ambushed them.

"I'd like to bring you both up to speed on the work we have done on Venture Point Holdings. Why don't you each get a refill on your coffee and join me in the conference room. I want to link in Latisha and Julian as they have both helped immensely on what we have found out up until now," said Marie, heading off in the direction of the room.

When Bill and Tommy walked into the room a few minutes later, Latisha and Julian were already online via Go To Meeting and their images were being displayed on the pull-down screen via the projector linked to the laptop.

"Good morning, Latisha, good morning, Julian," said Tommy as he walked in.

"So, Marie, kick this off and tell us what you got."

"I believe that y'all already know some of this, but to help with context let me go over it again.

"Venture Point Holdings, VPH, was formed in 2008. VPH consists of several components: The Venture Point Investment Fund, Deng Tang Corporation, Robertson Richards and Rodriguez Holdings. The chairman and largest stockholder of VPH is Garrison McMullen and the vice-chairman and second largest stockholder is Enrique Escobar Rodriguez.

"Let's start with the Venture Point Investment Fund. An investment fund is a financial vehicle that's designed to provide those who invest in the fund a high return on their money, far higher than they might otherwise enjoy with other, somewhat safer forms of investment. The risk might be higher, but the returns are very much higher. For example, a bank savings account today might offer one percent interest if you are lucky. Depending upon the investment portfolio and the risk, an investment fund might return eighty percent or more.

"An investment fund will raise the fund by pitching their portfolio to prospective investors. The portfolio is what the fund plans to invest in. Again, as an example, some investment funds might only invest in early-stage technology startup companies. The risk of failure here is very large, as only one in ten of these startups ever succeed. However, if one of them is a Facebook or a Google, then the return on investment could be huge.

"Investors who invest in funds like the Venture Point Fund are what are called qualified investors. They go through a pre-qualification to ensure that they understand the risk and have done this before. They are typically referred to as the *Limiteds*. They are large investors with limited liability on their investment. They could be pension funds or large blocks of investors who have formed a trust together.

"After the recent banking collapse and its impact on the global economy, federal government legislators have been using forensic accounting techniques to try to track down and close illegal offshore investment trusts, many of which were being used to launder drug money for the large South American cartels.

"One of the limited investors in the Venture Point Fund is Texas State Retirement (TSR). TSR has an investment portfolio of more than $25 billion and they have hundreds of investments designed to balance risk and reward. TSR is a legitimate investor.

"We have also determined that there are several large offshore trusts that also have large positions in the Venture Point Fund, and it will take us a long time to be able to track down the investors in these trusts. It is likely that some of these offshore trusts will be crooked.

"In conclusion, the Venture Point Investment Fund only invests in construction and regional development through Venture Point Holdings, and VPH focuses exclusively on development of the land that was originally the McMullen Ranch.

"Any questions so far?"

"This is already way above my head," said Bill.

"Mine too," said Tommy, "But carry on, Marie, I'm sure that you, Julian and Latisha will help us make sense of all of this!"

Julian chimed in, "It does sound complicated, guys, but it's relatively straightforward, believe me. I can help y'all put this in layman's language when we have the full picture. The real issue is to find out if there is anything illegal in all of this that ties back to Mike's killing, and we haven't found anything for sure yet.

"Just as you guys have a sixth sense for what you do, I have a sixth sense for financial vehicles, and this one smells."

"Thanks, Julian, carry on, Marie," said Tommy.

Marie continued. "Let's now talk about Robertson Richards."

"Robertson Richards is a huge design and construction firm headquartered in Houston. For example, they designed and built the Travis Tower in downtown Austin, the building where Garrison McMullen has his residence. Robertson Richards had its roots in the oil boom in Texas.

"Oil was first drilled out of Spindletop Hill south of Beaumont in Jefferson County in 1900. In its first year Spindletop produced more than 3.5 million barrels of oil; in its second, production rose to 17.4 million. Spindletop ushered in a new era in Texas-based industry and was enormously influential in the state's future development. New oil companies were formed along with the refining and support organizations needed to make the fledgling oil industry successful. Robertson Richards was one of these support organizations, designing and building much of the infrastructure: roads, bridges, warehouses and the like."

"They later branched out and created a residential and commercial division building new planned communities of homes and commercial buildings to meet the needs of the burgeoning Texas immigrant population that flocked to the state in search of jobs created by the 'Black Gold.'

"Venture Point Holdings has agreements in place with Robertson Richards to be the prime contractor for all design and building work. They designed the new marina and the rail link to Cedar Park, and they are currently awaiting approval from city and state planning authorities, including the Capital Area Metropolitan Planning Organization, CAMPO.

"There is also a contract in place between Robertson Richards and JR Construction Services. JR provides all of the construction workers to Robertson Richards. Jimmy Rodriguez owns JR Construction."

"Can you go back, please, to the slide you just shared on JR Construction?" asked Tommy. "Yes, that's it! The JR logo is red and blue on a white background, and I saw a photograph you presented earlier showing a construction site and there were white pickup trucks with the red and blue logo on the door. The manager at Gold's Gym said that Mike Muguara had an altercation in the parking lot with guys who drove a white truck with a red and blue logo," concluded Tommy.

"Okay we need to follow up on Jimmy Rodriguez as we discussed, but first let's get to another part-owner of Venture Point Holdings - Enrique Escobar Rodriguez.

"Enrique Rodriguez owns the huge Colinas Verde Ranch, the third largest ranch in Texas, with close to 500,000 acres. The ranch is located south of Pecos, in Brewster County and Presidio County, and the south side of the ranch runs along the Mexican border. Enrique Rodriguez is the elder brother of Jimmy Rodriguez, the owner of JR Construction Services.

"Enrique Rodriquez and Garrison McMullen go back a long way and have common business interests. They both own huge ranches, breed cattle and horses, and each has significant oil drilling operations on their land. Enrique launched a transportation business in the '60s to transport cattle and feed. Garrison McMullen helped him do that by taking a twenty-five percent stake, and the trucking company is now one the largest in the U.S., providing trucking services to every industry. Rodriquez Trucking is headquartered in El Paso.

"Rodriguez Trucking has a contract with Venture Point Holdings to provide all haulage and storage services.

"Finally, there is Deng Tang Corporation.

"Eddie Tang is a Chinese billionaire. He amassed his fortune after he inherited Deng Shipping Lines from his father. He diversified into manufacturing, primarily high-end consumer package goods, and then he branched out into construction and operation of casinos in Hong Kong and Macau.

"Deng Tang companies have contracts with Venture Point Holdings for the supply of domestic appliances and fixtures and fittings. They also plan to operate casinos in the marina vicinity if VPH manages to secure the necessary planning approvals. There is also a contract in place between Deng Tang and Rodriguez Trucking for the transportation of all Deng Tang products for the VPH development from the Port of Long Beach, California, to Texas.

"That's the full extent of our research to date," said Marie. "We are continuing to work on this, but suffice to say this is a huge operation and their master plan goes a lot further than a simple marina and a few upscale homes. They plan several hotels, a conference center and at least one casino. There will be a heliport that will bring high rollers from the airport and from the Circuit of the Americas. The rail link is primarily to bring in workers to run the hotels and casinos. The revenue to Travis County from taxes will be immense, so they have full-time lobbyists working the state legislators in the state capitol to ensure they have support for their plans."

~

"This is fantastic work!" said Tommy.

"I agree," said Bill. "However, as Julian has said, there is nothing yet to suggest that this is in any way linked to the killing of Mike Muguara. Having said that, if Mike got in the middle of this in some way and had begun to rock the boat, I could see why he felt he needed weapons."

"We need to keep at it," said Tommy. "Marie, I would also like to give you the additional task of finding out all you can about Jimmy Rodriguez's limo driver. When Bill and I visited with Martha and Jacob Goldman in Houston, we discovered a piece of information that we could potentially leverage to put the squeeze on him. We need to know his background and his connection to Jimmy Rodriguez, but we need to do it without spooking him."

"Okay, boss, I can do that," said Marie.

The meeting ended and Bill and Tommy left Marie to wrap up with Latisha and Julian.

~

"So what do you think, Dad?"

"Marie and the team have done great work but, as we discussed, we need to get back on the road that Mike traveled. We need to see if along that road there is a detour he took that put him in the middle of this nest of vipers. I suspect there is, and when we find it the pieces will start to fall into place. Our first step on the road is to get up to Oklahoma. I will set that up and get back to you."

Bill went off to call the Corbin, Clayton and Anderson law firm in Lawton.

Chapter 23

Last Will and Testament

"GOOD MORNING, CORBIN, Clayton and Anderson, how may I direct your call?"

"I'd like to speak with Bob Corbin, please. This is Officer Bill Ross of the Travis County Police Department in Austin, Texas."

"Hold the line, please, and I will check if Mr. Corbin is in his office."

"Bob Corbin here, I've been expecting your call, Officer Ross!"

"Oh, I guess Claudette Weiss has already been in touch then?"

"Yes, she has, she called me and then she sent me an email with your name and contact details. If I hadn't heard from you by this weekend I was going to call you, so it's good we are now connected."

"My boss, Detective Sergeant Tommy Ross, and I would like to come visit with you. When might it be convenient for us to do that? By the way, Tommy is my son, if you were wondering why we have the same last name."

"Yes, I'm aware of the family connection as well as the working relationship. The email from Claudette was quite comprehensive. Very efficient is Miss Weiss. I will make myself available to meet your schedule, Officer Ross. By the way, you should plan on being with me for a full day, so I suggest that you stay overnight. I can recommend the Hilton Garden Inn on 281, it's just around the corner from our offices on West Gore Blvd."

"A whole day? Why do we need a whole day?"

"It will be clear when you get here, but just let me say that Mike Muguara left a lot more with me for safekeeping than just a *Last Will and Testament*."

"Okay, I'll talk with Tommy and get back to you, Mr. Corbin."

"Just send your travel details to Betty and please, Officer Ross, call me Bob. Betty is my personal assistant. She can also make a reservation at the hotel for you both if needed. I look forward to spending a day with you, Officer Ross. I am sure that you will find it very interesting and worth your trip up here."

Bill went off to find Tommy and brief him on the call. A whole day! What did Mike Muguara leave with Bob Corbin that will take a full day to explain?

~

The following day they flew from Austin to Wichita Falls and then rented a car to drive the 50 miles to Lawton. They checked into the Hilton and went off to bed. They woke bright and early and arrived at the law offices at 9 a.m. just as Betty was opening the office for business.

"Good morning, gentlemen, I trust you had a good flight and slept well last night. Go right on into the conference room and I will get a fresh pot of coffee going. I also brought some doughnuts so you can keep your blood sugar levels up. Low blood sugar can be very dangerous," said Betty as she went off to get the coffee.

They drew a look at one other. It was obvious based on her build that Betty was diligent in keeping her blood sugar up.

A few minutes later Bob Corbin arrived. He was well over six feet tall, slender build, with salt and pepper hair. Tommy reckoned that he was in his early sixties, and based on his build probably played basketball when he was younger. As it happened, he had played for the North Carolina Wolfpack in 1974 when they defeated UCLA, earning the first national title in school history.

"Bob Corbin, good to meet you both, and thanks for making the trip up here."

The three men shook hands and helped themselves to coffee and a doughnut.

"We're going to be here a while, so make yourselves comfortable. Betty will get some sandwiches brought in for our lunch; she'll come take your order later. I've also taken the liberty of making reservations for the three of us at Luigi's for dinner tonight. Nothing fancy, just good Italian with pasta and pizza, hope that works for you boys."

"Works fine for us," said Tommy.

"Great then, let's get right into this," said Bob Corbin as he bent forward, grabbing his coffee mug in both hands. He began to tell them about the life of the late Mike Muguara.

~

"My law firm, of which I am one of three partners, is retained counsel for the Comanche Nation. The Comanche Nation complex is located about ten miles north of here. What do you know about the history of the Comanche? I ask this as to understand what I'm about to tell you. It will be helpful if you know some of the history."

"I know virtually nothing," responded Bill.

"That goes for me too," said Tommy.

"Okay, then, let me try to give you some of the history by way of context."

"The Comanche Nation were lords of the plains and their original homeland, Comancheria, occupied an area 600 miles from north to south and 400 miles from east to west. Today this region makes up the West Texas Llano Estacado, the Texas Panhandle, the Texas Hill Country, eastern New Mexico, and western Oklahoma, including the Oklahoma Panhandle, the Wichita Mountains, southeastern Colorado and southwestern Kansas.

"I won't go into the entire history of the Comanche as that would not be productive for our meeting today. The most important part of their history as it relates to Mike Muguara began when Texas won independence from Mexico in 1836."

"The Comanche were still in control of the Texas plains. They frequently conducted raids on frontier settlements from San Antonio to northern Mexico. In May 1836 a particularly destructive raid occurred at Fort Parker, a settlement near the Navasota River in East Texas."

"The Comanche attacked the blockhouse, killed several settlers, and took five hostages, including nine-year-old Cynthia Ann Parker, who then lived with the Comanche for the next twenty-four years. Parker became the wife of Chief Peta Nocona and the mother of Quanah Parker, the last great Comanche chief."

"In an effort to stop Comanche destruction on the Texas frontier, Sam Houston, the first elected president of the Republic of Texas, instituted a policy aimed at establishing peace and friendship through commerce. Houston's peace efforts were hampered because the Texas Congress refused to agree to the one Comanche requirement for peace: a boundary line between Texas and Comanchería."

"Peace commissioners did succeed in negotiating a treaty with a band of Penateka Comanche led by Chief Muguara, but the Texas Senate never ratified the treaty. When Houston left office in late 1838, Texan-Comanche relations were rapidly deteriorating."

"Mirabeau Lamar, who succeeded Houston as president, abandoned the peace policy, which he considered a failure, in favor of waging war on the Comanche Nation. Lamar's policy culminated in the Council House Fight, a tragic incident that occurred in San Antonio in the spring of 1840 when Texas officials attempted to arrest a Comanche peace delegation. Fighting broke out, and thirty-five Comanche, including their leader, Chief Muguara, and eleven other chiefs, were killed. The remaining thirty Comanche, primarily women and children, were imprisoned by the Texans.

"That's the brief Comanche history lesson. Any questions at this stage, gentlemen?" said Bob Corbin as he walked across the room to refill his coffee and grab another doughnut.

"So I'm guessing that Mike was a descendant of this Chief Muguara who was killed in the council house fight?" said Bill.

"Right first time, Bill! There's a reason why you're a detective," laughed Bob.

~

With fresh coffee and more sugar treats at hand, they sat back around the conference room table.

"I first met Mike Muguara a couple of years ago when he came to visit with the elders of the Comanche Nation. I happened to be visiting with them at the same time and we grabbed a coffee together. I then invited him to have dinner with me."

"He told me that he was trying to establish who his birth parents were. His grandfather and grandmother on his father's side of the family had raised him, so he knew he was of the Muguara lineage. They gave him love and taught him some of the history of Comanche and the sub-tribe called the Penateka—the honey eaters. Chief Muguara was a chief of the Penateka Comanche who live in the southernmost regions of Comancheria, what is today the Texas Hill Country, including the area that is now Austin.

"He was also told that, being a descendant of Muguara, he had inherited the power to speak to those who had passed on. Muguara meant spirit talker. His grandparents took him out each night to look at the stars and listen for anyone from the past who wanted to communicate with the living. He believed completely that he had these powers and, as he said while we drank coffee together, he talked to the spirits every day. He said that he had talked to them each night in the desert of Iraq and that they had kept him safe and helped him in his work there.

"His grandfather told him that he and his wife had left the reservation only one time and that they had taken their three children with them. In 1952, the federal government initiated the Urban Indian Relocation Program. It was designed to entice reservation dwellers to seven major urban cities where the jobs supposedly were plentiful.

"Relocation offices were set up in Chicago, Denver, Los Angeles, San Francisco, San Jose, St. Louis, Cincinnati, Cleveland and Dallas. Bureau of Indian Affairs (BIA) employees were there to orient new arrivals and manage financial and job training programs for them. Grandfather Muguara and his family went to Dallas. At the time Mike's father, Achak, was only one-year-old. When Achak was eighteen his parents decided to return to the reservation and Achak didn't want to do that. He stayed in Texas and worked various jobs, eventually getting a good job working on the McMullen Ranch outside of Austin."

"He did a little bit of everything on the ranch, working with the cattle and the horses, and in return got a paycheck and a place to stay. Life was good."

"Over the years Mike's grandparents lost touch with Achak. The next time they saw him was when he turned up on the reservation with his wife and a nine-month-old baby boy. They asked the grandparents to look after the boy until they got on their feet. In the native Indian tradition, the grandparents accepted this obligation no questions asked. That was the last time they saw their son and his wife. They never heard from them again. That nine-month-old baby boy was Mike Muguara."

"Mike told me that his grandparents knew nothing about Achak's wife; all they knew was that her first name was Alyana and, as that was a native Indian first name for a girl, they assumed that she was first nation."

"Any questions about what I have just told you?" asked Bob.

There were no specific questions and the three of them just sat around the table going over all of what Bob Corbin had explained.

~

Betty took their orders for lunch. The sandwiches arrived soon after and they had a pleasant lunch, with Bob reminiscing about his youth and the excitement of being on a basketball team that had won the national championship. Bill talked about his life growing up in Scotland and his love of Kilmarnock FC.

When Tommy said that he was an Oakland Raiders fan, Bob Corbin put his arm around him playfully and said, "I feel your pain, buddy!"

"And now to the main event," said Bob, wiping some mayonnaise from the corner of his mouth. "Let's hear from Mike Muguara!"

Tommy almost choked on his last mouthful of pastrami on rye. A projector screen slowly dropped from the ceiling, and with the touch of a button Bob Corbin brought Mike Muguara to life. Mike was seated in the same conference room where they now sat and, at his side, Bob Corbin.

Today's date is Friday, January 10th, 2014 my name is Mike Muguara. Bob has agreed to be witness to this recording and he is now sitting beside you there today. You must be from some branch of law enforcement as Bob is only authorized to share this recording in the event of my death with those who seek to solve my murder. I want to tell you what I know and also what I don't know and can only speculate. You can then take it from there and find and bring to justice those responsible for my death.

For some time now I have been trying to track down my birth parents. It's my belief that they are now both dead. Part of what I will say here will explain why I think this is so, as I don't have absolute proof of their passing. I believe that they were both murdered and that, including my own death, there are three killings for you to solve.

My father's name was Achak Muguara, and he worked for Garrison McMullen on his ranch outside Austin, Texas from 1968 until his death. He worked primarily in the cattle and horse-breeding part of the business, and in doing so he had reason to interact on many occasions with workers from the Colinas Verde ranch in southwest Texas. This ranch is owned by Enrique Rodriquez.

Enrique Rodriguez and Garrison McMullen are close friends and business partners. They both have huge herds of cattle and horses. Some horses they raise to be used by the cowboys who work the ranch, some they race and some they sell. They raise beef cattle and cattle to be used for milk production. The Colinas Verde ranch is the exclusive supplier of cattle to the huge milk-producing facilities in and around El Paso.

In 1964 before my father became employed on the McMullen ranch, Enrique Rodriguez and Garrison McMullen created a trucking company

*to haul their animals to market and, when needed, to bring in feed.
Rodriguez Trucking, is now one of the largest in the nation and has
diversified into hauling every type of product, not just livestock and feed.*

*Enrique Rodriguez has a younger brother, Jimmy Rodriguez. Jimmy
was appointed as the first general manager of Rodriguez Trucking;
however, he hated living on the Colinas Verde Ranch and wanted to be
closer to the bright lights of Austin. Garrison McMullen suggested that he
come live on the McMullen Ranch and help run the place in addition to the
trucking line. Jimmy agreed and moved into the McMullen Ranch in
1965.*

*In 1966 Garrison McMullen met the love of his life at a rock concert
in Zilker Park in Austin. Alyana Reyes was the daughter of Fernando
Reyes, a very successful Hispanic businessman in Houston. They fell madly
in love and married in the spring of 1967.*

*Alyana quickly realized that Garrison McMullen had a dark side.
He was given to fits of anger and frequently would be physically abusive of
Alyana. My father arrived on the scene in the spring of 1968 and, in
addition to his many tasks, was given the responsibility of looking after the
two horses that Garrison McMullen had bought for his wife to ride.*

*On many occasions he would see the bruises on her face and arms and
he would see her wince when trying to mount her horse. He would fetch ice
for her to apply to her injuries and over time he became a shoulder to cry
on. A physical relationship soon developed and they fell in love.*

*Alyana fell pregnant in the fall of 1968 and in May of 1969 she
gave birth to a son. Garrison McMullen was over the moon and he chose
the name Gavin for the child, as he thought that his family had originally
come to the U.S. from Scotland and that Gavin was a good Scottish name.
The boy had dark black hair similar in color to Garrison McMullen's
and he had olive-colored skin from his mother.*

*A year later Garrison McMullen fell from his horse and sustained
severe injuries to his lower abdomen. One result of the injury was that he
was impotent and could never father another child. He decided at that
moment that all of his power and fortune would be channeled for Gavin's
success in life as his sole son and heir.*

*You probably are now guessing where this might lead, and my guess
is that you are right. Alyana became pregnant again during the time when
Garrison McMullen was bedridden with his injuries. He had no idea who
the father was and didn't really care; he just wanted her out of his house,*

and Alyana was banished. Soon thereafter he officially divorced her, and by that time my father had quit the job on the ranch and he and Alyana were living together in Houston where my father got a job working in the oil industry.

I was born in April 1971 and my parents were having a tough time financially. In November of 1971 they drove to Oklahoma and left me with my grandparents and returned to Texas.

After Alyana was banished from the ranch, the responsibility for raising young Gavin McMullen fell on the McMullen ranch housekeeper, Antonella Aguilar. I tracked Antonella down and it was she who gave me much of the information I am sharing with you today.

Garrison McMullen never married again and he devoted his energy to ensuring that Gavin would have the best education; he eventually graduated UT Austin with a Ph.D. in Law and Comparative Politics.

Garrison McMullen has been a major contributor to the Republican Party for many years and, with the help of others in the party, he architected a plan for Gavin to enter the political arena, first in local and state government and then hopefully in the future at the national level. The fact that he had a Hispanic mother was a key component of the strategy, as with the changing regional and national ethnic mix the party saw a huge need to find a charismatic white/Hispanic leader.

Although my mother was banished from the McMullen home, I can't imagine that she did not try to make contact with her first son, Gavin. My guess is that Antonella Aguilar would be able to help shed some light on this, but since my first meeting with her at her home in Round Rock, she has disappeared. I feel also that she may be key in finding my mother's family, the Reyes, and they might know something also.

I ran recon on Jimmy Rodriguez to see if I could find a connection through him. He has a driver named Pepe Vivar. Vivar is Honduran and a real piece of work. He has a scar down his left cheek, and I've followed him and seen him extort money from the hundreds of Mexican workers who frequent the cantinas in the Venture Point, Leander and Lago Vista neighborhoods. He lives in a wing of the home of Jimmy Rodriguez.

I followed Jimmy Rodriguez and Pepe Vivar on two occasions when they drove down to the Colinas Verde Ranch and saw them meet with Enrique, Garrison McMullen and a bunch of other high rollers I didn't recognize. After the first time following them, I decided to set up the surveillance equipment that my buddy Joe Nichol got me in Boston. I recorded them all celebrating Christmas at the Colinas Verde Ranch. It was a huge barbecue and again there were many high rollers in attendance.

One group arrived in a convoy of five vehicles with front and rear security vehicles. When they arrived the muscle got out of the front and back cover cars and formed a security perimeter for their bosses to make an entrance to the party. All these cars had Mexican tags and two were official Mexican police cruisers.

These recordings are on a backup hard drive that you will find in my U-Haul locker in Houston. Claudette Weiss has the information on the locker and can get you access. You can get the contact details for Claudette from Bob if you do not have them already.

The primary reason I have recorded this at this time is that I have been given a warning. They are on to me and I have two choices, I go back to Germany and forget this, or I continue on. Pepe Vivar delivered this warning. He met me outside the Gold's Gym on Lamar Blvd in Austin where I work out sometimes. He told me that if I continued to upset his employers, I was a dead man. I propose to continue on. I have adequate ordnance for a firefight; however, I doubt that if they come for me it will be head on. My guess is that they will have done their homework on me and realized that that would be a bad idea.

That's all I know. If you find my body, I would like to be buried on Comanche land. Bob has the instructions for this. If you find the bodies of my mother and father, I would like that they be buried with me. There are adequate funds to cover all of the expenses for this to be done.

Good luck. My spirit will be with you. These are dangerous people; please tread carefully. My guess is that there is a lot we don't know and if drug cartels are involved, which I suspect they are, they won't lie down easily.

~

When the video ended, there was total silence in the room. Bill and Tommy just shook their heads and stared at each other in almost total disbelief of what they had just seen and heard. It was Bob Corbin who broke the silence.

"So it was worth the trip?" said Bob Corbin.

Bill Ross was immediately focused on the content of the dead man's speech.

"So where's the hard drive? It wasn't in the storage unit. We now know that the driver's name is Pepe Vivar and that he's Honduran. We suspect that Jimmy Rodriguez was present at the killing and that he ordered Pepe Vivar to take care of the details. I think we now have enough to move on Pepe Vivar. Mike said that Pepe gave him the warning outside the Gold's Gym, so we can re-interview the manager at the gym and see if he recognizes Vivar. We need to see if Marie has made progress and if there's a photograph of him on file."

"I agree, Dad, and we can talk to Chief Dunwoody about how we move on him when we get back to Austin. My suggestion will be to get a search warrant for his home immediately. He lives at Jimmy Rodriguez' place so that would give us the chance to see what we might discover in the process of the search that might implicate him."

"The issue is still the motive and who ordered the hit and why make it look like a lynching? Was it Garrison McMullen who ordered it? Was it the cartel people? If it was the cartel people they would have done it themselves and not made it so elaborate; it would have been pop, pop and you're in the lake. This was not a cartel hit, I'm sure of it."

"So if it was Garrison McMullen, what was he trying to protect? What is most important to McMullen? His son and his rise to political stardom? His business dynasty, his money and his reputation? So how did Mike threaten any one or all of these things? That's what we need to find out."

"We also need to find Antonella Aguilar and see what she knows. Before we go to dinner tonight I'd like to give Marie a call and find out if she's made progress on her research work on Pepe Vivar. Based on what we learn from her, we can then call Bill Dunwoody and ask him to get a search warrant issued for Jimmy Rodriguez' place so that we can access the apartment in his home where Vivar lives."

~

Bob Corbin left the conference room so they could make the call to Marie. Marie picked up on the first ring.

"How goes your visit to Oklahoma?"

"Great, Marie, we can give you a full report later but we've made a real breakthrough here, which is the reason I'm calling. Have you made any progress on background on Jimmy Rodriguez' limo driver?"

"Yes, let me pull it up on my laptop. There's quite a lot of background on this guy and he's in our system.

"His name is Pepe Vivar and he's from Honduras. Enrique Rodriguez sponsored him as he is the son of Enrique's brother. Enrique has six brothers, by the way, and this brother married a Honduran and moved home to Honduras. As it happens, he was the son of the woman that Rodriguez' brother married. She was a single parent when the Rodriguez brother met her; hence, his last name Vivar. If he was not the son of a U.S. citizen, it raises the question about how he got into the U.S. in the first place."

"Since his arrival in the U.S. in 1978 he has accumulated a criminal record as long as my arm. Mainly bar fights and other assaults. He went to jail for a year in 1994 for sticking a broken bottle in a guy's face. He has been joined at the hip with Jimmy Rodriguez since he came out of jail in 1995 and has the same address as Rodriguez, so maybe he rents a room there or something. Jimmy Rodriguez has never been married. so maybe there's more going on there than meets the eye, but at any rate that's where he lives."

"I can email you the details if you want."

"Yes, do that, Marie, and copy Bill Dunwoody and tell him that I'll be calling him later to ask him to get a search warrant for Vivar's place, as he is now a prime suspect in the murder of Mike Muguara," said Tommy.

~

After a nice Italian dinner at Luigi's, they thanked Bob Corbin for all his help and assured him that they would keep in touch and update him on progress. Bob said that he would brief the Comanche elders on their meeting. Bob had already informed them that it was very likely that Mike Muguara was dead. They had asked him to update them regularly on the progress with the case.

When they arrived back at their hotel they got on the phone with Bill Dunwoody.

"I got the email from Marie and I have already called the DA. He said we will have a search warrant for Vivar's place in hand for your return tomorrow. So update me on the day with the attorney."

Tommy gave the sheriff a full report and then he hit the sack.

Chapter 24

Pepe Vivar

THEY ARRIVED AT THE 34TH Street HQ at lunchtime the following day and went straight to the conference room, where Marie was sitting and talking with Bill Dunwoody.

"Here's your search warrant. When do you plan to go search his place and what additional backup do you need?" asked the chief.

"My plan is to do it at 6 a.m. tomorrow. Marie and I will hit the front door with the warrant. As a seconded civilian my dad will have to stay back in the vehicle, and then he can join the search once it's underway. I would like another team of two to come in the front with us to help us with the search.

"We will then need a second team to cover the rear of the residence by the deck in case they try to throw things off the cliff into the lake. It would be a real pain in the ass if we ended up needing to deploy dive teams to go looking for stuff."

"Good plan, Tommy. I'll get the teams lined up and we'll meet here at 4:30 a.m. and then drive on out there. I suggest you two get yourselves home and get some rest; you'll have a big day tomorrow," said the chief.

~

The following morning the team assembled in the parking lot at 34th Street. The duty officer checked that everyone had the necessary bulletproof vests and that all weapons were checked to ensure they were fully functional. If they needed to engage in a shootout they wanted no mishaps. The three cruisers then set out for the residence of Pepe Vivar and Jimmy Rodriguez.

It was still dark when they arrived. In early December sunrise is about 7 a.m. so it was still an hour or more away. Although the home was spectacularly large, for some reason they didn't have any security gates that needed to be opened by the resident, so they were able to drive up the long driveway right to the front door. They could see security cameras in the trees. They may have triggered some kind of warning; however, it was impossible to tell. They were in stealth mode, no lights and no sirens. They gently coasted up to the steps leading to the front door.

Team Two exited their vehicle and took up their position at the rear of the home on the deck, preventing any exit to the lakeside. Tommy, Marie and Team One climbed the steps to the double-hinged metal front door and rang the bell.

A few seconds later the intercom sprang to life.

"Who the fuck is it at this time in the morning? Someone better have died or I'll shoot you myself, you fuckers!"

Jimmy Rodriguez had obviously not checked his security system or he would have seen the cruisers in his front yard.

"Travis County Police Department, can you open the door, please? We have a warrant to search your property!"

The front door opened and Jimmy Rodriguez, obviously still drunk or at least significantly hung over, stood in front of them wearing a long silk robe. He had made an attempt to look like Liberace and failed miserably. Marie concluded that perhaps her earlier suspicions of the relationship between Jimmy and his driver did indeed extend to the bedroom.

Tommy had been wise to have Team Two on the deck. The sliding patio doors flew open and an apparition that was Pepe Vivar burst out on to the deck, his arms full of packages of cocaine and marijuana.

"Thanks for bringing us your stash, Pepe, and we didn't even need to ask," laughed the two officers with their guns drawn. "Is that a weapon you have sticking out under your robe or are you just pleased to see us?"

The deputies led Pepe back into the residence and had him put all the drugs on the coffee table. Jimmy Rodriguez was beginning to focus and the realization hit him that he was in deep shit.

Tommy took the lead.

"Jimmy Rodriguez and Pepe Vivar, we are arresting you both for being in possession of controlled substances, namely, cocaine and marijuana, with the intent to distribute. There may be further charges that we will bring at a later date. We have a warrant to search this residence."

They cuffed them and the officers from Team Two took them off to the cruisers parked outside. As they walked out of the house they passed Bill Ross walking in, and Jimmy Rodriguez recognized his golf partner immediately. All he said was "You!" and he walked on by to be put into the back of the police cruiser.

~

The drugs were a godsend. It enabled Tommy to arrest them immediately and get them out of the house. They began their search.

It was a treasure trove. They found many more packages of cocaine that they estimated had a street value of a couple of million and over $500,000 in cash stacked on the bed in one of the spare bedrooms. There were hand guns, shotguns and four AK47 rifles configured for automatic fire. Boxes of ammo, crates of liquor and boxes of Cuban cigars completed their haul.

In Vivar's bedroom they found the Hugo Boss leather jacket, and when they checked the right sleeve they found Jacob Goldman's signature patch. On the nightstand at the side of his bed was a solid silver money clip with a two-diamond inlay and an engraved insignia that looked like the ace of spades. Propped up in the corner of the bedroom was a Louis-ville Slugger baseball bat.

Bill took out his cell and dialed Claudette Weiss' number in Heidelberg. She answered immediately.

"Guten tag, wer anruft?"

"Guten tag, Claudette, Bill Ross calling from Austin."

"Oh hello, Officer Ross, how can I help you today? Are you making progress with the investigation?"

"We are, Claudette, we are making *significant* progress. Tell me, did Mike own a solid silver money clip?"

"Yes, he did, Detective Ross. It was made special, one of a kind, and my grandfather gave him two diamonds to inlay. It was engraved with the Special Forces Marine Corps insignia, the same as the tattoo under his right arm. Have you found it? I would so much like to have it back!"

"Yes, we have it, Claudette, but we'll have to keep it for a while. I assure you that it will be returned safely when our work is done here."

"Oh, that would be wonderful, Officer Ross."

"Enjoy the rest of the day, Claudette. I will be in touch again soon.

"Got you, you bastard!" said Bill when he hung up the phone.

~

There was so much stuff in the home that they had to call for a truck to come and haul it back to 34th Street. When everything was loaded and dispatched, they drove back to start the interview process, beginning with Pepe Vivar.

Vivar had been processed and was in a holding cell. On the way back to the office they stopped by Gold's Gym and showed Alan Archer the mug shot of Vivar that the desk officer had sent to Tommy's cell phone earlier. Alan Archer confirmed that Pepe was the man he had seen arguing with Mike in the parking lot.

They had Vivar brought from his holding cell into the interview room. Marie, Bill and Tommy sat opposite him. The side of his face where the scar was twitched uncontrollably, and his eye occasionally twitched as if he were winking at them.

Each time it happened they winked back. He was a seething cauldron ready to explode.

"I bet yesterday at this time you never thought that 24 hours later you would be having breakfast in this fine establishment, eh, Pepe?" said Tommy, opening up the interview.

"I want to call my lawyer," barked Pepe.

"Oh, come on, this is just a quiet chat. You are under caution, of course, but is there anything that you would like to say about all the toys we found?"

"I want my fucking lawyer!"

"That was a real nice bathrobe you had on this morning and the Viagra was obviously working. This fucking lawyer you refer to, is that a lawyer you fuck? Can't imagine that a limo driver can afford a big-city lawyer."

Pepe exploded right then, yelling every obscenity imaginable and straining at the chains that secured him to the chair and to the floor.

"Let me get you a phone and you can call your lawyer."

~

While Pepe was calling his attorney, Bill Dunwoody was calling the Travis County DA's Office and spoke with assistant DA Bobby Brown. Bobby arrived 30 minutes later and sat in Bill Dunwoody's office awaiting the arrival of Pepe's attorney.

A couple of hours later, the lawyer arrived. It was Julien Boudreaux of Boudreaux and Simon, one of the very best law firms in town. He typically billed out at $800 an hour. They had rattled the cage of the big money; no way back now.

"I want to speak to my client. Alone please! I would like a cup of coffee, one sugar, and a glass of sparkling water, no ice," said the attorney, wiping the seat with his silk handkerchief so as not to soil his ten-thousand-dollar suit.

"I'll get you a coffee from the vending machine. I'm afraid the water is a *no can do* as we have a water conservation policy here in the office and the sparkling water truck broke down on its way here this morning," said Marie with a smirk.

"What's your name, officer? I will see to it that Chief Dunwoody hears about this!"

"I've already heard, Julien," said Bill Dunwoody as he walked into the room. "Now, don't be a horse's ass, just do what you need to do, then we can all get on with the rest of our lives."

The door closed and Julien Boudreaux spoke with his client.

A short time later Julien said that they were ready and that his client would not be answering any questions. Julien wanted to be clear on the charges.

Bobby Brown now joined them and they all sat down in the interview room, Pepe Vivar now looking like the cat that got the cream and Julien poised over his leather-bound notebook, peering over his half-rim gold-frame reading glasses, his Monte Blanc fountain pen in hand ready to take notes.

Bill Dunwoody stood in the corner while Bobby Brown read the charges.

"We have possession of Class A narcotics with intent to distribute and we have possession of cash and firearms. Oh, by the way, Julien, are you representing both Mr. Vivar and Mr. Rodriguez?"

"Yes, I will be representing both, but I wish to concentrate on Mr. Vivar at this time. I will be insisting on an expedited hearing with the judge and I will be seeking bail as Mr. Vivar is a fine, upstanding member of the community."

"Oh, I think that you better keep your powder dry on that one, Julien, as I haven't finished reading you the charges. *We are also charging your client with capital murder!*

"On or about January 15th of this year, a Mr. Mike Muguara, aka Raul Hernandez, was dragged behind a truck, his head was beaten to a pulp with a baseball bat, and his hands were severed.

"The murder took place in the Whispering Hollow neighborhood of Leander and the body was dumped next to a burning cross. Doubt if the judge will be up for bail on that one, old buddy.

"I guess you need more time with your client, as he's suddenly looking a little pale. We can now offer you some water based on the stressful circumstances."

To use another Sherlock Holmes quote, "*The game was afoot.*"

"What evidence do you have to charge my client with such a horrendous crime?" demanded Julien, with beads of sweat now beginning to form on his forehead.

"Our evidence is considerable and it will all be made available to you and then presented at trial. We have the jacket of the deceased recovered from your client's bedroom. We have a solid silver money clip belonging to the deceased, also recovered from your client's bedroom. We have a Louisville Slugger baseball bat taken from his bedroom that we suspect was used in the crime, which is now in our forensics lab and is providing more fingerprints than a whorehouse doorbell. We have eyewitness testimony, and the list goes on."

"I would like a short adjournment while I talk further with my client," said Julien, the beads of sweat now forming small rivers as they made their way to the attorney's chin.

They left the room, and a few minutes later Julien asked to meet with them again.

"By way of clarification, will you be bringing the same charges against Mr. Rodriguez?" asked Julien.

"No, we will not. At this time, Mr. Rodriguez will be charged on the drugs with intent to distribute and firearm possession only."

Julien Boudreaux looked relieved but Pepe Vivar looked terrified; he was being hung out to dry. Old Sparky would have only one new customer. As it happens, in Texas execution is by lethal injection, not by the electric chair, but for Pepe it didn't much matter as he was going to die. In the end it doesn't matter which door you use to leave; the destination is the same.

"Okay, Bobby, I will be in touch in due course. I would like to see my other client now."

~

As Pepe Vivar was being led back to the cells, he was shaking like a leaf and twice his legs went out from under him. Thankfully, however, he stayed in control of his bowels.

After conferring with Jimmy Rodriguez, Julien Boudreaux told Bobby Brown that he and his client were now ready to meet with him. They all sat together in the interview room that an hour earlier had been used to present the charges to Pepe Vivar. After Bobby Brown had read out the formal charges regarding the drugs and firearms, Julien responded on behalf of his client.

"Mr. Rodriguez had no knowledge that the illicit drugs and weapons were in his home. As Mr. Pepe Vivar is his nephew, Mr. Rodriquez has allowed him to rent rooms in his house and has also provided him with a job as his driver. Mr. Vivar has had trouble getting his life together since coming to the U.S. from Honduras and has had several run-ins with law enforcement, but he is family all the same. Mr. Rodriguez felt an obligation to try to help in any way he could, and unfortunately it would appear that he has strayed from the straight and narrow yet again.

"I request a hearing with the judge as soon as possible, at which time I will request that all charges against Mr. Rodriguez be dropped."

"Good try, Julien. Your position is that your client is the salt of the earth. I understand; let's see if the judge agrees. I will work on getting the hearing set up and get back to you ASAP," responded the assistant DA.

~

They were all back in the conference room after the events of the morning.

"Latisha Williams is chomping at the bit to get the story of the arrest into tomorrow's edition of the *Statesman*," said Marie.

"She can do that but she still needs to stick to her agreement with us. This is just the beginning, the first step in getting to the truth. She cannot divulge any of the other suspicions we have. She can simply report on the arrests made and that Pepe Vivar has been charged with the murder—that he was arrested in a dawn raid on the home where he lived in Venture Point," said Tommy.

"I think it's likely that Rodriguez will walk," said Bobby Brown.

"Julien is a smart SOB and he will make Jimmy Rodriguez look like a saint for trying to help his brother's kid. Vivar is truly screwed; they will let him go down for this and, in doing so, make sure that there is no connection to the person who ordered the hit. My guess is that Julien will even help us with a motive, saying that new information has come to his attention about a previous altercation between his client and Mike Muguara. He will try to get the death penalty off the table. That's unlikely, but in my opinion that's what he will try to do, because that's what I would do," continued the assistant DA.

"So let's assume that it unfolds in this way. We can play along. Jimmy Rodriguez gets to walk and he thinks he's dodged a bullet. He will relax and we can use this to our advantage," said Bill.

"We need to start building a case to go after Jimmy Rodriguez and the way to do that is to work on Pepe Vivar. We need to have Pepe understand that he is being set up to take the fall on this and that his attorney is constructing an argument to protect Rodriguez. If we can begin to drive a wedge between him and Jimmy and assure him that we think that he is just the fall guy, we might be able to get him to talk. We might need to offer to take the death penalty off the table. Is that something that your boss the DA would go along with, Bobby?"

"Not sure, Bill. Let me get back to you on that. I do think that your approach is the right one, however, so let's start to drip water on Pepe Vivar and in the meantime I will talk to the DA."

Chapter 25

Antonella Aguilar

EVERY YEAR IN AUSTIN THERE are violent swings in tempera-
ture as fall gives way to the onset of winter. One day it might
be 80 degrees and humid and the next day 50 degrees and
windy. Trees that a few days earlier were covered in fall colors
were now laid bare by the buffeting winds.

Bill sat in the heavy traffic on FM360 in the late evening as
he made his way home, the normal rush-hour congestion made
even worse than normal by shoppers heading to the mall to
hand over their hard-earned cash for overpriced gifts for
Christmas. They would stand in line so their kids could tell
Santa what they wanted for Christmas, and have their photograph taken with an overweight guy in a red suite who smelled
and a couple of weeks earlier had been out of work and living
under a bridge.

Elaine was hard at work changing the décor of their home
when Bill walked in. Every year Elaine would decorate with
orange and black for Halloween, then transition to red, yellow
and gold for Thanksgiving, and finally to the crimson red and
white for Christmas. This was her annual ritual each year,
hauling each batch of decorations down from the loft, only to
return them back to storage a couple of weeks later as one
holiday transitioned into the next.

It was a tradition in the Ross home that at Christmas time,
when the tree was to be set up and decorated, the family

worked as a team, each in turn choosing just the right colored ball or garland to place on the tree while Nat King Cole and Bing Crosby sang "Deck the Halls" or "White Christmas" in the background.

So it was to be that night. Tommy was on his way over with Claire, and Elaine had baked her famous Scottish shortbread, ready for their arrival. Claire would have hot chocolate, Elaine a glass of sherry, Tommy a Coke as he was driving back home, and Bill his Glenmorangie as they ate the shortbread, sang along with Nat and Bing and got the Christmas season kicked off in the traditional manner.

"One wrong move and we could blow this thing," said Bill as he and Tommy sat in his office after the tree decorating had been completed.

"You're right, Dad, and we're going to have to think two and three steps ahead."

"If it was Garrison McMullen who ordered the hit, which I suspect it was, he will be nervous about the arrests and will be calling the shots with Julien Boudreaux. His biggest risk will be if Pepe Vivar starts to talk, and he will know that. They could just take Pepe out—have someone get to him while he's in the holding cell. We need to ensure that Bobby Brown is sensitive to this possibility and that he gets the DA to go along with our plan to take the death penalty off the table. If we get Pepe to talk, then we will have to protect him.

"We also need to expect that Garrison McMullen might call in markers from those he has helped along the way. We know he is a shaker and mover in the Republican Party and that his son is the governor-elect. The governor's office might put some undue pressure on the DA or on the chief. If McMullen is smart, which I'm sure he is, he will not want to show his hand completely. For example, if he gets the governor involved on his side, he will show his hand and he will know that he has shown us that he is the guy pulling the strings. It will have to be subtle, but we should expect it and be ready for it," said Bill.

~

The following morning, they were in the office early. Marie was at her desk reading the editorial in the Statesman written by Latisha Williams. She had done what was asked of her and limited the editorial to the arrest in the slaying of Mike Muguara. She had done a really good job on the backdrop to support the piece, describing Mike Muguara as a war hero whose life had been extinguished by a two-bit hoodlum.

"Marie, can you take the assignment to try to track down Antonella Aguilar, the retired housekeeper from the McMullen Ranch? We need to find out what she knows," said Tommy.

"Will do, Boss."

"Dad, let's you and I go over to the holding cells and see if we can get Pepe to talk without his attorney being there."

~

Pepe was in his cell, head in his hands, when they arrived.

"Sleep well last night?" asked Tommy.

Pepe barely raised his head, but as he did so he let out a low-pitched growl and bared his teeth just like the caged animal he was. However, also like every animal when cornered, he was looking for a way out, an escape route, to be able to live to fight another day. Bill and Tommy began to sow a seed of hope. They hoped Pepe would recognize that it was his only real chance for survival.

"You're being thrown to the wolves, Pepe. Your boyfriend Jimmy is going to ensure that he comes out of this squeaky clean, and to do that he needs to give you up. The drugs, the money and the guns all belong to you and you killed Mike Muguara on your own. He had nothing to do with it. While you're sitting there with your head in your hands, why don't you stick your head through your legs and kiss your ass good-bye. You're dead, Pepe, you just don't know it yet."

"Go fuck yourself!" yelled Pepe. "Jimmy would never do that to me."

As they left the cell with these words ringing in their ears, Tommy and Bill knew that Pepe Vivar was trying hard to convince himself that this was true. They also knew that he wasn't succeeding.

Marie Mason had arrived at the Round Rock address, the last known location for Antonella Aguilar. She talked with neighbors but no one had any idea where Antonella had gone after she moved out of the small three-bedroom home she had owned for the past ten years. Some of the neighbors expressed surprise at the speed of her departure; one day she was there and the next day she was gone. The house was then put on the market and a moving company came and took all of her stuff away. The house sold fast as it was listed at a price well below fair market value.

The neighbors gave Marie the name of the Realtor who sold the property and she headed off to find her office.

"I'm looking for Dawn Summers," said Marie as she walked into the Keller Williams agency on East Main Street in Round Rock.

Dawn Summers looked like a poster child for the real estate industry. She was tall and slim with long blond hair. Her makeup was perfect. She moved like a top class model on the runway, gliding rather than walking across the floor.

"Dawn Summers," said the Realtor, extending her hand to Marie, holding it in place for just a microsecond to ensure that Marie saw the diamond and sapphire ring and matching tennis bracelet. "How might I help you today?"

"I'm Detective Marie Mason of the Travis County Police Department. Is there somewhere we can talk privately? I need to get some details on a home you sold recently."

"Travis County Police Department," said Dawn with some trepidation. "I hope there wasn't a dead body buried in the garden," joked the Realtor.

Marie was not impressed by the joke.

"A place where we could talk, *please*!"

Dawn led Marie to the conference room at the rear of the office. They passed by the scoreboard on the wall. Every Realtor company has a scoreboard in full view with the sales for each agent displayed. Being number one on that board was what they lived for. The money was great, but being the top dog on that board was what really gave them their jollies. It was no surprise to Marie that Dawn Summers was number one on the board. She also saw the notation on the board for the sale of Antonella Aguilar's property on Brushy Creek.

"You were the listing agent for the Aguilar property on Brushy Creek, is that correct?" said Marie.

"Oh yes, three-bedroom, two-bath, 2200 square feet. Real nice little property. Got a sixteen-day close on that one, then the title company screwed around with the disbursement of funds."

"What was the reason for the sale?"

"Not sure, something about wanting to be closer to her son in Florida."

Marie found that confusing, but didn't share her thoughts with the Realtor.

Antonella Aguilar didn't have a son!

"Do you know her son's name and also do you have a copy of the closing documents? I'd like the information on the bank account used to receive the proceeds of the sale."

"Not sure that I am allowed to give you that information," said the Realtor, now feeling that she was out of her depth. She was in shark-infested waters and needed to get help.

"I think you need to talk with the owner of our agency. His name is Bill Mitchell; let me go get him, if you don't mind."

A few minutes later, she was back with Bill Mitchell. Marie explained what she needed and why she needed it, and the owner of the agency understood and instructed Dawn to provide the information from the file.

"Okay, I have it here. The son's name is Gavin and the bank account is with the First Bank of Sarasota, Sarasota, Florida."

"Do you have a forwarding address?" asked Marie.

"Yes, it's a PO Box 2722, Martin Luther King Way in Sarasota."

Later, in her car in the parking lot of the Realtor agency, Marie concluded that someone wanted Antonella Aguilar out of the way. She had no son, but her fictitious son had the same first name as the boy she raised when his mother was banished from the McMullen Ranch. Had Antonella run, or was she pushed? Was Gavin McMullen also wrapped up in all of this?

Chapter 26

Spill the beans

"HE WANTS TO SEE you, Tommy."

It was the deputy from the holding cell on the phone. "Pepe Vivar wants to see you."

Marie was still out at Round Rock, so Tommy and Bill went to the holding cell to meet with Pepe Vivar.

"What can I do for you, Pepe?" said Tommy as he entered the cell. It looked like Pepe Vivar hadn't moved since the last time they saw him. He was still sitting at the back of his cell with his head in his hands.

"I was just doing as I was told," said Pepe, shaking his head in despair.

"And what were you told?"

"If I tell you, I don't want the needle and I'll also need protection as Jimmy will arrange to get me killed. He's done it before with others who have opened their big mouths."

"The problem with that, Pepe, is that I'm not going to go stick my neck out for you unless I know what it is you have to tell me. You're just going to have to trust me that I will do what I can for you. That's better than what you've got right now, which is nothing."

Pepe waited for a moment but soon realized that he had little option but to spill the beans.

"Jimmy asked me first to tell him to back off. He said that this guy Raul Hernandez was trying to muscle in on our business and bring in his own cheap illegal labor. He was also going to give the illegals that work for us more money and try to tempt them away to work for him. It was going to really screw up what it had taken us years to build, and if he got too close and found out about our drug business, then the shit would really hit the fan."

"Jimmy asked me to follow Hernandez and find out where he lived. I saw him come out of his hotel and head over to the gym on Lamar a couple of times a week, and I got in his face one night and told him that if he didn't back down he was a dead man."

"He wouldn't stop, and we saw him talking with a group of electricians who appeared to be agreeing with what he said. That's when Jimmy said that we would have to make him disappear. We could make it look like he was an illegal, and if we could do that the cops wouldn't spend too much time looking for the killers."

"We sat in the limo in the parking lot at the gym, Jimmy and I, and some of the illegals who worked for us, in a couple of our trucks and a beat-up old Taurus. I hit him from behind and we bundled him into the trunk of the Taurus. I took the remote from him for the BMW and looked to see what I could find in the car. There were a couple of handguns in the trunk and a nice leather jacket in the back. So I took them."

"We drove out to Whispering Hollow where the others we had paid to help get the job done had cleared the area of a couple of homeless guys and made sure that the coast was clear when we arrived."

"When we got there we hauled him out of the truck and I tied a rope around his wrists and secured it to one of the pickups. I took his wallet and money clip out of his back pocket; I just saw it when I was fastening the rope so I took it, and then I gave the signal for him to be dragged."

"When it was over I took the baseball bat to him and Jimmy cut off his hands. We cleaned up the drag site, threw the hands in the back of the truck and dumped them in the lake later."

"The cross had been set up and Jimmy poured gas on it and set it alight. He then took out the sign from the back of the limo, which he had written earlier, and nailed it to a tree. That was it, we were out of there and we drove home."

Pepe had coughed the lot.

"Well, the thing is, Pepe, it's your word against his. I doubt that your compadres who helped are going to suddenly get a conscience and tell us what happened. Nope, it's a *he said - he said* thing, Pepe. I need more than what you've just given me."

Pepe paused, staring at the ceiling for a moment. It was as if he was trying to decide to jump off the cliff or not. If he played his final card, there was no going back. As it stood right now the cops could say that they found out what had happened in the course of their investigation. They could construct it to hide the fact that Pepe had grassed. But if he played his final card then it would come out in the trial that he was the one who had given them the evidence. He decided he had no option but to get them to play along with his scheme to hide the fact that he had grassed.

"Okay, I'll give you the evidence you need to prove that it was Jimmy who asked me to do this. Now you're going to have to trust *me*. Before I tell you where the evidence is, I want it in writing from the DA that I won't get the needle and that I'll get protection. I don't want to involve that slime ball Julien Boudreaux, so no talking with him. You get me a letter and I give you the evidence - deal?"

"Okay, Pepe, I'll see what I can do." Bill and Tommy left the cells to go brief the Chief and Bobby Brown.

~

Marie returned to the office after her trip to Round Rock. It was just after two in the afternoon and she looked up the telephone information for the post office on Martin Luther King Way in Sarasota. She found it and made the call.

"Can I speak with the person in charge of your PO box rental facilities?"

"Hello, Angelina Rocha here, I'm in charge of the PO box rental. Do you wish to rent a box?"

"No, Angelina, this is Detective Marie Mason of the Travis County Police Department in Austin, Texas, I need some information on a current renter."

"I can't give you that information over the phone, Detective, but if you send me an email with the box number, outlining why you need the information, then I can get you the information immediately."

An hour later Marie had what she needed. The box had been rented by a Shirley Simpson of 17 Longmeadow Circle, Sarasota, a very expensive neighborhood on the outskirts of the city.

Shirley Simpson, why do I know that name? thought Marie. It came to her in a flash. Shirley Simpson was Gavin McMullen's campaign manager for his election bid for the Texas governor race. What the hell was going on here?

Tommy's cell phone rang as he and Bill were headed back to the office from their meeting with Bobby Brown. It was Marie. "Where are you guys? I've uncovered some interesting information about Antonella Aguilar. Are you coming back to the office soon?"

~

They met in the conference room at Hudson Bend 20 minutes later and Marie brought them up to speed on what she had found.

"Gavin McMullen is in the middle of this. He is risking his entire political future; why would he do that? Did Gavin McMullen give the order for the hit because Mike was getting too close to uncovering his involvement? Mike had met with Antonella, and if she told Gavin about it and the fact that Mike was digging around in the family business, perhaps Gavin lost it and had him taken out," said Tommy.

"The pieces don't fit," said Bill.

"Gavin's name has never come up. Mike never mentioned seeing him during his surveillance activities. Mike simply said that Antonella raised Gavin, so Gavin must have a strong bond with her. Are we suggesting that he has killed Antonella in addition to ordering the hit on Mike? If he was concerned about Mike digging dirt up on the family, it's likely that An-tonella knows more about where the skeletons are buried than anyone. Why involve his campaign manager to set up a PO box for communication with the Round Rock Realtor regarding the sale of her home? No, Gavin is not a bad guy in this, I'd bet my life on it, but he is involved in some way. The real issue is, why is he involved? That's what we need to find out."

"Marie, can you get hold of Shirley Simpson tomorrow and try to get to the bottom of this? We need to talk with Antonella Aguilar. Bill and I need to get back with Pepe Vivar; the DA has given us a green light to take the death penalty off the table provided that he can give us solid evidence that Jimmy Rodriquez orchestrated Mike's killing."

~

The following morning Bill and Tommy were back in the holding cell with Pepe Vivar.

"I have your letter from the DA, Pepe, but read it careful-ly. If what you give us as evidence of Jimmy Rodriguez's involvement is useless, then all bets are off. If, on the other hand, if it's golden and we get a conviction, then the DA will go to bat for you with the judge and not seek the death penal-ty."

Pepe spilled the beans.

"Okay, here's the deal. You need to search the limo. Below the driver's side seat, tucked up inside the lining, is a metal clip. The clip holds a micro-recorder. Most of the time when Jimmy talked with me about dirty work he wanted me to do, we did it in the limo. He's paranoid that his house is bugged and he thinks the limo is secure. We drive out into the middle of nowhere, miles away from any cell towers, and have our little talks.

"For my own protection I've been taping our conversa-tions. If it's still there, it will have the conversation recorded when he told me to make the hit on Raul Hernandez and how he wanted it set up. When you find it, I want you to contact Julien Boudreaux and tell him that your continued investiga-tion, including the search of the limo, has turned up additional evidence and that you want to bring him up to speed. At that time, you can say that unknown third parties have been bugging the limo and that might convince him that it wasn't me who recorded the conversations and snitched on him. Agreed?"

"Sounds like a plan, Pepe. No idea if Jimmy will buy it, and he may still come after you. We'll do our best to protect you, but *you* got yourself into this."

~

They left the holding cell and called the chief to get a search done of the limo. That night they had the recorder and they all sat in the conference room and listened to Jimmy Rodriguez set up the hit.

Jimmy Rodriguez speaks - *So he won't listen to reason! We're gonna have to make this motherfucker disappear, Pepe. I want it done in the next week. I'm tired of this shit. If he starts bringing in his own people, like the fucking Guatemalans or, worse still, the Salvadorians, then there will be a war in the street.*

We can pick him up and take him down by the lake at Whispering Hollow, kill him there and then just fade into the sunset. Everyone is used to seeing our trucks running around at night in the 'hood, it will be no big deal. Where's the best place to hit him, Pepe?

Pepe Vivar - *He goes to the gym on Lamar a couple of times a week. We can whack him there in the parking lot and put him in the trunk of a car and bring him out here. How do we kill him, Boss? Just put a bullet in him and throw him in the lake?*

Jimmy Rodriguez - *No, we need to send a message! We lynch him, string him up or something, no let's just tie him to a fucking truck and drag his ass! We also need to make sure he can't be identified, so we need to cut off his fingers and take his teeth out. Can you get a team together, Pepe, not too many, say ten, and give them a hundred bucks each and tell them that we need to get rid of a guy trying to bring in South American shitheads to steal their jobs. Tell me when it's set up."*

"Now let's do a couple of lines and get outta here!"

That was the end of the tape. They had the smoking gun. Bobby Brown picked up his cell phone and called Julien Boudreaux.

~

"Julien, Bobby Brown here, can you be at the Sheriff's office tomorrow morning? We need to meet with you and your client Jimmy Rodriguez. There's been some new developments."

"I was just about to call you, Bobby. My client has been held now for 36 hours and I want a hearing with the judge as we discussed. Are we on his schedule and if so, when?" replied Julien, trying to take control of the conversation.

"I've spoken to the judge, Julien, we're getting it on his schedule. Just be there tomorrow at nine!"

Bobby hung up the phone.

Chapter 27

Turn it off!

THE FOLLOWING MORNING MARIE CALLED Shirley Simpson, Gavin McMullen's campaign manager. It was Shirley Simpson herself who answered the phone. *Probably in her office early before her staff get in,* thought Marie.

"Shirley, this is Detective Marie Mason of Travis County Police Department. Do you own a PO box in Sarasota, Florida?"

"Yes, I do, Detective, what's this about?"

"Why do you have a PO box, Shirley?"

"Because I live there, Detective, and I prefer my mail going to a PO box and not my home. What is this about, please?"

"Do you know why your PO box would be listed as the mailing address for an Antonella Aguilar regarding a real estate transaction for the sale of her home in Round Rock?"

"There has obviously been some mistake, it's probably a clerical error and they have the wrong PO box number, that's all I can think of."

Marie knew that Shirley was lying, she could hear it in her voice, so she pressed forward.

"So why didn't you send back the closing documents for the property that were sent to this PO box over three months ago? They must have arrived in your box and you would have realized that they were important papers. Why did you not send them back, Shirley?"

"I don't remember any papers, Detective. If I had received them in error, I would have sent them back. Again, it must be a clerical breakdown. I wish I could help further, Detective, but I have a meeting with my staff in two minutes."

"Thanks for your help, Shirley. We may get back with you as our investigation continues."

The conversation ended and Marie knew that Shirley Simpson and her boss, Gavin McMullen, were both in this up to their eyeballs.

~

While Marie was having her call with Shirley Simpson, Julien Boudreaux had arrived at the holding cell and was meeting privately with his client Jimmy Rodriguez prior to the meeting with the assistant DA.

At nine the meeting started with Julien Boudreaux and Jimmy Rodriguez seated across the table from Bobby Brown and Tommy. Julien again tried to take control.

"I have met with my client this morning. This has gone far enough, Bobby. My client needs to be released. His business is being adversely affected by his absence and he is suffering significant loss of income. We need to get in front of the judge so that my client can get back to his normal life. We will cooperate in every way with your investigation of Mr. Vivar, the real guilty party in all of this."

"As I said last night, Julien, new information has come to light. We have been continuing the search of the residence at Venture Point and of the limo that was driven by Mr. Vivar. Did you know that your limo was bugged, Jimmy? Some people trying to keep tabs on you, are they? Who might they be?"

The blood drain from Jimmy Rodriguez's face, and for the first time Julien Boudreaux looked flustered. Jimmy was about to say something but Julien stopped him.

"Please stop posturing, Bobby, and tell us what new information you have," said Julien.

Bobby Brown looked to Tommy and Tommy laid the micro-recorder on the table.

"Amazing little device this, made in China, of course. It's total wireless. I can call it on my cell phone and retrieve the contents remotely, just like this."

Tommy dialed the number of the wireless micro-recorder using his cell and put it on speaker.

So he won't listen to reason! We're going to have to make this fucker disappear Pepe. I want it done in the next week I'm tired..."

"Turn it off! Turn the fucking thing off!" yelled Jimmy Rodriguez.

"We need to take a brief recess. I need to talk with my client," said Julien, desperately trying to do damage control before his client lost it completely.

~

"Well, I think that went well!" said Bobby as they all sat in the conference room, having left Julien with Jimmy Rodriguez.

"Jimmy will be terrified. He won't want to go down for this alone. He will want to give up the people who ordered the hit so he can save his own skin. Julien will be trying to calm him down," continued Bobby.

"I think that we should try to keep tabs on Julien after he leaves here today. He knows now that bail will be impossible and that Pepe *and* Jimmy will be charged with the killing. Whoever is calling the shots here will feel completely exposed. Pepe and Jimmy will need to be protected. We need to keep them away from other prisoners," said Chief Dunwoody.

~

Julien told them that he was ready to meet again.

Bobby Brown read the charges.

"In addition to the previous charges of drug and weapons possession brought against you, Mr. Rodriguez, we are now bringing the additional charge of capital murder—that on or about January 15th of this year you ordered the killing of a Mr. Mike Muguara, aka Raul Hernandez, and that you actively participated in that killing."

Jimmy Rodriguez was returned to the cells. Bobby and Julien had a brief discussion and then Julien left.

"What did Julien say?" asked Tommy.

"He said he would see me in court," laughed Bobby.

Chapter 28

Antonella's story

BILL, TOMMY AND MARIE were having a coffee in the break room after the excitement of the morning when Tommy's cell phone rang.

"Am I speaking with Detective Tommy Ross?" said the female caller without any introduction.

"This is Tommy Ross."

"Detective Ross, I am calling from the office of the governor-elect, Gavin McMullen. The governor-elect would like to meet with you today if possible. Can you be in our offices here in South Congress at 3 p.m.?"

"I will be there."

"Who was that?" said Marie, picking up on the strange expression on Tommy's face.

"Gavin McMullen wants to see me at three o'clock today and you're coming with me, Marie."

~

They arrived on time for the meeting with Gavin McMullen. They were offered coffee, which they declined, and were told that Gavin McMullen was finishing up a call and would be ready to see them in a few minutes. Forty-five minutes later they were led into the conference room.

The room was huge, dominated by a long conference table that could seat at least twenty. At the end of the room, through huge bay windows, the dome of the capitol could be seen in the distance. On the sidewall hung the state flag of Texas and the U.S. flag, and a photograph of the current governor, Raymond Shaw.

Gavin McMullen entered the room.

"Good to see you again, Tommy, thanks for coming. You must be Detective Marie Mason I've heard so much about!" said the governor-elect.

"Y'all need some coffee or water? I can have Valerie get you what you need."

"We were both offered coffee, Gavin, thank you, we're both fine," replied Tommy.

"Okay, let's get started. I'd like you to meet a couple of people."

As if choreographed, the door opened and two women walked in.

"This is Shirley Simpson, my campaign manager, and I would also like you to meet Antonella Aguilar. I think you've been trying to locate Antonella, so here she is."

Tommy looked agitated and annoyed. Marie looked shocked, and it was Tommy who spoke first.

"You're going to have to explain what's going on here, Gavin. You were obviously well aware that we were looking for Ms. Aguilar and you've been keeping her from us. You're interfering in the course of a murder investigation," said Tommy, making sure that Gavin McMullen realized the seriousness of the situation.

"Fully understand, Tommy, but give me a chance to explain and perhaps you will appreciate why I needed to do what I did."

"As I am sure you are aware, Antonella raised me after my father and mother divorced and when my father prohibited my mother from having any further contact with me. My father was in my life, of course, but his business interests dominated his time and it was Antonella who was primarily responsible for raising me. She is my rock." Gavin smiled across the room at Antonella and she returned his smile.

"Antonella was very close to my mother before she was banished from the ranch. My father was and still is a very violent man. He built an empire and he didn't let anyone or anything get in his way. He was never violent with me and was very committed to my education and to my career, but he frequently beat my mother, and Antonella tried to help her deal with her pain."

"Antonella has told me over the years that things happened in the past that she cannot talk about. She is still very scared of my father, and if he thought for a minute that she might have talked about the past to a stranger, he wouldn't hesitate in causing her physical harm."

"She left her job on the ranch a few years ago and bought a little house to be closer to her sister in Round Rock. Her sister has now passed and she was hoping to spend what time she had left living quietly on her own with her three cats. That's when a man called Raul Hernandez came to visit with her."

"Raul Hernandez was trying to track down his birth parents, and when he told Antonella that his real name was Mike Muguara, she knew immediately why he had tracked her down. Mike's father had worked on the ranch and she had known him very well. Mike Muguara was obviously the baby that had been born to my mother, Alyana, and the reason why my father sent her away. Mike Muguara was my half-brother."

"Alyana told Mike Muguara about his mother and father and the love they had for each other that began as a result of the constant beatings she received at the hands of my father. She knew that my mother's maiden name was Reyes and that they were from Houston, and she also told him that, contrary to my father's wishes, she would meet off the ranch with Alyana so that she could see me and let me run around in the park. While my mother was walking with me in the park, Antonella would wait with the baby in the stroller. The baby in the stroller was Mike Muguara."

"After Mike had visited with her, she knew that he would keep digging until he found the truth, and she became scared for her life. That's when she called me for help."

"We agreed that she needed to disappear and we designed a plan to sell her house and have her relocate using a different name. Shirley agreed to help by using her bank account and PO box for communication with the Realtor. A superficial check on the sale of the property would result in a trail of the funds to Florida and the conclusion that Antonella had moved there to be closer to her son, when in reality she was still here, living in Round Rock under a different name."

"Given the current situation, Antonella wanted to speak with you to tell you *all she knows*. I agreed that I would help make that happen by setting up a meeting with you and your team. The call that Marie made to Shirley was very timely."

"So that's the background, that's why I did what I did. My father is still my father no matter what he's done, but he is not a nice person and if he is guilty of a crime he must be brought to justice."

~

So Bill Ross had been right, Gavin was not the bad guy in this; in fact, Gavin McMullen was a good guy, a very good guy!

"I think we should take a break and get some water and coffee. Antonella, you can meet with the officers privately in this room and Shirley and I can go get on with our work," said Gavin.

For the first time since she had walked into the room, a rather frail Antonella Aguilar spoke.

"I would really like you to stay, Gavin; there are things that I'm going to tell the detectives that I would like you also to hear."

They got coffee and water. Shirley left and Gavin, Marie and Tommy sat together to hear what Antonella had to say.

~

Antonella was very nervous and when she began to tell her story she made a couple of false starts, and then finally regained her composure after taking a sip of water.

"I started working as a housekeeper at the McMullen Ranch in 1962 when I was just twenty years old. Garrison

McMullen's father had died a few years earlier, and after a long illness his mother passed away in the winter of 1961. He needed help in running the household and he hired me."

"Back then Garrison McMullen was a wild man. He was a larger-than-life figure and he was going to grab life by the scruff of the neck and build an empire. With him it was always about money and power."

"He would have wild parties at the ranch and he developed a close friendship with Enrique Rodriguez, who owned the Colinas Verde Ranch in southwest Texas. Enrique had five brothers, and one of them was Jimmy Rodriquez. Enrique and Jimmy would always be at the parties at the ranch."

"Enrique and Garrison talked about business all the time. Jimmy, on the other hand, was all about partying. When I met him he said he was twenty, but my guess is that he was a lot younger, maybe sixteen or seventeen. Jimmy Rodriguez got drunk at one of the parties and raped me!"

"I wanted to leave, but I guess I was a slave to the money, and if I just closed my eyes to everything that went on and just did my job, life would be okay. Things did get worse, however, when Jimmy Rodriguez moved into the ranch. Garrison built a separate cabin for him and he ran everything, other than the household that I ran. He was always competing for Garrison's affection and he saw me as competition. He would always talk about the great things he was doing on the ranch, and constantly criticized my work."

"Jimmy had a real run-in with Garrison one day. Garrison was looking for him and found him in the barn having sex with one of the ranch hands. I guess it didn't matter to Jimmy, male or female; it was about domination and power. Garrison realized that he now had something he could leverage. He was sure that his brother didn't know what Jimmy was doing with both men and women, and I used to eavesdrop on some conversations and hear Garrison often say, "Now, you don't want me to tell your big brother, do you?""

~

"Garrison McMullen met Alyana at a concert in Zilker Park. For him it was love at first sight, for her he was a larger-than-life figure, an owner of one of the largest ranches in Texas. She did love him initially, but not as much as he loved her."

"The beatings started soon after they were married and I would console her and bathe her to try to ease her pain. She confided in me about her feelings for a particular ranch hand, and it was during this time that I began to have suspicions about her. She was from a very good Hispanic family and her father was very influential in the community, but there was something about her that didn't seem right. It was the way she moved and the way she talked."

"It was after one of the beatings when she was in the tub and I was washing her hair and dressing some of her bruises that she told me. The Reyes family had adopted her after her mother and father were killed in a house fire in Houston. The Reyes were the next-door neighbors and they applied to the courts to adopt Alyana and their application was granted. Alyana Reyes' birth name was Alyana Parker' the daughter of Aponi and Pallaton Parker, direct descendants of Quanah Parker' the last great chief of the Comanche. Alyana was not Hispanic' she was first nation, she was one hundred percent Comanche Indian!"

Tommy looked over at Gavin; he was sheet white. He grabbed the glass of water in front of him on the table and with a quivering hand drained the contents.

"I'm sorry, Gavin, I should have told you when you were young, but I was scared of your father. I'm sure that to this day he never knew," said Antonella, the tears streaming down her face as she looked across the table at Gavin.

Gavin had won election to be the next governor of Texas primarily by carrying the majority of the state Hispanic vote. He had a Hispanic mother, and this had been a cornerstone of his campaign. How was he going to do damage control on this?

Gavin was still shaking and got up from the table to get another glass of water. When he returned he asked Antonella if that was it or if there was any more that she hadn't told him. As more tears rolled down her face, she asked Gavin to sit down, that she wasn't done.

"I had sensed that she was not Hispanic, but I couldn't have been sure until she confided in me that night."

"When you were born, Gavin, things got a little better for Alyana. The beatings subsided and Garrison was over the moon about the fact he now had a son and heir. Then he fell off his horse."

"He almost died. He had been riding down some stray cattle and while riding at full speed his horse stumbled and rolled forward. The immediate injuries he sustained in the fall were not particularly serious, as he had managed to roll rather than go into the ground headfirst. The main damage was done when one of the stray steers ran over the top of him. He suffered major internal organ damage that left him impotent, and from then on he walked with the help of a cane."

"Nine months later your mother fell pregnant again. I knew who the father was, but Garrison didn't know and didn't care. His wife needed to get out of the house, never to return. The father of her child was the ranch hand she had fallen in love with, Achak Muguara."

"Achak quit his job and he and Alyana lived in Houston, where he got a job in the oil industry. It was heavy manual work with long hours and paid poorly. She still managed to make a trip up to Austin by bus every so often to see you, Gavin, and I would pay for a hotel for her and then she would get the bus back the next day."

"She told me that she was going to confront Garrison and try to get him to help; after all, she was the mother of his son. She told me that she planned to leave her new baby with Tommy's parents in Oklahoma until they got back on their feet. It was several weeks later when I heard a telephone conversation between her and Garrison. Hearing his side of the call, I heard him say for them to drive up that weekend and they could talk over it and see how he might be able to help."

"They arrived in an old Chevy pickup and Garrison let them in. I stayed close by and tried to listen to their conversation because I had a bad feeling about the situation. Knowing

Garrison as I did, I knew that he would never help them. Never in a million years!"

"Alyana thanked him for letting them come see him, but when he saw Achak, he flew into a rage. "You!" he screamed at the top of his voice. "You'll never get a penny from me. You're nothing but a two-bit whore!" Achak put his arms around Alyana and motioned her to go. Garrison dashed forward, pushed Achak out of the way, and as Alyana was falling to the ground he brought down his heavy walking stick with the solid silver ball top on her head and crushed her skull."

"Achak threw himself on the floor and cradled his dying wife in his arms. Garrison brought the stick down again on Achak and beat him with it in a frenzy; there was blood everywhere and two people lay dead."

~

Gavin was now in need of some fresh air. He asked Tommy to walk him outside, which Tommy did. While they were gone, Marie sat down beside Antonella and put her arm around her as she wept. "I had to tell him, I had to!" she sobbed.

"It's okay, Antonella, you did the right thing, you got it all out now."

"No, there's more, Marie, he needs to hear it all."

Marie went outside and found Tommy and Gavin sharing a cigarette together. "I don't know how to tell you this, but Antonella isn't done, there's more."

~

Having regained some composure, Gavin returned and sat down. Antonella continued on.

"Garrison sat in his chair and stared at the bodies for what seemed like an eternity. I was frozen to the spot. He then started yelling for Jimmy Rodriguez. Jimmy was not in the house so he came to find me. I had returned to the kitchen, pretending that I hadn't seen anything, and he screamed at me to get Jimmy and have him come to the house and for me to stay out of the way."

"I found Rodriguez and told him that Garrison needed him right away, and then I stayed out of the way but managed to position myself so I saw everything that happened next."

"Garrison brought Jimmy into the room and when Jimmy saw the bodies he threw up. "Well, you're going to have to clean that up as well!" yelled Garrison.

"I want you to get the two of them back into their truck, the old Chevy in the driveway, and drive it to the cliff at the edge of the lake. Put them in the driver and passenger seats and push it off the cliff into the water. It's a good 150 feet down; make it look like they lost control at the curve and went over the side. Make sure there are no boats around on the lake before you do it, and then come back here and get this place cleaned up."

"Jimmy did exactly as he was asked. That truck will still be down there at the bottom of Lake Travis."

"A week or so later, Garrison called Enrique Rodriguez and told him what he had done and that he needed his help to lay a false trail, as it were. He wanted to create a story that his wife and her lover had been killed in a road accident in Mexico. He wanted Enrique to work with his Mexican police buddies and build the story. Enrique did what Garrison asked, and a couple of weeks later Garrison leaked the story to the *Statesman*, flew down to Mexico to bring back the body of his dead wife, and buried her in the family plot."

"This is why I was so scared, Gavin. If Mike Muguara had continued to dig and found some connection to the truth, then Garrison would put two and two together, find out that I had met with him, and I would end up sharing the same grave as your long dead mother."

"Is that it all now, Antonella?" said Gavin, almost pleading that it be over.

"That's it all, Gavin!"

~

Marie was still sitting next to Antonella and again she put her arm around her, and the seventy-year-old went limp and cried uncontrollably, the burden of secrets that she had carried over the years now lifted from her shoulders.

Gavin sat with Tommy.

"I'll need to get divers out to the lake, Gavin, and if we find the wreck you know where we go from there," said Tommy.

"No, Detective! I know where you go from here whether you find the wreck or not! I heard what Antonella said, I will arrange for my people to have her go through it all again on camera just in case by the time a trial rolls around she is either too frail to testify or has passed. You do what you need to do to prepare to arrest my father. I need just a few days to brief my people and my supporters in the party. I know you will not like this term, but we will have to spin this in some way. Garrison McMullen is my father, but I am absolutely not like Garrison McMullen."

"You are not like your father, Gavin. I have seen that here today and it's reinforced by the actions you took to try to help and protect Antonella. You have what time you need, and you call me when you are done. I won't get divers out to the lake until we arrest your father, as that will spook him that we are already on to him."

"We have Jimmy Rodriguez in custody and charged with the killing of Mike Muguara. I am sure now that Garrison McMullen ordered that killing. If we can get the skeletal remains from the lake then we can match DNA with your mother's remains and be able to finally identify that the dead man is Mike Muguara."

"Let me know when you're ready for us to move."

~

Tommy went over to the still weeping Antonella Aguilar.

"We have to be on our way, Antonella. You have been very brave here today and your actions will see very bad men brought to justice."

Antonella managed to get to her feet and Tommy and Marie both hugged her. They shook hands with Gavin McMullen and then left the South Congress office to head back to Hudson Bend. On the way Tommy called the chief.

"We're on our way back to the office after our meeting with Gavin McMullen. We all need to meet in the conference room tonight. Can you also check if Bobby Brown can join us? What we uncovered today will blow your mind. My dad was right. Gavin had nothing to do with any of this, and I will explain it all when we get there," said Tommy, and was getting ready to end the call.

"We need to talk about something else in the briefing tonight, Tommy," said the chief. "Governor Shaw has been to see me and he wants to make sure that none of this shit going down is going to stick to him. Latisha Williams is better connected in the governor's office than we thought, and she's been shooting her mouth off. The long and the short of it is that the governor wants this wrapped up and Rodriguez and Vivar taken down for the killing, and he wants it to end there. Latisha has spilled the beans that we may have some evidence that connects Garrison McMullen in some way. McMullen has backed Shaw with significant funding for his run for the White House and he doesn't want McMullen tied into this thing."

"Well, sir, that might not be possible. I will explain when we meet. Latisha has let me down and gone back on our deal. This might backfire on her also. See you later tonight, chief," and Tommy ended the call.

Chapter 29

Dirty Laundry

THEY WERE ALL THERE IN the conference room and it was just after six in the evening. Tommy Ross presented his report on the meeting with Gavin McMullen and Antonella Aguilar. Bobby Brown was typing on his laptop as fast as he could and every so often shaking his head with incredulity.

"This will have an impact of seismic proportions across the political spectrum," said the assistant DA. "Here we have one of the biggest shakers and movers in the business world in Texas, if not the entire nation, soon to be arrested for multiple murders. His son is the governor-elect of Texas and some say is on a path to the White House. I need to make a call to the DA right away," said Bobby, and he left the room to make the call.

"I will need to call Governor Shaw," said Bill Dunwoody. "The shit he was trying to avoid is rolling downhill fast in his direction. He will want his spin-doctors working on this throughout the night. This might impact Gavin McMullen's future White House expectations, but it will certainly impact Raymond Shaw's current White House bid. He will need to distance himself from Garrison McMullen. I need to go call him right now."

"Marie, we need to get hold of Latisha. Let's go to my office and we can call her from there. Do you want to join us, Dad?" said Tommy.

"Yes, I'll tag along. We need to think through what we are going to say to her and I have some ideas," said Bill.

~

They sat down together in Tommy's office. "Okay, Dad, how do you think we should handle this with Latisha?"

"When we tell her what we know she will have egg on her face. She will know that she has pulled the trigger too quickly and tried to leverage her governor's office connections to endear herself to Governor Shaw. She has done this in a calculated way. She may think that being the eyes and ears of a future President inside the press might advance her career. She might also be angling for the press secretary role. Who knows? One thing is certain; she didn't spill the beans to Raymond Shaw out of the goodness of her heart."

"We need to take the approach that she has put herself in the shit and we can help her climb out. We can say that we are now briefing the governor on the truth and that she was not in full possession of that latest information. We can tell her that we will tell the governor her actions were with the best intent. We then get something in return; we don't need to be specific about what that is, simply that she owes us one," concluded Bill.

"Holy crap, Dad, you should have been a politician!"

"No. I need to be able to sleep at night with a clear conscious, son."

~

They called Latisha and adopted Bill's approach. It worked perfectly. Latisha Williams was forever in their debt; at least that's what she said.

Assistant DA Bobby Brown returned thirty minutes later.

"The DA wants to have us conference him in; let's get back to the conference room," said Bobby.

All of them, including the chief, assembled in the conference room.

"We're all here now, sir," said Bobby, kicking off the call.

"Hey, everyone, this is Tom Morton here," said the DA. "Bobby has kept me up to date every step of the way on this and has briefed me on the latest developments of today. Chief Dunwoody, I have to congratulate you and your team for their exceptional work in getting this to this stage. We now need to work together very closely as a team to take it over the finish line and see that all guilty parties get their just desserts. I'm sure that you would agree, Governor Shaw."

The DA had already linked the governor into the conversation.

"I completely agree," said Raymond Shaw.

"I also took the liberty of bringing the governor-elect into the call this evening, and although he was very appreciative of the consideration that Detective Ross offered him today, after discussing the issue with Tom and me he is in agreement that we need to move now and arrest his father with all due haste. Would you like to say a few words, Gavin?"

"Thanks, Raymond. Yes, I agree with everything being said and I do want to say here for the record that Detective Sergeant Tommy Ross was in no way out of line today, and that it was I who asked for the delay in taking action. I now realize that the public good would be best served by making the arrest now and that I will need to deal with political fallout as best I can."

Bill Ross sat in awe at the speed with which these politicians and senior elected officials moved to circle the wagons and protect themselves. In what was in effect less than an hour they all were on the same page. Each could claim that their actions tonight were collectively designed for the public good. It was impressive!

"Thank you both for taking the time to be on the call tonight. I think that Bobby and I should now work through the details on next steps with Chief Dunwoody and his team. Thanks again."

The governor and the governor-elect left the call.

~

The DA was now calling the shots. He moved the conversation to the next phase.

"It's now eight-thirty and I am at a Make-a-Wish Foundation dinner at the Four Seasons. I believe that we should make the arrest tonight," said the DA.

"Do we have any idea where Garrison McMullen is? It may take us some time to organize the team needed to make the arrest," said Bill Dunwoody.

"Garrison is about 200 feet to my left. He's at the same event as I am. We should make the arrest when he exits the event and is picked up by his driver," said Tom Morton.

~

Now it all made sense to Bill, the need for speed. The DA saw the opportunity for a photo op. Based on the "who's who" attendee list at the Make-A-Wish Foundation fund raiser, the press would be crawling all over the place. It would be on all national news channels in a micro-second.

The sheriff made the call. Tommy Ross would make the arrest with Marie Mason by his side and supported by several deputies. Chief Dunwoody, the assistant DA and the DA would make themselves available for the media to answer questions after the arrest was made and the suspect was secure.

Everyone went off to ready themselves for the event, and Tommy and Marie went off to make another call.

~

"Latisha, we need to talk with you again. There have been some further developments," said Marie, kicking off the call.

"Marie, there is no need to rub it in. I fucked up. Please stop gloating. As I said in the call a few minutes ago, I owe you one," replied Latisha.

"Latisha, this is Tommy, you need to shut up and listen. Get your ass down to the Four Seasons as fast as possible. Get all support you need to get what will happen there out in the public domain. You can get the drop on this, Latisha, and this is further evidence of our good faith and willingness to continue working together. In about forty minutes Garrison McMullen will be arrested outside the Four Seasons."

The phone went dead. The Rottweiler was on her way!

~

Exiting the fundraiser, Garrison McMullen was surrounded by his normal supporting entourage. Following on behind were the guests from the table for ten that Venture Point Holdings had purchased. They included Enrique Rodriguez, Finlay Robertson of Robertson Richards and his wife, Eddie Tang and his wife, and Charles Haywood of the Venture Point Investment Fund and his wife.

The limos pulled up to the curb and the driver jumped out of the lead limo and opened the door for Garrison McMullen. He stepped from the door of the hotel and then did a 180 to say goodbye to his friends and business associates and wave to the press. When he turned back around to move to the car, Tommy and Marie stood in his way.

"Garrison McMullen, I am arresting you in connection with the murders of Alyana Reyes and Achak Muguara. When we reach the police office, more detailed charges will be made and you will be Mirandized. I strongly suggest that you simply step this way and not create the need for us to arrest you forcibly in front of the national press," said Tommy.

Garrison McMullen did as they asked, but as he walked with them to the waiting cruiser he whispered in Tommy's ear. "Your life as you know it is over you son of a bitch!" Tommy looked him in the eye smiled and winked and said, "I think you got it the wrong way around, you arrogant asshole!"

~

There was total chaos at the entrance to the Four Seasons. Garrison McMullen's guests and business partners scurried across the parking lot looking for their limos to *exit stage left* out of the melee. Reporters, there to cover the fundraising event, were on their cell phones with their bosses trying to get instructions on what to do to leverage the coverage of the chaos for their news outlet. It was pandemonium.

Off to the side of the main entrance two men stood with a mobile news team from KXAN, the NBC affiliate in Austin. The cameras rolled, transmitting a live stream to the local Austin community and to NBC New York, which had been given a 25-minute warning that a huge news story was breaking in Austin and to be ready for the feed.

The Travis County District Attorney, Tom Morton, with Sheriff Bill Dunwoody and Bobby Brown at his side, made a brief statement.

"This evening officers from the Travis County Police Department, led by Detective Sargent Tommy Ross, the head of the cold case unit, arrested Mr. Garrison McMullen in connection with the death of his ex-wife, Alyana Reyes, and her partner, Mr. Achak Muguara. Due to the lateness of the hour, Chief Dunwoody and I will give a more detailed statement tomorrow afternoon at 3 p.m. Central time. Thank you."

The throng of reporters was now firing questions at them, but no answers were forthcoming. They made no further statement and left.

Standing in the parking lot of the hotel, Bill Ross watched all of this go down. He was humming a tune, remembering the words of the song "Dirty Laundry" by Don Henley:

> *I make my living off the evening news*
> *Just give me something-something I can use*
> *People love it when you lose,*
> *They love dirty laundry*
>
> *Kick 'em when they're up*
> *Kick 'em when they're down*
> *Kick 'em when they're up*
> *Kick 'em all around*

Chapter 30

The Scottish genius

JULIEN BOUDREAUX WAS AT THE sheriff's office bright and early.

"We're going to have to give you an employee badge if you keep this up, Julien! How come all of your clients are suddenly getting into so much trouble? The good thing, of course, is that based on your hourly rate your kids should get some expensive Christmas gifts this year!" said Bill Dunwoody, laughing.

"I want to see my client!" demanded the Cajun attorney.

"Let me see now, which one would that be, Julien?"

"Chief, take me to Garrison McMullen immediately, please!" said the lawyer now irritated by the chief's lack of respect.

~

Tommy arrived in the office at the same time as Marie.

"Good work yesterday, Marie! I see that Latisha was on the ball. She had a full page in the *Statesman* this morning with the report on Garrison McMullen's arrest. There's also a nice group photo of all of us as we get him loaded into the car. She was obviously right on the ball was Latisha. I wonder how that happened," said Tommy, grinning from ear to ear.

When Tommy reached his desk there was a note waiting for him that Jimmy Rodriguez wanted to see him the minute he got in.

"Marie, we need to go take Jimmy Rodriguez his morning coffee!" yelled Tommy before Marie had a chance to check her own messages.

"Good morning, Jimmy, don't tell me you missed me and couldn't wait to say hi the minute I got in. That's so sweet of you. I brought you a latte, well, actually it's just a white out of the vending machine with two sugars, but we can call it a latte this morning just to give our meeting a little more ambience."

Jimmy was not amused at Tommy's little joke.

"I need to talk to you without my lawyer present. Can we do it now, please? I have something very important to share," said Jimmy.

"Sure thing. Let's you, Marie and I take the lattes to the small conference room over there and let's hear what you have to say."

The holding cell deputy led Jimmy across the hallway to the conference room and secured him to the chair.

"Your show, Jimmy, fire away."

"I understand that Garrison McMullen was arrested last night; is this true?"

"Yes, it's true, Jimmy."

"I will give you information that will help you put him away if you take the death penalty off the table."

"You and Pepe are always negotiating," said Tommy, knowing that the comment about his boyfriend would not be lost on Jimmy. "What evidence do you have, Jimmy? I can't go to the DA without a solid understanding of what's on offer."

"You think Garrison McMullen ordered the hit on the Raul Hernandez dude and told me to put it about that it was because he was muscling in on our business. That wasn't the reason. It was because the dude was asking too many questions about Garrison's dead wife, and I will testify to that. I will also testify that McMullen asked me to clean up the mess at the ranch after he killed his wife and Achak Muguara. I can also tell you where the bodies are as I was asked to get rid of them."

"Okay, Jimmy, I appreciate your fine offer. I'll take it to the DA and see what he says. I'll get back to you on it. This fine deputy will take you back to your cell now and you can enjoy your morning coffee in peace."

~

Tommy got back to his desk where Bill Dunwoody and Bobby Brown were waiting on him.

"Good work last night, Tommy. Julien Boudreaux wants to meet us with his client Garrison McMullen. Want to sit in? You can just stand in the corner with the chief; I think you've earned it. If they ask you to leave then you have to get out of there."

They arrived at the interview room that had become very familiar to them over the past couple of weeks. Julien spoke first, of course.

"I have gone over the charges with my client and he denies any knowledge of any murder. There was no murder! His wife and Mr. Muguara were both killed in a road traffic accident in Mexico. My client flew down there and identified the body of his wife, brought her home, and she is now buried in the family plot in Lago Vista.

"These charges are a complete fabrication and the accusers must be persons looking to take political advantage from my client's demise. I request a hearing with the judge immediately. I will request complete dismissal of all charges."

Julien sat back, pretty satisfied with his opening salvo.

"Were you ever on *Saturday Night Live*, Julien? You're hilarious! We plan to exhume your client's wife's body and check it with his son's DNA for a match., My guess is that will not work in your client's favor. We have an eyewitness who saw the killing of both people take place. Oh, in addition, there are likely to be further charges brought. Certain individuals currently in our custody claim that your client ordered the killing of Mike Muguara, Achak Muguara's son. That was the body found out at Whispering Hollow earlier this year, the murder that two of your other clients have been charged with. It sounds to me, Julien, that you might have been drinking too much holiday cheer!"

Julien was so red in the face that Bobby thought he might self-combust at any moment. Garrison McMullen stared at his attorney like he wanted to tear his head off right in front of them.

~

After the meeting with Garrison McMullen and his attorney, Tommy was back at his desk with Bill bringing him up to speed on latest developments.

"When there is blood in the water, predators come from miles around!" said Bill. "Tell the DA to wait and not to force the pace too quickly. It's Christmas and Julien knows that everything slows down to a snail's pace at Christmas; that's why he's trying to move it along," he continued.

"Why don't you tell him yourself, Dad? He wanted to meet you, and here he comes right now."

Bill turned around and saw Tom Morton striding purposefully in his direction.

"Bill Ross, the Scottish genius! I can't tell you how much I have been looking forward to meeting you. I wanted to officially thank you for the great work on the Luther Fisher case and also for the insight and support you continue to provide your son and his team every day. I don't mean to embarrass you, but since you are not compensated for your incredible service, I wanted to wish you the joys of the season."

Bill hadn't seen the guy at the back of the room arrive with the DA, and he now stepped forward with a box and placed it on the desk in front of Bill. Tommy had never seen such a look on his father's face; he stared at the box and then he held on to the side of Tommy's desk for support.

"*The Pride '78!*" he seemed to whisper the words under his breath.

Lying on the table was a box of two bottles of Glenmorangie Single Malt Scotch, with a current retail value of $5,800 per bottle.

Gaining his composure, Bill explained why he was so overcome.

"Glenmorangie Pride 1978 is a limited edition. Only 700 bottles of the single malt were made available worldwide. Only five casks were laid down, making it extremely rare, and only 180 bottles of the limited edition whisky was made available for purchase in the U.S. Two bottles are now resting in front of me. I don't know what to say."

"Say nothing, Bill!" bellowed the DA. "You deserve this for your continued service to the good people of Travis County - Enjoy!"

~

"In the conference room now, please!" The DA had now moved on and was barking instructions at the Chief, Bobby and Tommy.

A group of about a dozen suits sat in the conference room awaiting their arrival. They were PR people from the county, city and state administrations. Seated at the head of the table was Governor Shaw and to his right Gavin McMullen.

The DA took the floor.

"This afternoon at three o'clock we have our first formal statement on this. My team advises me that the nation's press is descending on Austin. I am also advised that there are state and national politicians already giving interviews on national TV, spinning this story every which way. The left is having a field day and licking their lips at the potential demise of a major Republican contributor, second only to the Koch brothers. The right is claiming a conspiracy by liberals to try to tarnish the good name of a business leader committed to the creation of thousands of new jobs.

With all due respect to the governor and the governor-elect, we must try to stay out of the politics of the moment and focus on clear and concise communication with the media on the facts of the case. Before any statements are made by anyone in this room, or by the staff of anyone in this room, it must be first cleared and approved by the communications team I have assembled, led by Jane Brewster. Any questions?"

There were many questions, but the meeting ended and everyone was clear on who was in control. The DA was going to ensure that no one was going to damage his opportunity for his moment in the sun.

Bill and Tommy were both incredibly impressed by Gavin McMullen. The possibility existed for him to be destroyed by all of this, but he was resolute that justice should prevail and that his father should be held to account for his actions.

~

"Julien Boudreaux is on TV!" It was one of the PR team yelling as she ran toward Bobby Brown, who was helping himself to his fourth black coffee of the morning.

Everyone then huddled around the TV in the break room to listen to what Garrison McMullen's attorney had to say.

"This morning I met with my client, who is innocent of these scurrilous charges. Due to the impending holiday season, we will be requesting that an initial hearing with a judge be expedited, at which time I will be requesting a dismissal of all charges."

A barrage of questions followed as Julien Boudreaux made an attempt to leave. He deliberately stopped in mid-step and in a very planned maneuver turned again to the cameras.

"This entire charade is politically motivated. There is not one shred of truth in any of this. Thank you."

He then disappeared into the sea of humanity as the on-scene news teams fired up the lights for their reporters, who were making last minute adjustments to their makeup and coiffures. The circus was in town and the clowns were first up!

Chapter 31

Lake Travis secrets

AT LAKE TRAVIS, NO one paid particular attention to the inflatable with three men aboard heading across the lake in the direction of Whispering Hollow. On any given day there are many boats of every shape and size on the lake, so nothing looked particularly out of the ordinary.

The inflatable slowed and then stopped below the cliffs by Venture Point. They could see above them a very impressive home with a cantilever deck protruding out over the lake. The two divers slipped silently into the water, leaving the third man to control the location of the boat.

~

Back at the Sheriff's office the receptionist was being inundated with calls from the press wanting to speak with Detective Tommy Ross - the arresting officer. There were reporters camped outside the building trying to ambush him and get in his face for a comment or two. Tommy felt like a rock star, but not in a good way. "Now I understand what it must be like to be hounded by paparazzi," he said.

"There's a call for you, Tommy."

"Well, tell them to go screw themselves!" said Tommy.

"Doesn't sound like a reporter."

"Okay, put it through"

"Is this Detective Tommy Ross?"

"Yes, who's this? And if you're with the press I have nothing to say."

"I am not with the press, Detective Ross, my name is Enrique Rodriguez. I am the owner of the Colinas Verde Ranch and I understand that you have my brother in custody."

Tommy motioned Bill and Marie to hook into Line 3.

"Oh, yes, Mr. Rodriguez, how may I help you?"

"I would like to fly up to Austin and meet with you, Detective. I believe that I may have information that could be helpful to you regarding your case against Garrison McMullen. Garrison is a good friend and a business partner, but it would be wrong of me not to come forward in the interest of justice being served. I have specific knowledge of events surrounding the death of Garrison's wife and her lover."

"Very interesting, Mr. Rodriguez. When would you like to make the trip?"

"I can fly up now, I have my Cessna Citation always fueled and ready to go. Perhaps I could buy you dinner tonight?"

"No dinner, Mr. Rodriguez, but if you wish to make the trip, be my guest. I take it that you will be flying into the Austin Executive Airport in Pflugerville; I can meet you there. There are conference room facilities at the airport that we can use. Let me know your ETA and I will be there with my colleagues to meet with you."

"I'm on my way. I will call you in flight and give you my estimated arrival time. I look forward to meeting you, Detective Ross!"

He hung up the call.

"As I said, there's blood in the water and the sharks are now circling. One of them with a veracious appetite is now headed in our direction," laughed Bill Ross as he slapped his son on the back.

~

They met at the airport as planned. Enrique Rodriguez, flanked by two Antonio Banderas lookalikes, walked into the conference room. He didn't look anything like Tommy had imagined. He looked like an older version of the guy from the

Dos Equis beer commercial, the difference being that this guy probably *was* The Most Interesting Man in the World. At least in his own mind, that is.

"Thank you for agreeing to see me, Detective."

Tommy, Marie and Bill shook hands with the man who was probably responsible for the trafficking of the majority of cocaine coming into the U.S.

"So what is so important that you would make the trip up here to meet with us?" asked Tommy.

"What I have knowledge of, Detective, needed to be shared at the earliest opportunity," replied the drug lord.

"But before I share what I know, I must first have assurances that my brother's fate will not result in him being put to death. He has told me that he was involved in the unfortunate death out by the lake, but that it was Garrison McMullen who had coerced him into the crime by threatening to tell me about my brother's proclivity for male bed companions, something that has been known to me for many years now."

"So you're telling me that you flew all the way up here to tell me that Garrison McMullen ordered the killing and had Jimmy do it? If that's the case you've had a wasted trip; we already knew that," said Tommy.

"No, Detective Ross, I have much more information than that, and I'm willing to share provided that there is a bargain to be made regarding my brother's fate. You can be assured that the information I possess will guarantee that you get a solid conviction of Garrison McMullen for the killing of his wife and her lover."

"Oh, I see. Well, in that case you're going to have to give me more detail so I can convince the DA that it's worth trading for your brother's reduced sentence."

"Don't try to play me, Detective, I am not a person you want to make an enemy of."

The two thugs shifted a little in their seat to reinforce the drama of the moment.

"Don't try to threaten or intimidate me either, Mr. Rodriguez. My selling abilities with the DA might be adversely affected, and that wouldn't be in the best interests of your brother's fate."

"Okay, let's not get too agitated, Detective. I can share this—and this is not all that I know, it's just a part of what I know. Garrison McMullen's wife did not die in a road traffic accident. The body that lies in the family plot is not that of his wife. I know this because I facilitated the provision of a body for him at his request. The dead woman was someone who had died of natural causes and was about to be buried by her family in Mexico. I simply gave them some monetary compensation in return for the body."

"And you would testify to that effect, Mr. Rodriguez?"

"I would, Detective. In addition, my brother and I have further evidence of the actual killing of his wife and lover, a crime that was perpetrated by Garrison McMullen at his ranch in Leander."

"Very interesting, Mr. Rodriguez, and thank you for flying up here. Sorry for the little bit of confusion earlier. I *will* take your offer forward to the DA and I will be in touch regarding his decision."

They shook hands and *The Most Interesting Man in the World* and his henchmen flew back to the Colinas Verde Ranch.

~

Meanwhile at Lake Travis progress was being made. It was the second day of searching for the Chevy truck with its two occupants, and they had located what looked like a vehicle semi-submerged in the silt at the bottom of the lake. The lead diver, with his powerful underwater searchlight, cleared the silt away from the passenger side door and window. As he did so the outline of a human skull began to appear. The skull of Alyana Reyes lay sideways across the dashboard of the truck.

The divers sent up the marker to the surface indicating that they had found what they were looking for. The other diver in the inflatable threw out the buoy as the other two divers broke the surface and climbed into the boat. They got on their cell phone and reported that the search had been successful. They were instructed to retrieve a piece of bone from each skeleton and bring both back to HQ for forensic examination.

They did as instructed and returned to the Sheriff's office with the bone samples, each one in its own separate plastic evidence bag. The medical examiner took that samples and headed off to the lab that had been put on standby ready to run DNA tests.

When the news of the find in Lake Travis been reported earlier in the day, the medical examiner had dispatched one of his assistants to the office of Gavin McMullen to retrieve samples of blood, saliva and hair to be used for DNA matching. As he had been all along, Gavin McMullen was fully compliant with the request and he provided that lab technician with what she needed.

~

The following morning the phone rang on Tommy's desk; it was the medical examiner.

"I suggest that you get everyone together. I have the preliminary DNA results," said Sven Stevenson, the Travis County medical examiner.

Tommy had worked with Sven on many cases, including the Luther Fisher case, and he was known for his almost stoic personality. On this call Sven Stevenson sounded like a kid on Christmas morning having just opened a present from Santa.

Twenty minutes later they were all in the conference room awaiting the arrival of Sven: Tommy, Bill, Marie, Bill Dunwoody and Bobby Brown. A breathless Sven Stevenson burst into the room after his drive up from central Austin.

"A glass of water, Sven, or would you like something stronger?" joked Tommy as the medical examiner began assembling his props on the conference room table.

"Water will be fine, thank you, Tommy," said the ME, now getting his breath back.

Sven had a couple of mouthfuls of water and then began his report.

"First, I have to say that these are preliminary findings, but I would speculate with a fair degree of certainty that these findings will finally prove out to be indeed correct.

"The specimens used for the matching were:

1. Blood and hair samples retrieved from Gavin McMullen.

2. Bone sample #1 retrieved from the submersed truck in Lake Travis.

3. Bone Sample #2 retrieved from the same submersed truck.

4. Blood, tissue, hair and bone samples taken from the deceased found at Whispering Hollow, assumed at this time to be Mike Muguara.

"We ran only nuclear DNA tests at this time. Mitochondrial tests typically take longer and may not even be necessary given the results of the nuclear DNA."

Test One Results - Gavin McMullen samples were a match for Bone Sample #1

Test Two Results - Mike Muguara samples were a match for Bone Sample #1.

"We can therefore reach the preliminary conclusion that Bone Sample #1 is Alyana Reyes, the mother of Mike Muguara and Gavin McMullen."

"*Yes!*" The call was almost on unison as it echoed around the room.

"May I continue?" said Sven Stevenson, back in his normal stoic character.

Test Three Results - Mike Muguara samples were a match for Sample #2.

Test Four Results - Gavin McMullen samples were a match for Sample #2."

There was now a collective gasp around the room and the medical examiner verbalized the reason for the gasp.

"We can therefore reach the preliminary conclusion that Bone Sample #2 is Achak Muguara, the father of Mike Muguara *and* Gavin McMullen."

"Holy crap!" said Bobby Brown. "This means that Gavin McMullen is not the son of a megalomaniacal killer. He's going to be happy about that!"

"Yes, that's correct, Bobby," said Marie, "but it also means that the new governor-elect of Texas is a full blown *Comanche*! He's a direct descendent of Quanah Parker, the last great Comanche chief. It will be celebrated in the Comanche Nation as the rebirth of Comancheria!"

Chapter 32

And they all fall down

"WHAT A DAY!" announced Bill as he arrived home and kissed Elaine on the cheek. "I need a wee dram. Can I get you a glass of sherry? I'd like to tell you about my day. We've got him, Elaine! We've got what we need to put Garrison McMullen away, and there's more."

Elaine finished putting the pork chops for their supper in the oven, washed her hands, and joined her husband in the family room and took a sip of sherry.

Bill told her the whole story; it took a while, of course, and storytelling is thirsty work, so the contents of the bottle of Glenmorangie had been significantly reduced by the time they both sat down for supper.

"You're enjoying your work then, honey?" said Elaine.

"Aye, well, someone has to do it," said Bill, raising his Edinburgh crystal whisky glass into the air.

"I'm talking about the detective work, not the whisky consumption you old fool!" said Elaine.

"They both go hand in hand, my love, it's like the ying and the yan."

"It's the yin and the yang! I think you've had enough for one evening!" said Elaine and grabbed his glass.

~

As Bill was dozing off on the sofa after supper, his cell phone rang.

"Hello?" he said tentatively.

"How goes the fight?" said Joe Nichol.

"Ah, it's yourself, a little late there for you, is it not, Joe?"

"I'm just getting ready to go out clubbing," joked Joe. "I've been watching developments on the TV, you've got your man I see?"

"Ah, long way to go yet, Joe. In our opinion there is no doubt that McMullen ordered the killing and Jimmy Rodriguez and Pepe Vivar carried it out. Shit, I can't be telling you this," said Bill, realizing that his Glenmorangie-induced relaxed state had resulted in him telling Joe more than he should.

"Your secret's safe with me, just you and Tommy do your job and make sure that these assholes get the needle. Just thought I'd call to touch base; keep up the good work, Bill!" and Joe was off to go clubbing.

~

It was the following morning and Garrison McMullen was due to be arraigned by Judge Bonnie Lewis in the main courthouse in downtown Austin. The press and the public were both out in force and the police were doing their best to keep the entrance to the courthouse clear. Tommy, Marie and Bill wanted to be there to see McMullen arraigned and to see if Julien Boudreaux's no-doubt Oscar performance would have any effect on the outcome. They stood together off to the side of main entrance awaiting the grand arrival.

A Travis County transit van pulled around the corner followed by a Cadillac SUV. They both stopped in front of the courthouse and Julien Boudreaux was first to emerge from the rear of the SUV. He walked across to the transit van to witness firsthand his client emerging from the back cuffed to a Travis County deputy.

Garrison McMullen had dressed for the part. He wore a black Stetson, white cowboy shirt, blue jeans with a snakeskin belt and a huge buckle, and a pair of what looked like $4,000 black full-quill ostrich-leather boots. He obviously wanted everyone watching to know that a powerbroker Texan was in town.

Crack!

A single shot pierced the Stetson, and half the side of Garrison McMullen's head was vaporized. The deputy was unharmed but it looked like someone had just dumped a gallon of red paint all over him. The Stetson spun in the air and, as if in slow motion, gently settled on the ground. Julien Boudreaux had also been the beneficiary of some of the red paint, and he was trying to wipe it off his face with his white silk handkerchief that was now completely soaked in blood and brain matter.

Complete panic ensued. Law enforcement personnel tried to regroup, organize and get a location of the shooter. Sirens blared. Orders were being yelled.

"What just happened?" said Tommy.

"I guess someone didn't want to wait for the trial," said Bill.

"We need to protect Jimmy and Pepe. We need to get them out of the holding cells to a secure location!" yelled Chief Dunwoody. "I'll make the call! Now, you guys get back to the office; this is a mess, a fucking mess!"

~

Back at the holding cells they had received the orders to get Pepe and Jimmy transferred.

"What's going on?" yelled Jimmy as two deputies manhandled him out of the cell and down the corridor to the transit van parked at the rear of the building. Pepe, led by two other deputies, was a couple of paces behind. They exited the rear of the building to walk the ten yards to the waiting van.

Crack! Jimmy Rodriguez' head disappeared in a cloud of red mist. Pepe Vivar, walking a few steps behind, let out a scream. *Crack!* The scream was instantly silenced as Pepe's head was also vaporized.

Two shots, red mist, and two bodies with no heads lay on the ground.

At the two locations they found the sniper rifles and took them off to forensics, but they doubted that they would reveal anything. It was a logistical impossibility for one person to have committed both assassinations, so a team had to have been involved. They had operated with precision, predicting that after the killing of Garrison McMullen the police would try to protect Pepe and Jimmy.

~

The mood was somber when they all met in the conference room later that evening.

"What a mess!" said the DA, "Any ideas or opinions on what might have happened here?"

Chief Dunwoody was first to speak. "We did everything by the book, Tom."

"Well, someone misread the book, Bill."

"This was a very well-planned and well-coordinated assassination," said Tommy. "We have to ask ourselves, who would benefit from their deaths? They all had stories to tell, secrets that could damage others, creating a domino effect across many criminal organizations.

"As an example, the other night Enrique Rodriguez flew up to talk to us about secrets that he had and was willing to share about Garrison McMullen. That suggests to me that it wasn't just his brother's best interests he had in mind, but his own. McMullen could have traded what he knew about Rodriguez to save his own skin. The people Rodriguez works with are serious players. They would have the capability and resources to pull this off. I think we need to look at Enrique Rodriguez first." concluded Tommy.

"What are your thoughts. Bill?" asked the DA as he saw Bill leaning back and staring at the ceiling.

"I think Tommy is right—well, almost. The part that doesn't fit with Tommy's theory is that Jimmy Rodriguez was killed. Would Enrique take out his own brother? The answer is, maybe. He was a homosexual and it's well known that Hispanic red-blooded males don't like faggots. But kill his own brother?

Again I say maybe. I think we need to start with Enrique Rodriguez and see where that takes us," replied Bill.

"I have to leave. I have a meeting with the governor downtown and I'm not looking forward to it," said the DA. "I expect the governor-elect will also be there. Does he know yet what the DNA tests revealed?"

"No. not yet," said the chief.

"Well, that's fucking great!" said the DA as he stormed out of the room.

Chapter 33

Comanche

"GOOD MORNING, IS Gavin McMullen available? It's Detective Tommy Ross calling."

"Good morning, Detective Ross. It's Valerie Smith here. Gavin is in a meeting right now regarding the terrible events of yesterday. Is it something that I can help you with?"

"No, Valerie, I just wanted to try to get on his schedule. I know he has a lot on his plate right now and his head must be spinning with the death of his father and everything else that's going on. Can you tell him please that I need an hour of his time? I have some important information that I need to share."

"I'll try to catch him between meetings. The earliest I can see an open slot would be six o'clock tonight; would that work, Detective?"

"Yes, that would work, Valerie, just give me a call back if Gavin confirms that it works for him. Many thanks!"

~

When Tommy got off the phone, Marie was standing behind him like a praying mantis.

"Latisha Williams is going berserk. She demands to speak with you to get up to speed on what's going on," said Marie.

"Okay, let's get her on the phone."

"Latisha Williams!"

"Latisha, I have Tommy on speaker, do you have time to talk?" said Marie.

"Of course I have time to talk, Marie. Tommy, what the fuck is going on over there? Have you any idea who the shooter was? Can I now go with everything I know? You promised me, remember."

"I remember, Latisha. You have to keep quiet about all the research work that you, Marie and Julian have been doing on Venture Point Holdings. We don't know yet what the whole picture is there and how Enrique Rodriguez ties into it.

"On the shootings yesterday, you can write away to your heart's content. It will be announced soon, but we think it was impossible for one shooter to pull it off. We have no leads, so there is nothing to write about that right now. As soon as the smoke clears and I know something, I will let you know. Hang in there with us on this; I think there will be a great story for you to write when we have put all the pieces together."

"Okay, but no secrets, Tommy, or I'll nail your balls to the mast!"

~

They finished the call with Latisha as Bill walked into the room.

"I just got this package delivered to me by courier. There is no sender name but the courier said that he picked it up from the front desk at the Hilton downtown earlier this morning," said Bill, holding a box about the size of a shoebox in his hand.

"Well, let's open it. You don't hear anything ticking inside do you?" joked Tommy, but the look on Marie's face suggested that she didn't find the joke the least bit funny.

Bill opened the package and inside was a backup hard drive storage device. There was also a single sheet of paper with a typed message and no signature. It read:

You will find the contents of this drive of interest. Now that Garrison McMullen has gone to meet his maker, the FBI and the DEA should be briefed as soon as possible on what is contained here.

There are several video-recording files on this drive. They were record-ed by Mike Muguara as part of a surveillance operation that he was running on Garrison McMullen and Enrique Rodriguez. The equipment used for this surveillance was the IP-IRPTZ long-range camera with an integrated synchronized laser illuminator. It has a range of up to 3 miles at night, and in daytime the 1550 mm lens provides an extraordinary view from 5 miles away. The equipment was set up at a camouflaged location and complete with a self-destruct device that would trigger if it were tampered with. It was hooked up to a secure network link with a 10-mile range from the location of the equipment. If someone had detected the signal they would have thought that someone had just pulled off the road to talk on their cell phone. This enabled Mike to sit at a location outside the perimeter of the ranch, operate the surveillance camera and record the results. This meant that Mike could be physically 10 miles away from the target while providing a level of definition that could read a vehicle number plate. The FBI can validate its authenticity.

~

Bill went back to his desk to retrieve his laptop and returned to the room. He connected the backup drive using the USB port, and also connected the laptop to the video equipment in the room to enable everyone to see the contents of the video files up on the big screen.

On each of the five surveillance recordings Mike Muguara went into great detail on the voiceover as the images played on the screen. Two of the recordings provided the most compelling evidence of a complex organization that had taken years to put in place and was now in full operation.

Surveillance video #1 showed the group at a Christmas party, the party that Mike Muguara had mentioned in the video recording that he had left with Bob Corbin.

Mike's voiceover - *As you can see, Enrique Rodriguez and Garrison McMullen are clearly entertaining a bunch of other high rollers at a Christmas barbecue. There is another group arriving now in a convoy of five vehicles with front and rear security. The muscle is getting out of the front and back cover cars and forming a security perimeter for their bosses to make an entrance to the party. All these cars have Mexican license plates and two are clearly official Mexican police cruisers. Enrique and Garrison are now embracing the VIP who has just arrived. I can't identify him unless he turns around. Yes, got him, I think that's Pablo Zambrano, the head of the Zapata drug cartel. The FBI will need to confirm, but I'm sure that's who it is.*

In surveillance video #2, six men are seen loading cattle, people and packages of drugs into a Rodriguez Trucking eighteen-wheeler specially designed to segment the cargo so that in the unlikely event that they were stopped by law enforcement, a cursory inspection would show that the truck was full of cattle.

Mike's voiceover - *As you can see, they are unloading packages of cocaine and marijuana from pickup trucks with Mexican license plates. You can see the plate numbers clearly now, which should enable them to be traced. That is Enrique Rodriguez standing off to the side of the Rodriguez Trucking eighteen-wheeler and he appears to be upset about something. He has stepped over to where the illegals are being herded into the truck. My God, he just shot two guys in the head! The others are now running into the truck. He's now shaking hands with the driver of the truck and patting him on the back. The driver has climbed into the cab and the truck is now pulling away.*

"I need to go get the sheriff, He needs to see all of this and then make the call to the FBI, and they will bring in the DEA and other agencies as needed. This evidence is dynamite and it perhaps confirms our earlier theory that Enrique ordered the hit on McMullen, Pepe and his brother and had the drug cartel people arrange it. If they had spilled the beans on all of this to save their skin, then it would have been game over for Enrique and his cartel buddies."

Tommy then left the conference room to go find Chief Dunwoody.

~

"How is the analysis into the financing of Venture Point Holdings progressing, Marie," asked Bill as they sat together in the conference room after Tommy left.

"Julian Hernandez has been a huge help. We had found that there is both legitimate money and suspicious transactions flowing into the Venture Point Investment fund. An example of legitimate money is the Texas State Retirement Fund, and an example of a suspicious transaction is a one-time contribution of three hundred thousand that hit the fund last week from a bank in Grand Cayman. It was a pass-through transaction, it would appear, from a Chinese bank in Hong Kong. Julian thinks that what is happening is that dirty money from drug sales and illegal alien payments is being shipped out of the U.S. by Deng Shipping Lines into Hong Kong and then the Chinese are converting that at 70 cents on the dollar to clean money that then hits the Grand Cayman and bounces to the investment fund.

"If he's right then the principle bad players in this are Enrique Rodriguez, Eddie Tang and the now deceased Garrison McMullen. The good players are Finlay Robertson and Charles Haywood. These two probably suspect that something is going on but they're not active in the money-laundering scheme. Finlay and Charles could probably keep everything going legitimately if Eddie Tang and Enrique Rodriguez were removed from the scene and the money-laundering racket was closed down. At least, this is Julian's opinion," concluded Marie.

~

Tommy arrived back later that afternoon and announced that the chief was now up to speed. He had called the Feds and briefed them, and he was booked on a plane to FBI headquarters in Washington DC that night. Tommy then left again for his meeting, now confirmed with Gavin McMullen at his offices on South Congress.

~

"Thanks for agreeing to see me, Gavin. As I said to Valerie earlier today, your head must be spinning with all of this. How are you holding up?" said Tommy.

"I was under no illusions about my father, Tommy. I guess I just pushed it to the back of my mind. He needed to pay for what he did, and over the last twenty-four hours I have reconciled myself to the fact that perhaps it was best that he was killed rather than be put through the trial and go to jail for the rest of his life.

"He was a major figure in the Republican Party, so the party and I have both been damaged by what has happened. I will just have to suck it up and try to explain to the good people of Texas that I am not like my father and see how the chips fall."

"You may need to sit down, Gavin. I need to tell you something that will come as a shock to you. *Garrison McMullen was not your father.*"

"What!" Gavin McMullen stared at Tommy with a look of complete disbelief.

"He believed you were his son. But your biological father was Achak Muguara. who worked on you father's ranch. We've matched your DNA from the samples we took from you to the skeletal remains in the Chevy truck dumped in Lake Travis. Your DNA is a match for both; your mother is Alyana and your father is *Achak Muguara.*

"We have also determined that the man murdered at Whispering Hollow was Mike Muguara, the son of Achak and Alyana - *your brother*!

"The man you thought was your father killed three people: your mother, your father and your brother.

"Achak Muguara is also of first nation lineage. He is a descendant of Chief Muguara of the Penateka tribe, a sub-tribe of the Comanche. He was killed in the Council House fight in San Antonio in 1840.

"Gavin, you are of the Muguara lineage, a Comanche first nation Indian. Muguara means *Spirit Talker,* and your spirit talker line reaches back to the times when the buffalo herds roamed the plains of Comancheria. We also know that your mother, Alyana Parker, was first nation, so that means that you, Gavin, are one hundred percent Native American. You are a Comanche!"

~

Gavin flopped down into a nearby chair.

"I can't take this all in! Are you sure? There is no doubt about anything you have just told me?" said Gavin, slumped on the chair, head in hands.

"If this is true, my entire life has been a lie. I am not who I thought I was and I'm not the person that the people of Texas voted for when I won election to be the next governor of the state. Where do I go from here?" said Gavin, sounding totally devastated and spent.

"Well, if you want the opinion of one Texas voter who voted for you, you are no different from the man you were, the man who ran for the office and won. I don't think that suddenly you're going to change who you are inside or what you stand for. I would say that you need to tell the people of Texas that when you're ready.

"Only a handful of people know this, Gavin. You can deal with it in your own time and in your own way. I came here today because I believed that you needed to be told as soon as possible."

"Thank you for doing that, Tommy. I need time to think all of this through," concluded Gavin.

Tommy left Gavin McMullen to his thoughts and headed back to the Hudson Bend.

Chapter 34

The FBI

THE SHERIFF ARRIVED BACK FROM his trip to FBI HQ in Washington and briefed Bill, Tommy and Marie.

He had met with the director of the FBI, Sam Forester, and his team. They brought representatives in from the DEA and the director assigned Special Agent Dave O'Connell (Doc) from the Chicago office to take overall responsibility for the operation. Doc was to coordinate with other law enforcement agencies and put together a joint task force to take down Enrique Rodriguez and his associates.

After analyzing the Mike Muguara surveillance videos provided by the Chief, Agent O'Connell and his team determined that they needed to act fast to prevent possible leaks of information getting to the ears of Rodriguez that they planned to move in on his operation.

They also concluded that a human-trafficking and drug-trafficking business of this scale could not operate without the knowledge and support of border patrol and/or county law enforcement in the area, and therefore there was a distinct possibility that some of their people might be complicit in the illicit operation.

They decided that they would have to go it alone without the assistance of border or county law enforcement, and to do that they would need to brief the governor of Texas, the head of Homeland Security and the President. Director Forester took responsibility to do that and asked that Agent O'Connell proceed ahead with the preparation of a plan to make an assault on the operation at the Colinas Verde Ranch and have it ready for his review in 24 hours.

~

Immediately after the assassination of Garrison McMullen, Enrique Rodriguez had moved to take over the ownership of the entire business. He was elected chairman of Venture Point Holdings by unanimous consent and he also made an offer to Gavin McMullen to buy out all of Garrison McMullen's shares in the business for $1.2 billion in cash. Gavin was shocked at the speed of Rodriguez' attempt to seize control and he, like most in law enforcement, concluded that this was further evidence that Enrique had been behind the assassination of Garrison McMullen, Pepe Vivar and Enrique's brother Jimmy.

In researching the plan to attack the ranch, Agent O'Connell and his team discovered that Enrique planned another Christmas/New Year's BBQ at the ranch, and that this year it would be a double celebration of Christmas and Enrique's takeover of the entire Venture Point Holdings business. The guest list would be huge and would include all of the leadership and key players in the operation. It was the ideal time for the FBI to make their move.

The plan for the attack was presented on schedule to Sam Forester and he gave it his approval. There were several key elements of the plan that needed to be executed with precision for the operation to be a success.

Firstly, a false story would be circulated that DEA and FBI leadership planned to fly down to the border area to make a rapid onsite review of border security. This would be the cover for helicopters to be staged at the border with SWAT assault personnel ready to be called in to support the attack.

The second important element was that a Rodriquez Trucking eighteen-wheeler that made regular weekly runs to the ranch would be hijacked and the SWAT team loaded into the back so that upon arrival at the ranch they would exit the vehicle en masse and then call in the helicopter support.

The third and final element would be the *Eye in the Sky*, a remote-control drone with high-intensity infrared cameras and air-to-surface ordnance that would be used to ensure that assault command would have a bird's-eye view of the operation and that the ordnance could be used to disable any vehicles that managed to slip through the net.

They would time all of this to happen when the barbeque party was in full swing and when liquor and drugs were being consumed in large quantities, making them vulnerable to this type of full frontal assault.

Tommy, Bill and Marie were all very impressed with the speed at which the FBI and DEA had engaged in this, and hoped that the plan would be a success. They had only wished that they could have been there to see Enrique Rodriguez go down, but realized that it would not be possible for that to happen.

~

Meanwhile, out by Lake Travis, heavy cranes were being repositioned from the Venture Point construction work to the lakeside to assist with the retrieval of the Chevy truck from its watery grave. The operation went well and the skeletal remains were removed with care and place in coffins for transfer. The two coffins plus the coffin containing the remains of Mike Muguara were transferred to the Comanche Nation reservation in Oklahoma and held in a morgue there in readiness for the official burial ceremony.

Chapter 35

Fish in the net

SPECIAL AGENT IN CHARGE DAVE (Doc) O'Connell was sitting in the FBI Dallas field office briefing the members of the Critical Incident Response Group (CRIG) who had been selected for the mission.

Agent John Anderson had been selected to lead the main Swat Operations Unit (SOU) that would hijack the Rodriguez Trucking eighteen-wheeler on route from its depot in El Paso to the Colinas Verde Ranch. He would lead a team of 40 SWAT agents and they would be hidden in the back of the truck, ready for the assault. Agent Oscar Lopez was selected as a native Spanish speaker to take the position up front with the driver to ensure that he did as instructed when they arrived at the ranch.

Agents from the field office in El Paso had determined that there was a truck scheduled to leave the El Paso depot the day of the Christmas Party and that its ETA at the ranch was scheduled for 6 p.m. That was too early in the day to make the plan work, so Texas Highway Patrol was asked for assistance to pull the truck over and, in doing so, delay the arrival at the ranch until 8 p.m. when the party would be in full swing. This would not arouse any suspicion as their trucks did occasionally get pulled over for routine checks.

Captain Art Johnson would be the lead pilot for the Tactical Helicopter Unit (THU). There would be three UH-60 Black

Hawk helicopters with eight SWAT agents in each. The plan was to fly to the border checkpoint at Marfa for a spot inspection, and two Texas senators volunteered to fly in one of the helicopters to carry out the inspection. They would remain at the checkpoint when the choppers were called into the ranch for the real mission. The choppers were scheduled to arrive at Marfa at 4 p.m. the day of the party.

The drone for *Eye in the Sky* support would be controlled from the Dallas Office.

~

Enrique Rodriguez suspected nothing. He was high on cocaine and on the prospect of the vast sums of money to be made now that he was in sole control of the empire. Someone had done him a favor by taking out Garrison McMullen; it was unfortunate that his brother Jimmy had to die, but so be it.

His network of spies and informants had told him about the spot check that was happening that day at the Marfa checkpoint and that a couple of Texas senators were flying in. "They just want another fucking photo op!" had been his response.

~

By 6:30 most of the important attendees at the party had arrived. Eddie Tang and his entourage were in the west wing of the ranch and had already started partying. Pablo Zambrano and his Zapata people were scheduled to arrive at seven. The feast preparations were already underway and everyone could smell the pork and beef cooking on the spit. Enrique did another couple of lines of coke and a shot of tequila. He was ready to party.

By eight o'clock the party was in full swing. Zambrano and his people had arrived on schedule with several others from Mexican law enforcement who were on the Zapata payroll. Feliz Navidad was blaring out on speakers; the voice of Jose Feliciano was unmistakable.

The eighteen-wheeler with its cargo of SWAT agents had been waved through the security gates with no problem as the two guards sipped on their beers, wishing that they could be at the main ranch enjoying the party. They suspected nothing.

The eighteen-wheeler with its deadly swat team cargo parked in its usual spot, ready to be loaded up with its cargo of cattle, drugs and illegals the next day. It was parked about fifty yards from that main ranch house and Agent Lopez could see everything from his position in the cab of the truck. The driver, with his duties completed, had been handcuffed and was now in the back of the truck with the other agents.

"Go!"

Agent O'Connell gave the green light from his control center in Dallas.

The Black Hawk helicopters lifted off from Marfa to make the six-minute flight to the ranch. Two minutes later one of the circling drones fired a rocket into the desert to the west of the ranch, creating a huge fireball.

"What the fuck was that?" yelled Enrique as he and everyone else ran to the western side of the ranch to see what had happened.

The main SWAT team from the eighteen-wheeler had exited the parked truck and had already reached the main door at the eastern entrance to the ranch house. They took out the two security guards who had made a poor decision and tried to engage. At the same time, the helicopters landed and unloaded their teams.

~

It was all over in less than 30 minutes. The only casualties had been the two security guards at the front door. Everyone was rounded up. The key players—Rodriguez, Eddie Tang and Pablo Zambrano—were immediately transported by helicopter to Dallas. The others were herded into the eighteen-wheeler for a rather uncomfortable ride back to the El Paso field office where FBI agents stood ready to process them.

Special Agent John Anderson and his team were given the task to go over the ranch with a fine-tooth comb and gather all the evidence needed to support the prosecution of the leaders and particularly Enrique Rodriguez. The scale of the illicit operation was immense and the FBI and DEA joint task force removed all of the computer and communications equipment from the ranch offices and loaded it onto the helicopters for transport to Dallas and then on to FBI headquarters in Washington, DC.

They found the tunnels into Mexico and the staging area for the drugs and illegals that were brought through the tunnels into the U.S. In two huge warehouses they found over a ton of cocaine, and adjacent to that warehouse two bunkhouses containing over 60 illegals sleeping in conditions resembling those found in concentration camps during WWII. They spent a maximum of two days in these filthy conditions in transit from South America and Mexico.

~

In Washington, DC, back-to-back press conferences were held. The first was hosted by FBI Director Sam Forrester and Special Agent Dave O'Connell, who had flown in overnight from Dallas.

"Last night a joint FBI and DEA task force under the leadership of Special Agent Dave O'Connell carried out a successful operation to close down one of the largest, if not *the* largest, drug and human trafficking operation in the USA. The raid was on the Colinas Verde Ranch in southwest Texas. The owner of the ranch, Enrique Escobar Rodriguez, was arrested along with others suspected of being complicit in the running of this illegal enterprise, including Eddie Tang, a Chinese national and the CEO of Deng Tang Corporation, and Pablo Zambrano, reputed to be the head of the Zapata drug cartel.

"This operation was a direct result of the continuing investigation into the death of Garrison McMullen by the Travis County Police Department in Austin, Texas, and this extensive illegal enterprise would not have been uncovered without the diligent efforts of Travis County Police Department Chief Bill Dunwoody and his team.

"I must also thank Texas Governor Raymond Shaw and Governor-elect Gavin McMullen for their support."

The FBI director went on to describe the ongoing commitment to securing the borders and stopping the flow of drugs and illegal aliens into the U.S.

A statement from the President closely followed this news conference, and then the political dance continued. On-camera interview after interview followed. Senators and congressional leaders were each getting their moment to bask in the success of the operation and describe the key role that they had played in this as part of their undying commitment to the safety and wellbeing of the American people. It was the typical Washington tap dance after a successful operation.

Chapter 36

Gavin McMullen

TWO WEEKS LATER THE AUSTIN Convention Center main hall was packed to capacity for the inauguration of the next governor of Texas. Security teams were everywhere to ensure that nothing bad happened to the "Who's Who" of Texas society.

As the invited guests mingled together, dressed in their finest attire, looking for their table assignments and enjoying pre-dinner drinks, all the talk was about recent events and whether Gavin McMullen would be able to survive politically. They were waiting with unbridled excitement to hear his acceptance speech for any clues as to how he planned to defend his corner. Everyone loves a good fight, and to this crowd a political fight was to be savored and enjoyed.

After the dinner had been served and everyone was settling down with their drinks, the *main event* was about to start and the room went immediately silent when *the person from the red corner*, Gavin McMullen rose to address the crowd.

My fellow statewide elected officials, members of the judiciary, members of the House and Senate, friends and Texans, it's an honor to take the oath of office as your governor.

Before I look forward to the job ahead I must also reflect on the tumult of the past few weeks and months. The man I thought was my father was a stalwart of the Republican Party, but he was able to be in that position by fraudulent means.

It's important that I do not gloss over these events or attempt to put a spin on them to protect myself from the fallout. I must be honest, candid and forthright and only by being so will I be able to emerge from this with dignity and respect. Only then will the great people of Texas be able to trust this person who stands before you today, the person you elected to be the next governor of this great state.

The reality is that the man I understood to be my father was a liar, a cheat and a murderer. He was a despicable human being.

While he made public condemnation of the lack of action to protect our borders from the flow of illegal aliens, he ran the largest human trafficking operation, a super highway, if you will, exploiting those whose only desire was to get a better life to feed their families. While being critical of the current administration that there was not enough being done to stop the flow of drugs entering our country and poisoning our citizens, he ran the largest illicit drug business in the country, adding to and extending the misery of drug addiction.

To protect himself from being revealed for what he really was, he killed my mother and my real father and arranged for the killing of my brother.

This man was not my father. This man's blood does not run through my veins. I am not like this man in any way.

My father was Achak Muguara, a direct descendant of Chief Muguara of the Penateka Comanche. My mother was Alyana Parker, a direct descendant of Quanah Parker, the last great Comanche Chief. I am Comanche; I am a first nation Native American.

This explains my lineage, but it does not tell you who I am, what I believe in and what my vision is for this great state of Texas.

My brother was Mike Muguara, a Marine and a member of our Special Forces. He fought for his country as part of a Special-Forces team in the desert of western Iraq searching for and eliminating scud missile sites that were being used to rain down terror on Israel.

This team of six patriots and protectors of our way of life consisted of one Brit, one Australian, one Scots/Irish, one Hispanic, one Italian and my brother, a Native American. It was the sum of their parts that made them strong. They did not focus on their differences but on their strengths. They watched each other's back. It was all about the team, the unity and the camaraderie.

This great state of ours is a melting pot of cultures. Like that team in the desert, it's the sum of our parts and our diversity that makes us strong; we all bring something unique to the table. We all have a strong lineage and, with the possible exception of my first nation brothers and sisters, we all came here from somewhere else; we are all immigrants.

If you come here legally and you want to work hard and contribute, we welcome you. If you come here illegally and try to game the system or sponge off the efforts of others, there is no place for you in Texas. We are a diverse state, a rich state, and we will be made richer by the influx of legal workers with special skills who will add to our wealth, our diversity and our prosperity.

I will focus on jobs and business investment that creates jobs. I will ensure that we have a state government that stimulates and supports innovation and entrepreneurship. I will be a champion of women in the workplace and will look to drive opportunity for more women-owned businesses.

As our forefathers did, I will fight for and protect religious freedom. Being a melting pot of cultures, we must recognize that these cultures have different religious beliefs. We are predominantly a Christian nation, but we must recognize that others will be of different faiths and we must be respectful of their beliefs and their customs as they are of ours.

It's not about exclusion, it's about inclusion. I will look to collaborate for the common good, not confront and look to win a point for some meaningless political game. With me it's about being united in a common purpose to make this great state the greatest place on earth for our children and our children's children.

When I leave office I hope that I will have done something of real value and will have earned the right to have had my name on the door - Gavin McMullen-Muguara, Governor of Texas.

May God bless you, bless this great state of Texas and bless the United States of America.

Thank you.

There was a standing ovation. He had touched their soul; they now knew why they had voted for him. Gavin McMullen-Muguara was a good man, potentially a great man, and he had the makings of a great governor.

~

In Washington, DC, members of the Republican Party national committee watched the speech live.

"This boy from Texas is quite impressive; he speaks from the heart. We need to watch his progress over the years. Might be just the ticket to have a strong, conservative Native American in the White House!"

The following morning The Austin *Statesman* published the first part of an exclusive three-part editorial written by Latisha Williams called "The Fall of an Empire." It described the empire built by Garrison McMullen and Enrique Rodriguez from its early beginnings in the cattle and horse business to drugs and human trafficking.

She described how the intoxicating lust for power had created evil men willing to do anything for their drug of choice (power) and how they met their eventual demise as a result of the unrelenting and diligent efforts of members of the Travis County Police Department's cold case team.

Chapter 37

Their journey to the other side

IT WAS A FREEZING COLD February day. The burial ceremony was scheduled for mid-afternoon to ensure that it would be completed before sunset. The remains of Achak Muguara, Alyana Parker and Mike Muguara had each been wrapped in a Comanche Indian blanket and then placed in separate coffins. The site chosen by the tribal council was close by the grave of Cynthia Parker in the Post Cemetery at Fort Sill, near Lawton, Oklahoma. It was within sight of the Chief's Knoll where many of the great chiefs of the southern tribes are buried, including Quanah Parker.

It was bitterly cold, and the assembled funeral party dressed accordingly with heavy coats and scarves to protect them from the wind that gusted across the plains. A place of honor by the graveside was reserved for Gavin McMullen and for the representatives from the tribal council and the elders. Gavin had his arm around Antonella Aguilar, who looked very frail and had a Comanche blanket wrapped around her. Chief Dunwoody, Tommy, Bill and Marie stood together with Yolanda and Julian Hernandez. Claudette and Saul Weiss had flown over from Germany and they stood alongside Bill. Bill handed Claudette the silver money clip that had belonged to Mike Muguara and kissed her softly on the cheek.

The three hearses navigated their way through the cemetery and slowly pulled alongside the gravesite. Eighteen young

Comanche men stood ready, six for each coffin, and they performed their duty with honor and respect, carrying the caskets to the graveside and lowering them into their final resting places.

Throughout history when great chiefs were buried, oftentimes young braves would cut off a lock of their hair and place it with the chief. At the end of the burial ceremony and before the earth covered the caskets, Gavin McMullen stepped forward. He took out a knife that he had brought with him for this final tribute and he cut off locks of his hair and placed one on each coffin. He then stretched out his arms wide and held them up into the air and looked to the heavens. Gavin McMullen-Muguara spoke with the spirits. They were all there stretching back to the time when the buffalo roamed the plains: Peta Nocona, Quanah Parker, Buffalo Hump and Chief Muguara of the Penateka. Gavin McMullen-Muguara spoke with them and asked that they watch over his family as they made their journey to the other side.

A hundred yards away, up on the hill by the Chiefs Knoll, a solitary figure stood unseen by the other funeral attendees. When the ceremony was over, Joe Nichol quickly left and headed back to the airport.

Chapter 38

The Parting Glass

I HAVE A SURPRISE FOR you but you're going to have to trust me," said Bill Ross.

Tommy had invited Bill and Elaine over for dinner. After the burgers, Tommy and Bill were sitting together on Tommy's patio watching the sun go down while Elaine, helped by Claire, cleaned up in the kitchen.

"Okay, I'm in," said Tommy, "So tell me what you have in mind."

It had been an intense few months and they had just returned from the burial ceremony in Oklahoma and were ready to draw a line under the "Burning Cross" case.

"We'll set off early Friday morning and drive down to Houston. That's all I'm prepared to say at this time, but you should plan to be gone Friday, Saturday and Sunday nights and be back in Austin on Monday. Claire will be staying over the weekend at *Mimi's house*. Where we're going will be cold, so pack accordingly," said Bill.

~

The day of the trip arrived and Tommy had packed as instructed, and he and Bill set off early in Bill's SUV for the drive to Houston.

"The first stop is to see Martha and Jacob Goldman and to buy them lunch at the deli on Market Street. We would never have made the breakthrough on the Burning Cross case without their help. I have everything arranged and they'll meet us at the deli," said Bill as they approached the outskirts of Houston.

After a nice lunch of borscht, latkes and cheese blintz, they said their goodbyes to the Goldmans and headed over to the Woodlands to have coffee with Yolanda and Julian Hernandez. Yolanda and Julian had also attended the burial ceremony of Mike Muguara and his family in Oklahoma, so Tommy and Bill had thanked them for their help when they met up with them at the ceremony, but Bill felt that it would have been rude of them not to at least stop by for a coffee since they were already in Houston.

"So now where are you taking me?" said Tommy as they pulled out of the Hernandez' driveway.

"Okay, I guess I should tell you now, we're off to Boston. I have two tickets for the playoff game between the New England Patriots and the Indianapolis Colts. I know you hate the Patriots, but I also have another reason why I want to make the trip to Boston, so I thought we would make a weekend of it and take in the game,"

~

The United flight touched down at Logan Airport on time at 9:30 p.m. Eastern and they grabbed a cab to their hotel. After check-in and a quick nightcap in the bar they went off to bed.

~

Bootsy Brogan's pub still smelled like a mixture of disinfectant and wood polish. Kathleen from Waterford was in her normal place behind the bar when Bill and Tommy walked in just before noon on Saturday morning.

Joe Nichol was seated at his normal place at the far corner of the bar, and he barely lifted his head when Bill and Tommy pulled up a stool next to him.

"All right?" said Bill, staring straight ahead.

"Just fine, and you?" replied Joe with barely a glance in Bill's direction.

"This is my son, Tommy Ross."

"Aye, I know who he is, you awe right son?" said Joe Nichol; no handshake. just an acknowledgement of Tommy's presence.

Bill ordered Joe another Guinness, one for himself and one for Tommy. Kathleen delivered the dark rich beer to them. They each stared at the three pints as they settled, anticipating the enjoyment that lay ahead when they had that first fully satisfying mouthful of the rich ale.

After a couple of mouthfuls of beer enjoyed in the silence of the moment, Bill launched right in to what he had to say.

"So it all turned out as you planned, Joe. *You set us up and used us!*

You suspected that if you had tried to follow the trail to the killers of Mike Muguara, you could have ended up dead just like him.

"*You* took the backup hard drive from Mike's storage unit before we got to it first. *You* used a custom program to clean the laptop. *You* put the crumpled piece of paper in the back of the desk knowing full well that we would find it and track down what lay behind the cryptic clues that you left for us.

"*You* tracked our progress, and when you called me the night before the assassinations. I had thought that you were calling from Boston, when in actual fact you were already in Austin, where *you* had set up for the assassinations the following day.

"After the hits, *you* popped the hard drive in a shipping box addressed to me and had the courier pick it up at the front desk of the Hilton, where you were staying under the name Jimmy Martinelli. Yes, I checked the guest register.

"The only thing I haven't figured out is how you managed to carry out the three hits. I timed how long it might take you to get from the place where we found the rifle at the courthouse to the holding cell building. It's possible to do it but it's a push and there was no room for error or you would have missed the chance to take out Pepe and Jimmy."

Bill Ross paused, took another mouthful of beer and waited for Joe Nichol's response. It took a few minutes and was short and to the point.

"You have a great mind, Bill Ross. Wish I had thought of doing all of that, it might have been fun!"

"I didn't expect you to admit it, Joe, but perhaps someday you might tell me how you did it and got the timing just right. I made this trip in the hope that you might tell me, but with the clear expectation that probably you would not. I do have another task I want to accomplish while I'm here with you, however."

Bill reached down and pulled something from the backpack he had brought with him. He put the bottle of The Glenmorangie Pride '78 on the bar in front of them.

"Now, that's possibly the best single malt that money can buy. I was hoping that you, Tommy and I might spend the rest of the day consuming the contents and toasting the life of fallen comrades. I have cleared it in advance with the owners of this fine establishment."

Only then did Joe Nichol turn his head and look Bill Ross straight in the eye. There were tears running down his cheeks when he said, "Now, that would be my honor, Bill Ross."

They broke the seal on the '78, undid the cap and threw it in the trash. Kathleen and Sean O'Driscoll appeared with crystal glasses that were kept behind the bar for special occasions. Three full measures of the golden elixir were poured.

"To fallen comrades!" said Bill.

The glasses were raised and they each closed their eyes as the whisky warmed them with each swallow.

They shared the contents of the bottle as planned, and by mid-afternoon a three-piece Irish band arrived to prepare for the regular night's festivities. Bill walked over to the young men and asked them to play a tune. The two fiddles and the Irish bodhran stood in readiness for Bill to lead them off. Tommy knew what was coming as he had heard his dad sing "The Parting Glass" many times. The song was written in Scotland in the early 1600s by an unknown hand and was sung in Scotland and Ireland at the end of an evening or at funerals before Auld Lang Syne, written by Robert Burns, took its place.

Of all the money that e'er I spent
I've spent it in good company
And all the harm that ever I did
Alas it was to none but me
And all I've done for want of wit
To memory now I can't recall
So lift to me the parting glass
Good night and joy be with you all

If I had money enough to spend
And Leisure to sit awhile
There is a fair maid in town
That sorely has my heart beguiled
Her rosy cheeks and ruby lips
I own she has my heart enthralled
So fill to me the parting glass
Good night and joy be with you all

Oh, all the comrades that e'er I had
They're sorry for my going away
And all the sweethearts that e'er I had
They'd wish me one more day to stay
But since it falls unto my lot
That I should rise and you should not
I'll gently rise and softly call
Good night and joy be with you all

By the time they all had reached the third and final verse, every single person in the bar was on their feet, holding their beverage of choice high into the air and blasting out the lyrics like their lives depended on it. It was an appropriate tribute. Aye, that it was.

~

When they had regained their composure and the band had received their customary beverages in thanks for their efforts, Joe turned to Bill and slurred, "So what are you plans for tomorrow, Bill, after you and Tommy sober up?"

"Oh, I have two tickets to the Patriots playoff game at Gillette Stadium."

"I'm going to the game myself. I have a friend who has one of those fancy sky boxes. I do some work for him from time to time. Let me make a call and see if it would be okay for you and Tommy to get into the box with me."

Joe left to make the call and returned a few minutes later.

"Everything is set. He would be happy for you both to be his guests in his box. Give me your tickets and I'll get Sean to sell them in the bar later today."

~

Sunday morning was painful. They both struggled with intense hangovers. They ate a late breakfast, and after a quick nap headed out to meet Joe outside Gillette Stadium. He was standing in the parking lot waiting for them.

"Everything good?" asked Joe as they headed in through the concierge lobby of the stadium to the main elevator to the skybox area. A very well-dressed young lady handed them a glass of champagne as they exited the elevator.

The box was huge, and with Joe leading them they headed in the direction of two men who stood with their backs to them, surveying the field below.

"Robert, I'd like to introduce my two friends I talked to you about yesterday."

Tommy Ross almost dropped his glass of champagne!

Robert Kraft, the owner of the New England Patriots and the chairman of the Kraft Group, stood in front of him, and by his side his son Jonathan, president of the New England Patriots.

"Glad you could both could join us," said Robert Kraft. "Please help yourself to whatever you need and enjoy the game!"

"You have very interesting friends, Joe," laughed Bill as they headed in the direction of the sumptuous buffet.

~

They were on the United Airlines flight back to Houston the following day.

"When did you know that it was Joe Nichol who carried out the assassinations dad?"

"My sense was that something didn't quite fit beginning at the storage locker that Mike rented in Houston. Claudette had told me that Mike was manic about data protection, keeping everything on an external hard drive and not even trusting the Cloud."

"We found the laptop in the storage locker but no hard drive, and then we found a piece of paper stuck at the back of the desk. A piece of paper! Why would someone so paranoid about data security write stuff down on paper? Didn't make any sense. It was too perfect, just like the sign next to the burning cross. Someone was deliberately trying to manipulate us; in this case it was for good reasons."

"If he left us this clue on paper, why did he do that? Why not just leave the hard drive? I concluded that there was stuff on the drive he didn't want us to see, well, not right away. He wanted us to concentrate on the list of cryptic clues, but why?"

"When the hard drive arrived by courier after the assassinations, the pieces began to fit. The person who had sent us the drive had either extracted the surveillance files from a single hard drive that Mike used, or there was more than one drive. Either way, this person had taken the hard drive from the storage unit because in the video that he left with Bob Corbin, Mike told us that the hard drive was in the storage locker.

Other than Mike, who knew about the storage locker? Joe Nichol of course!"

"I concluded that Joe had a plan. He wanted us to concentrate on finding out for sure who had killed Mike Muguara. The drug and human trafficking business was secondary to him and he didn't want us to be distracted by the surveillance videos of Colinas Verde Ranch. He wanted us to focus on who killed Mike because he had planned all along that he would kill the person or persons responsible."

"It was when I thought about the sequence of events that it all fit. The phone call to my house the night before the assassinations that I thought wrongly had been made from Boston. Then the killings, followed immediately by the delivery of the hard drive, that's when I knew that Joe was behind this. When I checked the guest register at the hotel and found the name Jimmy Martinelli, I knew then for sure."

"I checked and double-checked the timing of the shootings. That's the part that still doesn't quite fit. He could have done both, but the timing would have had to be perfect, He would have needed a motorcycle."

"I ran the sequence of events myself, and Joe is fitter than me so my guess is that he would have been a bit faster. I knelt in the place in the parking garage next to the courthouse where I speculated he had knelt to shoot Garrison McMullen. I simulated the shooting, got up and ran down the stairs to the motorcycle that I rented for the test. I chose the same day and time as the original shootings to try to get the most accurate traffic conditions, and I rode the bike to where he had set up for the second shooting. I had about four minutes to catch my breath, steady myself and take the shots."

"Joe didn't know precisely when Pepe and Jimmy would be led out of the holding cell to the waiting van for transfer. He speculated that they would move them, but he didn't know for sure."

"No, he didn't do both shootings. He needed a second shooter, someone he trusted and someone who would be already set up in place to take them out *if they were transferred*. If they weren't transferred he had a plan B; don't know what that was, but he would never have let them live. Rather he or his accomplice would have got to them somehow. some way."

"But shouldn't we arrest Joe Nichol then?" said Tommy.

"Your call, son. My opinion is that justice was served. I am not in favor of vigilante actions, but I can see it from Joe's point of view. Garrison McMullen had so much power and influence that it was likely that he would buy himself enough time that he could live out his life and die from natural causes before any execution could take place. Joe was not going to allow that to happen. We would also have had a tough time convicting him and we would have needed to find the other shooter. No, I'm okay with it. You have to decide if you are."

Bill then closed his eyes and slept for the remainder of the flight back to Houston.

Chapter 39

Sheep have feelings

QANTAS FLIGHT 108 LEFT LAX right on time for its 16-hour flight to Melbourne and had leveled off at its cruising altitude of 32,000 feet. The female flight attendant was delivering the first round of drinks and seasoned travelers were settling down for the long flight.

It was Billy Williams' first trip to Australia, and the young computer software salesman was super excited. He was seated in the combined first and business class section in seat F5 and was fiddling with all the gadgets in the sleeper seat cubical, operating the various seat controls and making the seat go up and down.

When he looked across the aisle, the guy in seat A5 was grinning at him.

"Having fun, mate?" he sniggered.

He wore a black tee shirt with "Keep Austin Weird" across the front, an old faded baseball cap, blue jeans and flip-flops. This was in stark contrast to Billy's GQ outfit of Ralph Lauren Polo and khakis.

"Sorry about that, my first flight to Australia!" replied Billy.

"Are you going down to Australia for vacation?" asked the salesman, trying to make polite conversation.

"No, mate, I live there!"

"You live in Melbourne?"

"No, I live in a little place called Ballarat, it's about seventy miles from Melbourne."

"You were in California over Christmas and New Year, then?" continued the software salesman, the adrenalin from the excitement of the flight pumping through his system and causing his mouth to spout forth meaningless cryptic conversation.

"Trip of a lifetime, mate, hunting in Texas with my buddy Joe and then a few weeks watching the babes work out on Venice Beach. Magic!"

"I've never been hunting. Did you shoot anything?"

"Bagged a couple, mate. The folks there did a really good job of flushing them out for us, so it was like shooting fish in a barrel."

"So what do you do in Ballarat, then?"

"Bit of this, bit of that, you know. I take folks on tours of the sheep shearing and around the old Ballarat Bitter brewery that closed down a few years ago. They still run tours. Great beer, Ballarat Bitter, now owned by Carlton, helps them with product balance, I guess, as the other stuff they brew is like rat's piss!"

"I didn't get your name, by the way. My name is Billy Williams, and you are?"

"My name's Carl. Carl Conrad."

"Well, good to meet you, Carl. Hey, Carl, do you know the best place is to have sex with a sheep..."

Billy was about to continue on with the only sheep joke he knew when in an instant Carl Conrad was up out of his seat and in his face.

"No sheep jokes! You hear me, no sheep jokes! Sheep have feelings! I hate sheep jokes!"

Not a lot was said between them for the rest of the journey. The Airbus A380-800 cruising en route to Melbourne with its 600 passengers, including a young software salesman and a tired ex-Special-Forces sniper and Spirit Rider.

Post Script

I hope you enjoyed the book. It was total fiction, of course, but the settings for the story are real.

The cities of Cedar Park, Lago Vista, Leander and Round Rock are about 90 minutes northwest of Austin. There is a Point Venture area by Lake Travis, and Whispering Hollow is a private gated park for the exclusive use of the residents of Point Venture. There's a small golf course in the area, nine holes only and no grill.

The area I chose for the location of the Colinas Verde Ranch is actually a national park. Big Bend National Park has national significance as the largest protected area of Chihuahua Desert topography and ecology in the United States.

The town of Ballarat is a real place and is located 70 miles from Melbourne. I spent a lot of time in Australia on business and I drove to Ballarat one day, visited the sheep-shearing demonstration and drank Ballarat Bitter - great beer.

My wife and I lived in Germany for a couple of years in the small town of Wiesloch in the Rheine-Neckar region. It was a short rail journey to Heidelberg. We love the city. Like Bill Ross, we stayed in the Crown Plaza Hotel, walked along Hauptstrasse and visited the Christmas market in old town. We also would walk across the bridge over the river Neckar to Neuenheim on a Saturday morning to visit the farmers market, drink coffee and eat croissants.

Most of the research for this book I did online. Wikipedia is a great source of information. I accessed the Comanche Nation website www.comanchenation.com and also obtained lots of historical information on the early days of the formation of Texas from the Texas State Historical Association website www.tshaonline.org.

Finally, a friend of mine was kind enough to buy me a copy of *Empire of the Summer Moon* by S. C. Gwynne on the rise and fall of the Comanche Nation. The content of the book helped me immensely - Thank you, Rich!